M

(1907–1966) was born in
of nine surviving children
Her mother, Mary Ann,   ...rt the
family when they ran into   ...es. Maura Laverty
went to the Brigidine Conve   ... ...low, from where at seventeen
she went to Spain as a governess. After four months, however,
she taught herself a form of shorthand and typing and became
private secretary to Prince Bibesco, husband of Princess Bibesco,
the writer. Later she worked for the Banco de Bilbao and wrote
for the Madrid newspaper *El Debate*.

She became engaged to a Hungarian and returned to Ireland
to say goodbye to her family. Here she met James Laverty a
journalist with whom she had corresponded when in Spain.
Within three days they were married and she returned to Spain
to tell her Hungarian fiancé. Afterwards she lived in Dublin with
her two daughters and a son.

Maura Laverty had always written: articles, short stories,
translations from Spanish etc., but her first novel *Never No More*
(also published by Virago) was published to great acclaim in
1942. This was followed by *Alone We Embark* (1943); *No More
Than Human* (1944); and *Lift Up Your Gates* (1946). Each of these
novels was banned in Ireland until the 1960s. She also wrote two
children's books, *Cottage in the Bog* (1945) and *Green Orchard*
(1949), and two cookery books for which she was renowned in
Ireland, *Kind Cooking* (1950) and *Feasting Galore* (1961). She
continued to contribute to newspapers, including the *Sunday
Empire News* (an English newspaper which was also banned in
Ireland). In the 1950s Maura Laverty began writing plays, which
were well-received. The first of these was a dramatisation of *Lift
Up Your Gates*, called *Liffey Lane*, followed by *Tolka Row* and *The
Tree in the Crescent*. During the 1960s she wrote a weekly TV
programme called *Tolka Row*, which ran for some years, and she
also contributed to a weekly radio programme.

Maura Laverty died of a heart attack at the age of 58.

VIRAGO
MODERN
CLASSIC

NUMBER
210

MAURA LAVERTY

NO MORE
THAN HUMAN

With a New Introduction by
MAEVE BINCHY

Virago

Published by VIRAGO PRESS Limited 1986
A print on demand book published by Virago Press in 2004

First published in Great Britain by Longmans, Green and Co Ltd 1944
Virago edition offset from Longmans, Green and Co Ltd 1950 edition.

Copyright Maura Laverty 1944
Introduction Copyright © Maeve Binchy 1986

All rights reserved

British Library Cataloguing in Publication Data
Laverty, Maura
No more than human.—(Virago modern classics)
I. Title
823'.912   PR6023.A91/

ISBN 1 84408 193 1

Virago Press
An imprint of
Time Warner Book Group UK
Brettenham House
Lancaster Place
London WC2E 7EN

www.virago.co.uk

INTRODUCTION

IT WAS like meeting an old friend when Delia Scully came staggering up the station platform in Madrid, dragging her dress basket with its two straps and handle of plaited wire. She wasn't sure whether it was the water or the soap or the wind but her hair stood up like a furze bush pushing her navy straw hat up in the air, her navy nap coat was far too small, her make-up applied for the first time with glaring cupid's bows was too garish, and she was about to set off on another adventure. What a relief for all those who thought that they had said goodbye to her in Ballyderrig.

In 1944 when Maura Laverty published *No More Than Human*, the big question on everyone's minds was whether it took up the story of Delia again, and when it was known that it did then its success was assured. Because there was something about the eager, excited, emotional Delia Scully feasting in her Gran's kitchen, pining in her boarding school, becoming involved in everything that stirred in Ballyderrig, that haunted the readers. It was almost like peeping through a window at a real life, and that is because to all intents and purposes it *was* a real life. Maura Laverty lived through the same episodes set against the same backdrop. She must have had the same busy brain in which ideas tumbled over each other so fast that they came out as a torrent of words and made others think she was giddy and irresponsible.

In Maura Laverty's own real life she went to Spain to be a governess with a good Spanish family, as many another Irish girl did at the time. The Spanish families who wanted their children to learn English had a far greater fear of English Protestant or atheistic influence communicating itself to *los ninos* than they had of the children developing Irish accents. Many a Spaniard learned to talk English in the tones of Tipperary or Cork and would phrase a sentence in a manner that was totally Irish. So if you came with good references from nuns and families back home, if you were Irish in Spain in the 1920s, this was the place for you.

So many young Irish girls must have gone out there without questioning the journey and why it was really necessary. They went because there were few other avenues. Unless they were very brainy and very determined there would hardly be much further education. They went, drawn by the noble-sounding names, the hint of aristocracy in the employers, the mention of castle, stately home or at the very least huge residence. They went to escape their mothers and their small towns. They went for heat and flowers and foreign smells and the notion of having travelled. They went often in hope of making a brilliant marriage, like the superbly confident Señora Basterra, Delia's first employer. Señora had once been Peggy Kelly from Baltinglass, Co. Wicklow in Ireland, a fact she was trying hard to forget. Yes, that would have been part of the rationale, to become a grand señora and be able to employ one of your equals from back home . . . Perhaps they went to learn a little about young children, which would be useful later when they married. Because this was the only way they could work with children; to mind them at home would be like being a maid, and that would never do.

A great many of them became beached and bitter. They passed their time in a continuous condemnation of the country where they had chosen to live. The women were vain and lazy . . . and all the men were fiends with only one idea — the ruination of women and Irish women in particular. And as they sat at their weekly tea in the Molinero or on a bench near the Murillo gate they fulminated to each other on how poor the situation was and how depraved the men. To the sharp young eye of Delia Scully it was interesting that the older and plainer the governess the worse things she had to say about Spanish men.

Anyone who followed young Delia's adventures in Ballyderrig when she was about to set out into life would know that she was not about to sit down on the Retiro with the other governesses and join in the wail. Her first and best friend is an older woman, a Miss Carmody, who tells her how to became a *duena* or one of the *professoras* who live in lodgings and hire themselves out to teach English and chaperone the girls. That way freedom lay and there was hardly any freedom in the Big House Spanish style; you were never off duty, you had no place in society. Your employers kept you firmly in your place, the maids were afraid to talk to you in case that meant they weren't being in *their* place and the *ex pat* English society living in Madrid had no place for you in their colony either. It was a limbo, lazy because of the heat, more luxurious than home because of the flowers and the parks and the sweetmeats, but lonely waiting in the hot passionate climate where very little heat and passion was being generated in their own lives.

As you might hope, young Delia generates her own from the word go. There is passion in her loneliness and her ache for everything that reminded her of the pale countryside she had left behind, with its light and shade and its quivering changes so different from the bright blue sky, the red roofs and white houses, the same every day of the summer with none of the fine tones she had grown up with in her own part of the world.

So much did she ache sometimes that her only respite was in poetry. And here Maura Laverty lets us see her own gentle, innocent approach to life ... she *quotes* the poems. Another author might have let us know that the heroine wrote but not what she wrote. But you come to know Delia Scully and therefore her creator much more intimately by reading her verse. Even when it is religious and deals with meeting the Virgin Mary, sewing cloaks back in Delia's heaven which is Dunmurry Hill, and places that border on Ballyderrig, she doesn't seem silly; such poetry is part and parcel of her.

She was wretchedly unhappy and it is felt through every sense, even the sense of touch:

The sight of the Basque peasants wakened little stirrings in me and a hundred times a day I found myself thinking of how the gorse would be scattering its golden sovereigns at home, and how the banks on the Monasterevan road would be cream splashed with primroses. At the thought of primroses my fingers would feel the sweet coolness of delving deep in the moss and leaves for the little darning wool stems of downy pink.

It's not all homesickness, however; she does learn to live shamelessly for the moment, pressed to the manly Spanish breast of Rafael, in private, having danced a tango with him in public and all this at the one upper-class function she *did* get invited to. The disapproval is frightening; she is almost dismissed and deportation is on the cards too. But the brave Delia with a toss of her black curls survives it, and hugs the memory of the kiss to warm her through so many arid days and nights afterwards.

Anyone who remembers Delia Scully in her youth moving delightedly around her Gran's kitchen will not be surprised that she headed fairly swiftly for the kitchens of Spain. Now the Señora who was once upon a time Peggy Kelly from Baltinglass did not at all approve of Miss Scully the governess fraternising with the below-stairs staff, but even the Señora had to accept that there was little future trying to suspend Delia between the two realms and perhaps it was better to let her in to experience the creations of the fearsome Juanita who hated all men since her own husband had disappeared to live with a widow who ran a lodging house. Juanita told the young Delia all her cookery secrets and even gave her an apron and a chance to stir and beat and blend, so not all the time in Spain was lost time.

Here Maura Laverty's fine philosophy that cooking is love comes over strongly. She has said that cooking is the poetry of housework, and we know how highly she rates poetry. Maura Laverty who was also a household name for her cookery books after she had become known as a novelist believed that cookery was to her what literature, music and painting were to others:

> It is such a kind friendly unselfish art, the art of cooking, and every little step in the preparation of even the plainest dish is an opportunity for self expression . . .

She thinks that it brings peace of mind and would be better than any tranquillisers or medication for those who are disturbed or upset:

> . . . rub butter into flour for scones — there is something that I would recommend to neurotic people as a better tonic than anything their doctors could give them. The purity of the flour, the cool velvety feel of it, the gentle incessant calm-giving motion of the finger tips could hold out against such homely comforting.

And Maura Laverty was a good advertisement for her own theories. In a complex life with highs and lows, successes and failures and many moves from poverty to riches and back again than most people see, she remained remarkably un-neurotic. She came home from Spain and decided not to marry Peter the romantic Hungarian she fell in love with there. She intended to, but once she came home and met James Laverty who had written her nice cheering letters while she was abroad, she decided that there was going to be no going back to the Hungarian, except once, briefly, to tell him she couldn't marry him.

James was not an obvious provider; his finances took a down-swing but possibly thanks to the inner calm she got from her hours cooking, Maura Laverty was able to take that in her stride and through her writings carved out a living for them all, herself, her husband and their two girls and a boy. It was not only the Power of Positive Cooking that kept her so calm and so successful at a time when employment of any kind was hard to get and she had the added stigma of being banned in her native country. It all seems funny now and almost an accolade but at the time it was bad for sales and bad for her reputation. She never fulminated about it but it did surprise her greatly. The book that was stopped temporarily by the censor was *Alone We Embark*, and I have seen a letter that Maura Laverty wrote full of puzzlement about this: "It won the Annual award of the Irish women writers club and when it was reviewed by *The Sign*, the national Catholic magazine of America, they said it was as wholesome as home made bread."

The comparison must have pleased Maura Laverty greatly since it would have been the highest compliment you could pay her, and she was also relieved when the ban was lifted thanks to the appeal of Sir John Keane, Dr R. Collis and Mr A. Ganley. She was very firm in her letter and anxious to ensure that nobody should think it had been permanently forbidden to her country-men and women. Since the reprinting of *Never No More* by Virago a great deal of interest in Maura Laverty has come to the surface again in Ireland. Many tales are being told about her, and unusually or uncharacteristically among us Irish who don't speak well of each other automatically . . . all these tales are of her kindness and how she took her fame very lightly indeed. Because she *was* very famous by the time she died in 1966. She was the author of the exceptionally popular television series *Tolka Row* which had men, women and children looking in every week. She was a nationally important Problem Solver on the radio, whose mail bag was filled with letters from people who liked her practical brand of advice. She never made fun of any listener's letter nor milked it for its emotional charge; instead she strove to find a practical solution. Not only by advising them to make scones but in many other ways she helped the anxious and the distressed. I have heard from many who still have her kind letters of advice and concern which were beyond the call of her duty, for no one could have expected her to enter into private corres-pondence with the nation. But when her heart was touched she did.

People who played cards with her recall how interested she was in all their little doings and how she never played the Grande Dame even though she was a widely acclaimed writer and known outside Ireland as well. Her family speak of her affectionately and mourn that she should have had to leave the world so young. At fifty-eight she still had many more years of busy and eager living to do. They say she was quick to put a kind explanation on almost everything. Nobody was condemned utterly; they always had a redeeming factor in Maura Laverty's mind. Again that was something fairly rare in Dublin, as gossipy a city as I have ever enjoyed living and gossiping in. She wrote once to her sister about their father long dead. She said that he had a hard life, leaving what he was good at, which was farming, and being forced to come and work in the town as a draper. Maura's reading of it afterwards showed that she believed "father loved mother so much he would do anything for her including giving up his farm and coming into a world he didn't choose or understand".

Such generosity of spirit to those who went before and to the young who came after have made her a loved and well-remembered author. Her spirit lives on best in the character of Delia Scully, a portrait of the artist as a young girl in Ballyderrig and Spain. That bundle of eagerness and sensitivity is what turned into the woman later, and it is a great sadness to know that we really do have to say goodbye to her on the last page of this book. Maura Laverty wrote about other people in her other novels but the day that Delia left Spain the door is closed on her revelations about herself.

Maeve Binchy, London, 1985

CHAPTER ONE

I WAS seventeen and a half when I arrived in Madrid that November morning in 1924.

From the moment the train sidled into the Madrid suburbs I was at the window watching for Señora Basterra. She had written to say how I would recognize her: "a mink coat, crocodile shoes and bag and a black felt cloche." I saw her long before she saw me. There was no mistaking that mink coat. Among all the fur coats in the Estacion del Norte it stood out on its own. There was such a natural sleekness in the way the glossy fur clung to those big curves that it seemed to be actually growing on them.

I started up the platform towards her, lugging my one bit of baggage—an antique dress basket with two straps and a handle of plaited wire. Still she did not see me. Her eyes caught me for a second, but they threw me away at once and continued their little darting runs among the other people who were getting off the train. Could I be mistaken? As I came nearer I knew I was not. There were the crocodile shoes, almost Chinese-small below the enormous pouffe of fur. There was the crocodile bag, gripped tightly at the clasp by both hands. There was the black cloche hat with side pieces that came down like a spaniel's ears along each plump cheek.

I stopped before her. "I'm Delia Scully from Ballyderrig," I said. It took her startled blue eyes a full minute to parse and analyse me and then her lips puckered as if she were sucking raw rhubarb. My heart sank, for I guessed she did not like the looks of her new governess.

Looking back now, I cannot find it in myself to blame her. To someone expecting "a refined, steady, ladylike girl"—which was how the references sent by the Wicklow

5

nuns had described me—I must have been a little dis-
appointing.

I was wearing the navy nap school coat which had been
Gran's present for my sixteenth birthday, and I had grown
plenty since then. At home that coat had looked grand.
There had been some talk of starting me out in the world
with a new coat, but when the navy nap had been well
brushed, everyone agreed it had years of wear in it yet and
that a new coat would be money thrown out. They were so
taken up with admiring the grand hard-wearing stuff in the
coat that they overlooked the way it did not reach my knees,
and that a good inch and a half of chapped red wrist showed
between the cuffs and my brown woollen gloves. I cannot
say that these details seemed important to myself, either, at
the time. It was only after starting out on my travels that
I noticed them. Before I was a day out from Liverpool the
coats of the other women on the boat had me wishing I had
not taken such good care of the navy nap. I wore the coat
unbuttoned to show off the finery beneath. I thought
Madrid deserved the best in my wardrobe, so before leaving
the boat at Santander I had put on the light blue satin dress
Gran had bought me for my first dance the Christmas before.
Well, it *was* my nicest dress. Of course, I can see now that
it was not really suitable for travelling on the Continent in
winter. Wanting my hair to look nice for my first meeting
with Señora Basterra, I had washed it the day before landing
and had dried it on deck in the wind. There must have been
something wrong with the water on that boat. Or maybe it
was the soap. It could have been the wind for that matter.
Whatever it was, it did something queer to my hair. It was
never what could be called tractable, but that shampoo
finished it entirely. It stood up on my head like a furze bush
and pushed my navy straw hat up in the air.

And as if all this were not hard enough on the poor
woman who had come to meet a refined ladylike governess,
there was my make-up as well. I had shared a cabin on the

boat with a Liverpool Jewess of my own age who was on her way out to Cuba to get married. Her gorgeous collection of scented powders and creams and pastes filled me with envy. Before we parted, she generously gave me a box of white powder and a lipstick. I demurred, of course, but she assured me the shade of the lipstick did not suit her. How was I to know it would not suit me either? I had applied it in the lavatory of the train, following—as well as the swaying of the train would allow—the design favoured by my Jewish friend: a heavy daub on the lower lip, and on the upper lip two half-moons that doubled its size and made my mouth begin right where my nose left off. A good floury dab of the white powder, right, left and centre, and I had a face which would, I felt sure, make up in chic what my coat lacked in length.

With Señora Basterra looking at me like that I began to have doubts. I felt the urgent need of conversation, so I said with more brightness than I felt, "It was good of you to come to meet me and the weather so bad."

"Not at all," the señora said faintly, giving me a hand which would have been limp if it had not been so tightly packed into the little black kid glove. She gave a quick sigh then, as if to say, "Well, now that you're here I suppose I'll have to make the best of you."

It was a very subdued governess that arrived at the Basterra apartment in the Castellana. I was rushed to my room so quickly that my first sight of a Spanish interior gave only a bedazzled impression of black and white, of gleaming surfaces and dull matt tones—gleam of silver and mirror and floors, cream of walls, and the heavy darkness of great black chests and presses and tables. There seemed to be no end to the corridors.

"This is your room, Miss Scully," the señora said at last. It was a lovely room. An electric lamp for reading stood on a table beside the bed and there was a basin with hot and cold taps. I was so impressed with the splendour that was now mine that I recovered my poise. "The running water's grand and handy," I said chattily. "At home your back would be broken carrying every drop from the pump. It is bad enough when you have the pump in the yard, but there are some who have to walk a mile and more for the spring water for the tea. We had a pump, but I remember poor old Granny Mack, the creature was nearly eighty and she——"

The señora cut short my reminiscences. Without putting a tooth in it, she told me to wash my face before coming down to lunch. "Make-up is altogether out of place on a governess, Miss Scully," she said. "A little powder, perhaps, but lipstick or rouge, never. I hope you don't mind my saying so, but I must say you don't look very steady."

I could not have both of us made unhappy by leaving her with such a mistaken impression. I put on what I hoped was the grave serious look of a girl as steady as the Rock of Cashel—though it could not have been very effective seeing that I still wore that floury complexion and those outsize lips. "Sure I wouldn't care if I never saw a bit of lipstick— it's only that my lips get chapped if I don't use it," I lied.

"In that case a white salve would be just as effective and far more ladylike. I'd like you to tidy your hair, too. Oh, and another thing. That dress is far too flimsy for this weather. Put on something quieter and heavier."

I promised to do all this.

"Lunch will be served at one o'clock," she said at the door. "I'll send a maid to bring you down."

I was feeling a little hurt when she left me. I did not mind the criticism so much as the unfriendliness. I thought it queer of her to be so stand-offish when we had so much in common. She was born in Baltinglass, County Wicklow, next door to my own county, and had once been a governess like myself. She had even been sent out to Spain by the same Wicklow nuns she had to thank for me. I had come primed with the latest Wicklow gossip, sure that she would love a chat about old times. I soon discovered that her big aim was to persuade herself and Madrid that those old times had never been. To this end, she had discarded her Irish accent and had cultivated the way of speaking of the English colony. She liked to pretend that her life began on the day she married her rich cork merchant, and that poor little Peggy Kelly had never existed. In a way, you could not blame her. Peggy Kelly had known hardship enough, by all accounts. As time went on, I discovered that she was not really so unfriendly as she seemed. It was just that she felt she must be always on the alert in case a soft word might make anyone forget what was due to her grandeur.

I looked at my watch—Gran's gold watch. It was really a pocket-watch but I wore it on my wrist in a leather case which, unfortunately, hid all the gold. Half-past twelve— I had thirty minutes to unpack and make myself fit to meet the family. I unpacked the dress-basket and hung my clothes in the wardrobe. That left me twenty-five minutes in which to deglamourize myself. Off came the blue satin. I washed off the lipstick and powder and plastered down my hair with a wet brush. Then I put on my brown tweed skirt and my biscuit-coloured jumper. When I looked at myself in the glass I decided that so far as appearances went I might be going to sit down to bacon-and-cabbage in Ballyderrig instead of high lunch in Madrid.

A little brisk maid with a lovely friendly smile and eyes as brown as bog-water took me to the salon. She glided so noiselessly along the corridor before me in her rope-soled canvas slippers that my own heavy-shod steps sounded like the Curragh of soldiers bringing up the rear.

The señora was watching for me with an anxious face. When she had a good look at me the anxiety went and she gave a little relieved nod. She was even fatter without the fur coat. Her knitted two-piece of fine beige wool clung to her hills and hollows in a way that made her appear to be wearing nothing beneath it. Just the same, it was plain that she had been lovely when she was young and slim. She still had the deep blue eyes and the fair skin and fluffy hair that Spaniards, surfeited with dark-complexioned women, often find irresistible.

I was introduced to the three little boys and to Señor Basterra, who looked a good deal older than his wife. He shook hands with me absent-mindedly, and then rubbed the back of his head and looked at his watch in the way a man will when he is being kept from something important by something unimportant.

Meals were very important to Señor Basterra. I never saw anything like that man's appetite. He would eat enough off one course to do four turf-cutters and then attack the next course like a man who has been on hunger-strike for a week. There is this to be said for him: he showed the value of his food. He was even fatter than his wife. A dumpling in shape and colour. The suety shade of his skin was relieved by a small red mouth and two eyes as big and as black as prunes. Most of his hair was lost and his face seemed bigger and fatter because of the way that suety complexion extended right up to the back of his head. His heavy chin was covered with talc—it could be seen and smelled a mile away—and a black stubble showed through the powder. In the four months I stayed with the Basterras I never saw the señor without a stubbly chin. I did not blame him. I knew that some men have beards that grow quickly. Mike Brophy at home was like that. He would shave himself for Mass on Sunday morning but, if he were going to a dance that evening, he might have to shave again. Judy Ryan, who was engaged to him, told me that his beard was so rough that often and often she had to chase him away when he wanted a kiss, though she might be dying for one herself.

The children were nine, eight and six, grave-eyed, dark-skinned little creatures dressed in long-trousered sailor suits and with their hair slicked down with eau-de-cologne. They were so much alike that I could tell one from the other only by their size. They were so thin and wiry that they looked like poor relations of their parents.

A gong sounded and we went in to lunch, the señores to the dining-room, the children and myself to the breakfast room. Well, there I was with the three beings towards whom, if I was to believe the warnings and counsels of the Wicklow nuns, I had a terrifying responsibility. "You will be in the place of a second mother to them," Sister Ligouri had said to me. "You must treat them like tender plants." The three tender plants were watching me with breathless interest. Their stares were so feverishly intent that I was embarrassed and found it difficult to start to eat. I tried staring them back, but the three pairs of black eyes were too much for me. I gave in and started on my soup with as nonchalant an air as I could manage. When I had swallowed a few spoonfuls, I heard Javier, the youngest, let out a long breath of disappointment.

"She doesn't do it," said José, the middle one, and his voice sounded cheated.

"What did I tell you?" said Manolo in a lordly way. "Only the old ones do it."

"Do what?" I asked.

"Take out their teeth," Manola told me. "Miss Rice always took out hers and put them in her handkerchief before meals."

"Not on Sundays, of course," José put in. "On Sundays we always have lunch with Papa and Mamma. She ate *muy poco* on Sundays."

"When you get old will you take out your teeth?" Javier wanted to know. I could see he was hoping I would be at hand whenever I came to the interesting stage of having spare parts.

I was hoping I would not. Not that this first glimpse of governessing in Spain had made me want to rush home immediately, but I certainly had no intention of remaining a governess all the days of my life. I had no very well defined plans for the future, but I had a simple and lively belief that my governessing was to be a prelude to something grand and wonderful. I think I had some vague notion that I would probably do as Señora Basterra had done and win the love of a wealthy Spaniard and his hand in marriage. Heaven help my head. I was not long in Madrid until I found out that a governess's chances of marrying any man— let alone a wealthy man—were about a million to one. Peggy Kelly had good reason to be proud and stand-offish. She had pulled off a coup that had no parallel in Spanish history.

· · · · ·

Miss Carmody was the first and the best friend I made in Spain. She had been a great friend of Miss Rice, and the children introduced us when we met in the Retiro one evening. She was from Wexford, a slim, pale, dark-haired woman with a severe mouth but very friendly grey eyes. I took to her at once. She must have liked me, too, for she asked me to have tea with her in the Molinero on the following Thursday.

The Molinero was a café at the beginning of the Gran Viá where the governesses had tea on their afternoon off. You could get a nice *té completo* there for one peseta and twenty-five cents, but I preferred the Spanish equivalent of tea, the meal they call *la merienda*, generally chocolate and churros. The chocolate was as thick as gruel. You mopped it up with your churros and then washed the whole lot down with a glass of sweetened water. The churros were gorgeous little sticks of batter fried to golden crispness in boiling oil and then rolled in castor sugar. You could buy them in the street too. White-coated men went around with steaming baskets of them, singing at the top of their voices: "*Churrero! Churros calientes!*" I used to love to stand in the street and watch the churros being made. The *churrero* kept his pot of oil seething over a brazier. When the batter was ready he poured it into a contraption that looked like a funnel with a handle at the side. The funnel was held over the oil, the handle was turned and out came a rope of creamy batter. By keeping the funnel circling round and round as he turned the handle, the churrero was able to make the rope of batter fall in coils that turned crisp and brown the minute the boiling oil received them. Then the lovely glistening gilded thing was lifted out—a spring for a giant's clock—and snipped into six-inch lengths with a scissors. For a penny you got three churros, well dusted with sugar. If you did not mind being thought common, you ate them—greasy and hot and sugary—as you went along. I minded being thought common, but then, as always, my lower nature triumphed over my desire for the good opinions of others, and hardly a day passed that I did not risk being thought common.

I enjoyed my evening with Miss Carmody. She introduced me to several governesses and I could see that they had a great respect for her. She told me about her job. It sounded a lovely one. Two hundred and fifty pesetas a month—a hundred more than I was getting, and nothing to do but accompany a girl of nineteen on walks and to the theatre, and to her friends' houses. She was with a family called Juanes, very wealthy people with a big house in the Paseo del Prado and a villa in Bilbao where they passed the summer. Miss Carmody had been with them for fourteen years, and Luisita, her charge, had made her promise that she would never leave them. From little things she said, I gathered that her own people were well off, and that she could have been living at home if she wished. I wondered that she should choose to stay in Spain.

That evening in the Molinero was the start of a friendship that lasted a long time. Though we never got beyond calling each other "Miss Carmody" and "Miss Scully," I have never been so intimate with any other woman. We met frequently after that. We went to the pictures a few times and when Miss Carmody was free, which was often, she would come for walks with the children and myself.

Seeing me in such good company made the other governesses more friendly towards me. Up to this, they had not
taken much notice of me, but now they let me walk beside
them in the Castellana, or, if the sun was warm and they
were sitting on a bench in the Retiro, they would make
room for me. I was grateful, for it was lonely enough that
first winter. I thought it was kind of these girls who had
been in Spain a good while and who were so well dressed
and smart, to talk to anyone so raw and shabby and awkward
as they made me feel. That was a thing that puzzled me:
With Miss Carmody—though she was smarter than any of
them—I did not feel at any disadvantage at all, but with the
others I always felt inferior. The navy nap coat was chiefly
to blame. That may sound snobbish and petty of me, but
I doubt if any girl could have kept her poise among a crowd
of women while wearing a coat like mine.

When I got in with the girls I was astonished at all they
found to dislike in Spain. I know now, of course, what was
wrong: the unfortunate creatures were all homesick and
discontented and this grumbling was only their way of showing how much they resented their exile. There was sound
reason for their discontent. Good food, a lovely home and
an easy time did not make up to them for their lonely un-
natural life. There was no social life for governesses, no
parties, no dances. The English-speaking colony cold-
shouldered them. Their aristocratic employers kept them
in their place. They were living in the most romantic country in the world and they might as well have been immured
in a convent for all the male society they had. Not even the
youngest and prettiest had a boy. There they were, their
youth curdling on them in a killing monotony that was
broken only by the weekly tea in the Molinero and the
monthly Children of Mary meeting in the Reparadoras Convent. Small wonder they were discontented. They did not
really believe the things they said, but to listen to them one
would think there was nothing good or lucky in the coun-

try. The women were vain and lazy, the food was uneatable, the shopkeepers were robbers and the climate was deadly. No one ever washed properly, three-quarters of the people were barbarians, and all the men were fiends with one idea —the ruination of women and of Irish women in particular. It was always the older and plainer governesses who had the worst things to say about the men.

At that time I did not know enough about Spain and Spaniards to argue with my betters. But, short though my time in the country had been, there was one thing I *did* know, and that was that the food was grand. I could not let it go with the governesses when they said Spanish food was un-eatable. I knew good well-cooked food when I ate it—it was not for nothing I had lived all my life with Gran and she the best cook in the County Kildare. When criticisms of the food started I forgot my navy nap and spoke up. It would have been better for my prestige had I kept silent. "You're easily pleased," they said shortly, meaning that they thought I had never been used to much. If they knew but all, it was they who were showing up themselves and their homes in a bad light. Gran had taught me to see that well-reared people who have been used to full and plenty in their homes will always eat what is put before them, and that it is only the unfortunates who have been brought up on the skin of an onion that give trouble at the table. You would not need to go further than Soup Dunne to see the truth of that. He was a farmer who belonged to one of the richest families in Ballyderrig, people who for all their money had a very poor way of living. He was at Naas Fair one day when he decided to treat himself to dinner at Mrs. Lawler's new eating-house. He had never seen the like of it—wait-resses with caps, and flowers on the table and all. A plate of lovely clear soup was put before him. Now, Dunne's only previous acquaintance with soup had been to get it in a bowl with half a dozen potatoes and a lump of meat. To him, soup was nothing but the water the meat had been boiled in. He took one look at the plate of *consommé* and made for the door. "Don't you like your soup, sir?" the waitress asked him. "You may take it away," said Dunne with spirit. "Let them that ate the meat drink the soup." From the minute that story got around he was never called anything but Soup Dunne. It seemed to me that many of the governesses might be christened "Soup."

However, as I said before, their grousing was not to be minded. Behind it, they were decent well-behaved women who would not do anyone a bad turn. I disliked only one of them—Miss Fanning, a middle-aged woman who had been a long time in Spain. She had hair the colour of dried blood and a long pale face. Some nervous trouble had affected the lid of her right eye, making it droop in a perpetual leer. My three boys did not like Miss Fanning. Manolo called her "*El Loro de Guatemala*"—"The Parrot of Guatemala." In his stamp collection he had a Guatemalan stamp which showed a parrot. Miss Fanning's hooked nose and drooping eyelid gave her a startling resemblance to the Guatemalan bird. Naturally, it was not because of her looks that I disliked the woman. None of us can help our faces for we are all as God made us. I disliked her because she hurt me sorely.

It happened through Patsy Curley's shoes. The winter before, Gran gave Patsy a handful of money to make me a pair of shoes that would last. He did not cheat her. He made me a pair of shoes in which you could walk through the whole Bog of Allen and never get your feet wet. They had the best of leather in them and iron tips on the heels. They made my feet look big, to be sure. Gran used to tease me about that. She christened the right shoe "28B" and the left "29B" after Tom Murphy's two canal boats. Apart from that, there was not a word to be said against them.

One afternoon shortly before Christmas Señora Basterra took the boys out shopping and left me free. I went off to the Retiro. On a bench near the Murillo Gate I found four of the governesses. Miss Fanning was one of them. I had barely sat down when she leaned over and took a good look at my shoes.

"That's a grand pair of shoes, Miss Scully," she said admiringly.

I surveyed the shoes, with new respect. "They're a good strong pair," I agreed modestly. "I'm after getting plenty of wear out of them and they never let in a drop." They were all looking at the shoes now and making little sounds of admiration. I was delighted. Praise for the shoes was praise for the man who had made them, the woman who had paid for them, and the place they had come from.

"You shouldn't be wearing them every day," Miss Fanning said. "You should take care of them. You won't be able to buy anything like them in Spain." The way her voice choked on the last word gave me a sudden warning and I looked up quickly. The woman's face was as red as her hair with suppressed laughter. She had been jeering me.

That is a hurtful thing—to discover you are being mocked by someone to whom you have been talking with your heart in your hand. It has happened to me a few times in my life and always it has given me a sick jolt of hurt and dismay. Of fright too, for it is surely frightening to come up against people who get their enjoyment out of hurting others. The experience has never hurt me so much as it did that day in the Retiro. I can still see the amused faces of those four women, but clearest of all is the convulsed face of Miss Fanning and she leering at me with that grotesque eyelid.

My cheeks blazed. I wanted to tell her what I thought of her but I had a horrid fear that if I spoke at all I would start crying. Miss Carmody came along just in time to prevent this ultimate humiliation.

"I have been looking for you, Miss Scully." Her voice was like the sudden lighting of a lamp in a black-dark room.

My face and the faces of the others made her sense that a scene was imminent. "Come on," she said, abruptly. "I want you to come home to tea with me." Without giving me time for another word she linked me off. She walked me quickly out into the Calle de Alfonso XII and down the Paseo del Prado, talking of anything and everything as we went. We were in her room in the Juanes house before she admitted having noticed anything. "What happened between yourself and Miss Fanning?" she asked casually.

It was then the crying started. I have always envied women who can cry quietly and with restraint, who can weep their hearts out without disturbing a feature or making a sound. I have never been able to cry like that. Not that I often cry, but when I do it is a stormy business of jerky sobs and torrential tears. Miss Carmody tried everything to make me control myself—eau-de-cologne, scolding, a glass of water. She might as well have tried to dam the Poulaphouca Waterfall. I had to have my cry out. In between the sobs I gulped out the story of the shoes.

"Well, upon my word, Miss Scully, I'm surprised at you. I thought you had more sense than to let poor Miss Fanning's ill-breeding upset you." The maid brought in our tea and Miss Carmody poured me a cup. "Here, dry your eyes and drink this. You're a very foolish girl to be crying for nothing."

I was not crying for nothing. I was crying for much more than the insult to Patsy Curley's shoes. Though I did not know it until that moment, I was crying for Gran and lost friends and the life I loved. Miss Fanning had merely opened the sluice gates for the tears that had been gathering in me since I left Ballyderrig. Names and words bobbed like flotsam on the rush of my grief. Miss Carmody salvaged them, and understood. She busied herself with the table. "This cake looks good," she said. "Have some."

I did. The cake was lovely. When I had eaten a slice and had taken the tea my sobbing abated to a mere snivel.

Those clear grey eyes looked at me, weighing me up. "You ought to go home to Ireland," she said at length.

"But I like Spain," I protested. "Even though I'm a bit lonesome, I love being here. Anyway there's no place for me at home since Gran died. And there's no way I could earn my living in Ireland for I wasted my chances at school." There was silence for a second and then I veered back to my grievance. "It wasn't so much her laughing at the shoes I minded. But why did she have to do it? I mean why should she want to hurt me? I never did anything on her."

"Of course you didn't." Miss Carmody cut me another slice of cake. "But, as you'll find out for yourself, governessing is a queer life. It does queer things to the governesses. The only ones who weather it well are the born old maids. The others become very bitter."

"Why do they stay here if they hate it so much?" I burst out.

"Because, like yourself, most of them have no place at home," she said quietly. "They have a smattering of education that wouldn't earn them their keep anywhere but here. They are delighted with the life during the first year. Then they discover its loneliness and humiliations and they talk bravely of going home to any kind of job as soon as they have a few pounds saved. But they never go. By the time they have their fare gathered the damage has been done. The luxury of life in a wealthy home has corroded their pride and their spirit, and they stay on. A few of them— those who have backbone—get out before the trap closes on them. But they don't go home."

In listening to Miss Carmody I was forgetting my troubles. Her voice was so easy to listen to, so calm and low and rich. "What do they do, Miss Carmody? The ones who stop being governesses, I mean."

"They become what they themselves call *profesoras*. They go into cheap lodgings and earn a living by hiring themselves out as dueñas. They call this giving English lessons. Actually, they are merely watchdogs for the girls they chaperon. They haven't an easy life, but at least they are free to be themselves once they have deposited the señoritas on their doorsteps."

"Do they go to dances and parties?" I asked eagerly.

Miss Carmody's eyes twinkled. "It has happened," she said. "Some of them even have sweethearts and get married."

"What age do you have to be before you can become a dueña?"

"A little more than seventeen," she smiled. I did not care. My mind was made up and I could wait. The luxury would not soften me. Nothing on earth would keep me from getting out of the trap.

Miss Carmody stood up. "But here we are talking and I haven't yet told you why I went looking for you this evening." A shade of embarrassment fell on her manner. "Look, Miss Scully, Luisita asked me as a favour to get rid of some things for her. They're new, really, but you know how these girls are with their clothes. They wear them twice and then tire of them. She is about your size. There's a coat—and a few dresses. Would you be offended?"

My face gave her her answer. "Wouldn't I be made up?" I stammered.

"Wait. I'll get them." She disappeared for a minute and returned with an armful of clothes which she dumped on the bed. "They're they are. Try them on. I only hope they'll fit you."

I tried them on. In ecstasy, I tried them on. They might have been made for me.

(Oh, Miss Carmody, Luisita never asked you to get rid of them! I know now that you begged them for me. And I'd go begging through Ireland for you in return for the happiness you gave me that evening.)

The blue dress first—a blue as deep and tender as the violets in Loughlin's Grove, the woollen stuff as fine and soft and warm as the coat of a newly dropped lamb—a square neck to the tight bodice and a pleated skirt. With trembling hands I fastened the little buttons at the side and looked in the glass. That was not Delia Scully! That was a girl out of a fashion book. Delia Scully's eyes were never so blue as that. Surely her figure was never so slight? Off with the blue and on with the red silk, a heavy gorgeous clinging silk with the brave exciting red of rowanberries. The Rowanberry Girl was even less like Delia Scully than the Violet Girl. If only Margaret Mary Dempsey of the Far Bog could see me now! The brown two-piece came next, a brown that put me in mind of Leadbeater's avenue in autumn. The deep matt brown of rich leaf-mould was in the skirt, the knitted top had a thread of gold woven through the wool—October sunshine on chestnut-trees. That two-piece almost made me look the ladylike person Señora Basterra had been hoping for. But there was no ladylike reserve in the way I carried on over the dresses. I stammered and stuttered and displayed my ignorance of the refinements of dressmaking by exclaiming in wonder at the bound seams and the beautiful stitching and the little snap-fastened gadgets under the shoulder seams which, Miss Carmody explained, were to keep my shoulder-straps in place.

But where am I leaving the coat? No other man-made delight has ever given me such joy as that lovely coat of thick oatmeal cloth. It had a small round collar of some short curled fur, light brown, the very shade of my hair. You could have worn that coat inside out and have held your head high, for the rich satin lining was as luxurious-looking as the cape Molly McDermot sent home from America for her mother to wear at Maggie's wedding—and that is saying much, for Mrs. McDermot's American cape has been the talk of Ballyderrig from that day to this. I tried the coat buttoned and unbuttoned. I buried my hands in the pockets. I caressed the fur collar with my chin. I viewed it from the right and from the left. I craned over my shoulder to get a back view. Whichever way I looked at it, the coat was perfect.

Miss Carmody had been watching me while I preened and pirouetted. "Well, are you satisfied?" she said at length. There was nothing I could say. Dr. Johnson himself would have been short of words. I would have liked to have hugged her, but from the very first I had sensed that reserve of hers, a reserve which even in later years never permitted more than a handshake between us. I managed to mumble something inadequate.

"When do you get paid?" she asked briskly. I had been paid the week before and had already squandered half my salary on odds and ends—sweets and a pink pearl necklace and a bottle of lovely perfume called *Jardines de España*. I had seventy-five pesetas left—about two pounds ten.

Miss Carmody nodded. "It will do. I'll call for you on Thursday and take you shopping. You'll need a hat and a pair of shoes. And now you had better go or you won't be in time for supper and then Señora Basterra will have something to say to you."

She put the clothes in a case for me and sent me sailing away on a rosy cloud. At the door I was halted by a thought which had been nudging me all evening.

"Miss Carmody," I said diffidently, "how is it that you never got bitter? I mean, how is it that governessing didn't do queer things to you like it did to some of the others?"

"Did it not, Miss Scully?" Her voice sounded pleased. The grey eyes looked away from me then, and she spoke more to herself than to me. "Maybe it's because those others came out here looking for love and were disappointed." There was a note of quiet surprise in it, as if she were realizing something for the first time. "I came out to escape from love and I succeeded."

Not even my curiosity as to what she had meant could take from my delight that night. When I had bathed the three boys and had put them to bed, I tried on the clothes again. They were even nicer than I had believed. I could not stop marvelling at the wonderful coincidence which had made Luisita Juanes decide to weed her wardrobe just when I most needed clothes. That is the kind of coincidence which has been happening to me all my life. God is nearer than the door, is an old saying, and I am always discovering the truth of it. Whenever I get reason to be miserable or to doubt the goodness of the human heart, someone comes along with a gift of warmth and kindness and generosity and then I know for certain that man is made in God's image and likeness, and that the world is a grand place after all.

Life seemed very pleasant that winter night in Madrid. There was great comfort in the thought that I need never wear the navy nap again.

CHAPTER TWO

AT the end of January I walked out of my job. Señora Basterra and myself had the father and mother of a row, and I made the grand gesture of walking out of her house with three and fivepence in my pocket. It rather spoiled things when Miss Carmody marched me straight back again, and made me apologize and ask permission to stay until I had found another post. The señora conceded my request with a fine show of magnanimity. She had planned a trip to Barcelona with her husband for the following week, and she would have been almost as awkwardly placed without a governess as I without a roof.

I had had a whole series of rows with the señora. There were two major tremors before the final earthquake and they were due to two distinct causes: a song called "Paddy

McGinty's Goat," and the low drop of blood which my
poor mother had always insisted was evident in me and
which she swore I did not get from her side of the family.
The immediate cause of the final eruption was Mr. Robertson's weak kidneys.

In those days I used to pity myself for the way she found
fault with me. Looking back now, I can see that she had
plenty to put up with. I was such an untutored young one,
unbiddable too, and very ready with the quick word if I
thought I was being scolded in the wrong. I doubt if she
would have put up with me at all only for the way the
children and myself got on together. Among the governesses, the Basterra boys had the reputation of being very
difficult. I was told that they had driven poor Miss Rice
nearly cracked before she packed her bag and escaped to a
job in Seville. I found them very likeable children and easy
enough to manage.

I enjoyed our walks abroad. These were illicit excursions,
for I was supposed to take my charges straight to the Retiro
and home again. But the park bored them and me, so often
we turned to the right at the Plaza Cibeles and dandered up
the Calle Alcala, across the teeming Puerta del Sol and into
Old Madrid. It had welcome and colour and excitement in
it, this part of the city. The rickety old houses with their
barred windows and crazy-looking stairs were so much more
friendly than the grand modern buildings on the other side
of the Puerta del Sol. The people were more friendly too,
mostly workmen and well-fleshed housewives. And, of
course, scores and scores of little dressmakers' apprentices
with brief neat skirts and tapping heels, so demure and
Madonna-like as to sleek centre-parted hair and black lace
mantilla, so cometherish as to glancing eyes and cheeky
walk. I felt at home among these people. They were the
common people. They were my own kind.

When I mentioned these excursions to the other governesses they were horrified.

"But the men, Miss Scully! Are you not afraid of those rough workmen?"

Now why on earth have some women such a terror of men? I have found them, on the whole, to be harmless, likeable creatures. And those Spanish workmen seemed to be no different from the men at home—only better-looking, maybe.

"But don't they say things to you, Miss Scully?"

Of course they said things, and I would have been very upset if they had not. I already realized that a woman would need to be as ugly as Poll Ash and as old as Granuaile not to have a quick flower thrown to her in the street. I realized that I might throw my hat at life on the day I failed to win a *piropo* from a Madrileño. The workmen said things, but they said nothing that a girl would not hear every day in the week from the well-dressed hot-eyed men who sauntered speculatively through the Retiro or along the Castellana. The only difference was this. When the workman whispered light-heartedly in your ear as he passed, "*Qué bien estás, rica!*" you felt grateful for the compliment and glad to be young and not a sight. When the pouchy-eyed scented dandy said it, there was something in his face and voice that made you feel it was the pity of the world that Mike Brophy and a few of the lads couldn't lay their hands on him. The workmen wakened something warm and glad and proud in me. The dirty-eyed gentlemen turned that something into a thing to be ashamed of.

The governesses thought I was doing very wrong in taking the children off the beaten track, but I could not see that it did them any harm. Far from it, indeed. They always came home in much better spirits than if we had gone to the Retiro, less ready to quarrel and with a better appetite for their supper. I think I was born knowing that the greatest harm can come to body and soul out of boredom, and that the places and things and people that quicken you are usually good and healthy. So we went on our excursions, the four of us. The boys told me where they wanted to go and I took them.

There was just one street through which I refused to take them, and that was the Calle Marqués de Cubas. Half-way down that street a blind beggarwoman with one arm—God bless the mark—had her pitch. Those Spanish beggars shocked and terrified me, the poor unfortunate crippled creatures. How was I to know that a world which held the loveliness of Ballyderrig, held too these frightening awful miseries? And the most terrifying thing about them was the way they displayed their afflictions for the compassion of their fellows. When I had to pass the man who sat on the ground outside the Teatro Novedades with his ragged trousers rolled up to show the withered limbs, my whole inside used to squeeze up into a hard hurting lump. And I always wanted to scream when the boy who haunted the Calle Barquillo came up to me and thrust his poor maimed hand right into my face. But the worst of them all was that creature in Marqués de Cubas. Not because of her terrible poor eyes which looked, God bless them, as if they had been put in back to front, not even because of that naked twitching stump of an arm. It was her voice that killed me, her high agonized whine of a voice. "*Una limosna por el amor de Dios . . . una limosna por el amor de Dios. . . .*" She whined it again and again and again, scraping her mendicant's saucer of tin against the wall as an accompaniment to her song of Purgatory. I have tried to bury that song with other frightening troubling things in the untended part of my memory, but sometimes it forces its way up like steam from a dunghill, and then I could nearly go out of my mind with sorrow for all the black misery that is in the world. It was wrong and selfish to me to have kept away from that poor woman. My Christian duty was to go back to her often and often and give her an alms. I could not do it. Such things were too new to be bearable. To have been able to vanquish horror with pity I would have needed the loving heart of Saint Francis himself.

The boys, the little fiends, knew how I felt. When they wanted to blackmail sweets or ices or other forbidden between-meals dainties out of me, nowhere would do them to walk but the Calle Marqués de Cubas. Sometimes the price they put on their mercy was beyond me and then, after a bit of haggling, they would agree to settle in return for a visit to our old Chinaman. Though I loved the Chinaman as much as they, and would have liked nothing better than to have visited him every day, I was wise enough to keep him in reserve for difficult occasions. He stood in the street outside the Telefonica Building in the Red de San Luis, selling his necklaces of pink and white pearls, which dangled from his right arm making a gorgeous gleaming maniple, as sumptuous as any Father Dempsey ever wore at Benediction. A little shrunken old fellow, our Chinaman, with scanty white hair, withered ochre cheeks and dim brown eyes. A shabby old fellow, but how neat and pleasant and tidy. There he was all day long, doing his funny little jig from one foot to another to keep himself from freezing, and looking so far from home among all those vital, warm-blooded, handsome people. He knew us well and would smile and nearly nod the head off his shoulders as we came up. Sometimes Juanita, the Basterra cook, gave us a parcel for him. How the dim old eyes would brighten, then, how the head would nod. He had a little Spanish wife who was as neat and as cheerful and as ancient as himself. We called him Señor Thley Pelleta. That was because his Chinese tongue could not manage the letters "r" and "s." He would hold up a necklace to a passer-by and pipe out the price in his thin reedy voice. Tres pesetas was the price, but our little Chinaman could only say "Thley pelleta." We had to watch the time when we went to see old Thley Pelleta. It was dangerous for us to remain in his vicinity after half-

past four. Miss Glennie, a friend of Señora Basterra, had a
job in the Telefonica, and she got out at five. It would
have been woe betide me if the señora was informed that I
was seen so far from the Retiro with her sons.

Good-bye, then, to Thley Pelleta, when the big clock in
the Puerta del Sol gongs the half-hour. Down with us
quickly through the crowds in the Gran Via and Alcalá,
and home with us more slowly along the safety zone of the
Castellana.

It is a suddenly disquieting place, this tree-lined Castellana, in the half-light of the winter's afternoon, a place in
which my own thoughts and my own feelings resent molesta-
tion from little chattering black-eyed boys, however likeable. There are so many things here to unsettle me, so much
to splinter my content.

A student and a modestilla sit hand-in-hand on a bench
under the bare trees, sheltered from the cold by the warmth
of each other's eyes. The joy of belonging is about them,
making me feel shut-out and alone, and I try not to hear
my heart's rebel cry for something I can't put a name
to.

A hawker pads along with his tray of Christmas toys.
Christmas, indheadh! Much the Spanish people knew about
Christmas. Next Monday they'll be holding the live market
at home in Ballyderrig. Talk about Christmas happiness!
Sport and joy and life they'll have, with the turkeys gob-
bling and the men in the best of humour and the women
spending the half-crowns like pence.

An old woman comes out of the church of San Ignacio
and crosses the road towards Jorge Juan. I notice the spare
little back of her and the brave set of her grey head and my
heart gives a sudden twist. I used to know someone who
had the same tidy busy little walk. But I mustn't let myself
think of her, not of the brave grey head nor the straight
little back nor of anything at all about her. If I let thoughts
of her in on me, I'll get beguiled down a road where there

is no Chinaman, no Miss Carmody, no new oatmeal coat—nothing at all to come between me and my loss.

.   .   .   .

For the two hours between supper and the boys' bedtime we used to have a great time bartering games and stories and songs. We had a preference for games with a rhyme to them, so I taught them:

> I am the wee falorie man,
> The tattered and torn Irishman.
> Will you do all that ever you can
> To help the wee falorie man?

and,

> I am a poor soldier
> Lately come home
> Blind of an eye,
> Lame of a thigh.
> What'll you give me to make me up?

and,

> Come beating Bellsie Bray
>   With a hey ro raddy O,
> And also cup of tay
>   With a hey ro raddy O.

In return I was taught such classics as:

> A los pieds de usted, Conchita,
>   Que tal sique, que tal sique la mamá?
> La mamá sique malita
>   Con ataques, con ataques que le dá.

And,

> Carta del rey ha venido
>   Para Maria y Dolores—Dolores,
> Que se vayán a la guerra
>   A defender su colonel,
>   A defender su colonel.

There was one little game we particularly liked. It had a lovely rhyme which went,

> Palomita blanca,
> Que lleves en el pico
> Aceite y vinagre
> Para Jesusito.
> Jesusito te dirá,
> De mentira o de verdad
> En esta, en esta, en esta mano está.
>
> Little white dove,
> Who carry in your beak
> Oil and vinegar
> For little Jesus. . . .

Religion entered into most of their games and all of their stories. Judging by those stories, Spain was very short of fairies, with not a pooka or leprechaun in the whole country. Instead, they had nature legends connected with the Holy Life and Death. I learned that the rosemary puts forth new leaves every Friday in memory of the first Good Friday, that forget-me-nots had been pale colourless little things until Our Lady made much of them one day by spreading her Son's baby clothes to dry on a bed of them, since when they have had the colour of her mantle. And periwinkles were unknown before the Carrying of the Cross: as *el buen Cristo* walked to Calvary the bitter tears that fell from His eyes sprang up under His feet as the flowers we call periwinkles. What else? That it is a mortal sin to kill a martin, because it was a little pitying martin that plucked the cruel thorns from His head, and that during Masstime in Valladolid on Ascension Day all the leaves on the trees fold themselves one upon another in the form of tiny crosses. There was no end to these legends.

I tried to repay the boys with Fineen the Rover and the banshee and Finn McCool. I sang all our own songs too.

That was the rock I perished on. I was summoned to the *salon* one evening to answer a charge of corrupting Manolo. His mother had asked him to sing for a roomful of visitors, and he had obliged with "Paddy McGinty's Goat." I had not seen anything wrong with a song that was sung by the best-reared people in Ballyderrig, but when Señora Basterra had finished with me she had reduced myself and the unfortunate goat to the lowest terms of vulgarity and double-meaning.

Her poor opinion of me might have been depressing if I had not made friends with the four maids—and this, by the same token, got me into worse disfavour. At home, when I had swapped books with poor Sarah Gorry or had gone gathering mushrooms with Paddy-the-Bag's daughters, my mother would upbraid me. "So the low drop is coming out in you," she would say, more in sorrow than in anger, meaning that some regrettable throwback in me was driving me into the company of people who should have been beneath the notice of the Scullys.

From the first, the low drop came out in me in Basterra's. Any governess worthy of the name would have been able to keep her place, which was half-way between the *salon* and the kitchen. My low drop dragged me down to the kitchen. Night after night, when the children were in bed, I went down and sat on the table and talked to Carmenchu the housemaid, and Flora the nurserymaid, and Pepita the parlourmaid, and Juanita the cook. I thank their friendship for the fact that in three months I learned more Spanish than a governess who knew how to keep her place would have learned in three years. Sometimes Gregorio the chauffeur joined us. The kitchen was forbidden to him as to me, but he was in love with Carmenchu, the girl from Vizcaya, and he could not keep away from her tall sinewy grace nor out of the line of fire of her narrow topaz eyes which pledged him over high cheekbones.

Flora was a Sevillana, full of southern languor and ease.

She had a sleeky indolent way of walking across the kitchen which made you think that at any moment now she would start rubbing her hips against somebody's legs and break into a lazy pleased purr. It was a delight to hear her speaking. The others lisped the slender "c" in the orthodox way but Flora gave it the liquid Andalusian softness which made every second word out of her mouth sound like a caress. She could sing too, tangos and coplas and Malagueñas. Her singing was always getting her into trouble, for in well-conducted Spanish houses the greatest crime a maid could commit was to sing at her work. That was hard on poor Flora who would have found it easier to wash without soap than without music. But she sang for us in the kitchen at night, very, very softly so as not to be heard in the *salon*. When she half-closed her heavy eyes and sang in that purple velvet voice of hers, Gregorio and Carmenchu would look down at the floor away from each other as if love and the pleasure of Flora's singing were too much to be borne together. Pepita would stop stitching and smile and sway, and Juanita would gently beat time with her pestle on the edge of the mortar in which she was crushing pine kernels. I learned any amount of songs from Flora. There was one tango I used to make her sing again and again.

> De donde, niña, vengo?
> De una casita que tengo
>   De bajo del pinar,
> De una casita
> Para una mujer bonita,
>   Que me quiere acompañar.

"Where am I coming from, girl?" the boy asks. "From my little house below the pinewood, the little house that is all for the lovely woman who will keep me company there." And then he goes on to entice her with a description of the furnishings—"and the set of blue delft that I bought at the fair." That tango appealed to me because it seemed to be a song that did not call for an Andalusian alone to sing. Word for word, you could put it into the mouth of any boy from any part of Ireland who would be coaxing a girl to marry him.

Pepita was my favourite. Pepita, the neat-bodied little housemaid who had been the first person in Spain to give me a friendly smile. There was no way out of loving that little girl, she was so gentle and obliging and good-humoured. *Simpatiquisima*—only the Spanish superlative for the unification of all lovable qualities can describe Pepita. And she was such a pleasant little thing to look at. It used to do my heart good to come down in the mornings and find her polishing the corridor. No getting down on all fours for floor-polishing in Spain. There Pepita would be with her foot through the strap of the slipper-like polisher—hands on hips, shoulders thrown back, left leg lightly braced and right leg guiding the polisher in lithe swift rhythm, like the smooth regular sweeps with which John Daly used to paint the chapel door. When she heard my step, she would turn her head with the quickness of a bird and flash me her welcoming smile. When Pepita's work was done, the needle was never out of her hand, for she was engaged to a mechanic in General Motors and intended to marry him as soon as her bottom drawer was filled. That bottom drawer was a revelation to me—such layers of exquisite underclothing, such piles of hemstitched bed and table linen. Every penny of her wages went on materials. By the same token, there was a thing I was noticing about Spanish girls: their fastidious personal ways. I hated admitting it even to myself, but those four maids—none of them earning more than two pounds a month—had a stock of handmade underclothes that would have taken the sight out of the eyes of many a well-off Irish girl. When I saw my own common shop-bought things of stockinette hanging on the line beside their beautiful garments, I was shamed into buying yards and yards of fine lawn which Pepita helped me to make up and embroider with *encrustacion* and other lovely Spanish stitches.

I remember Pepita with affection, but it is Juanita, the cook, that I have to remember with gratitude, for it was she who let me into the gorgeous secrets of Spanish cooking. Pepita and Carmenchu had a sweetheart apiece and Flora had five or six, but men had no place at all in Juanita's life. She hated men. It was an effort on her to prepare the special dishes that the señora sometimes ordered for her husband alone, and I doubt if she would have let Gregorio set foot in her kitchen at all if Carmenchu did not bribe her by doing far more than her share of the work in the kitchen. Poor Juanita's husband had strayed away from her to a widow who kept a lodging-house, and she took his desertion out on all his sex. She came from a village outside Madrid and she looked exactly what the unmotherly arid soil of Castile would produce, a stunted hardy olive-tree of a woman. You would say that she could thrive for months in the blazing sun without food or drink and not be the worse of it. Unlike most professional cooks, she was not stingy with her knowledge. As she stirred and mixed and blended and beat, she would give a patient answer to all my questionings. Sometimes she even lent me an apron and let me take hand a under her watchful guidance.

The señora discovered me at this one night. She ordered me upstairs and gave me a lecture which showed that she had the same exalted idea of the social standing of governesses as my poor mother had of what was due to the Scully family.

Señora Basterra might have saved her breath. I could no more have kept out of that kitchen than cattle that have tasted growing oats can be kept out of the crop. Anyway, what else was there for me to do? I was not wanted at the *salon* fire, and I would have gone daft up in my room with no one to talk to. I could have read, of course, but I preferred to do my reading after I went to bed—often I read until two in the morning. I had to have friendly company and the kitchen was the only place where I could get it. Even if the maids had not welcomed me, I would still have been drawn to the kitchen. I love kitchens. The preparation of food has always been to me what literature or music or painting is to others. It is such a kindly, friendly, unselfish art, the art of cooking, and every little step in the preparation of even the plainest dish is an opportunity for self-expression. That sprinkling of chopped parsley beaten into the mashed potatoes is so much more than the final touch demanded by the cookery books. It is the satisfaction of your natural craving for all lovely green-and-white things, things like the tips of grass spears piercing the snow on a morning in January. It is the expression of your wish to share these things with the people you are feeding. Glaze the top of an apple-tart and you are not merely adding sweetness and a deeper colour to the crust. You are voicing your love for all that is burnished and golden and gladdening in Nature and in people and in art. Cooking is the poetry of housework. But it is satisfying in twenty other different ways as well. There is a grand warm companionable feeling to be got out of the thought that every time you baste a roast or beat an egg, or do any other little ordinary kitchen job, you are making yourself one with the Grand Order of Homemakers, past, present and to come. And it does your nerves a world of good. Peel a basket of apples and watch the soothed feeling that comes over you as the knife slides smoothly between skin and juicy flesh—round and round, round and round, till each peel drops in a long unbroken curl. Or rub butter into flour for scones—there is something that I would recommend to neurotic people as a better tonic than anything their doctors could give them. The purity of the flour, the cool velvety feel of it, the gentle, incessant calm-giving motion of the finger tips—no tangle or turmoil could hold out against such homely comforting.

Juanita's cooking was wonderful. Those Spanish dishes! The rich soups and the melting omelets and the hot savoury casseroles of saffron-coloured rice and tomato-smothered macaroni; the fifty different kinds of milky fish with fifty different sauces for serving with them; the baked and the roast and the braised fowls, the turkeys stuffed with dried peaches and the chickens simmered to butter-tenderness in a delicate mushroom sauce laced with wine; the meats in haunting dark sauce and stewed in oil and roasted on the spit and grilled on the clean red-hot top of the stove, the desserts of orange-scented creams and smooth-fleshed custards, the light, fruity pastries and the little eggy *yemas* that were so delicate and airy that like all the keenest joys of life, they vanished as you tasted them. Every recipe in Juanita's repertoire was, as the Spaniards themselves say, "finger-licking"—*para chuparse los dedos*. The epicures insist that French food is the best in the world. They may have it all if they give me the Spanish food, spicy and fragrant and exciting and warm like the Spanish people themselves.

There was not a town or region in Spain that had not made its contribution to the national treasury of cooking—*Paella de Valencia, Bacalao à la Vizcaina, Queso de Burgos, Salchicha de Pamplona, Plátanos à la Granada*—the names of the Spanish dishes were a guide-book in themselves. It was through them I learned my geography of Spain, which may explain why my conception of the country was and is a bit lopsided. Those little soft creamy cheeses that came from Burgos and which you spread on biscuits and topped with a dab of runny cherry jam came between me and the wonderful cathedral for which the rest of the world esteems the city. Vizcaya's dried cod-fish cooked in a delicious tomato sauce seemed to me as important as any fishing fleet or historical Basque customs that the north had to offer. Granada's Alhambra was only trotting after the banana dish to which the Moorish city gave its name. That was a dream of a dessert. Juanita would split the bananas, hollow them out and stuff them with crushed pine-kernel candy. Then she would put the halves expertly together, roll them in egg

and breadcrumbs and fry them in boiling oil. Icing sugar
was sprinkled on them as a last touch and they were eaten
hot with a sauce made from gooseberry conserve.

It was the same way with every other dish. Valencia might
be the garden of Spain to tourists, but to me it was the
cradle of *paella*. How am I going to tell what that *paella*
tasted like? Imagine you have a fine plump chicken. Poach
that chicken and strip the white succulent flesh from it and
chop it small. Now cook handfuls and handfuls of rice in
good meaty stock, with the chicken bones thrown in for
extra savour. Season the stock with every appetite-arousing
condiment you fancy and don't, on any account, leave out
a bead or two of garlic. Drain your rice now and toss it in a
little hot oil or melted butter. Mix in the chopped chicken
and saffron, and shellfish of every description. Press the
steaming savoury mixture into a bowl to give it shape. Now
unmould it and decorate it with strips of red and green
peppers that have broiled to tenderness on top of the stove.
And now eat your *paella*. Have the orange groves of
Valencia ever given such delight as that? You could coax a
man back from the mouth of the grave with the smell and
the taste and the look of a dish of *paella*.

It was not only after towns and cities that those dishes
were named. The saints and the clergy had played a big
part in their christening too. There was a special dish for
the feast day of every saint in the calendar. Custards of San
Roque, cookies of Santa Clara, buns of San Antonio—when
Juanita read from her recipe book it sounded as if the
blessed in Heaven were having their annual Christmas treat.
The saints were not in it with the priests and the hierarchy.
The most sumptuous party dishes were always *à la Cardinal*,
or *à la Obispo*, and the richest soups and the finest desserts
seemed to be all *à la Jesuita* or *à la Dominicana* or *à la* some
order or another. It struck me that that cardinal and those
priests must have been well-fed men if such gorgeous things
had originated in their kitchens. But maybe the cardinal

and the priests had never tasted the dishes at all. Maybe they had been dedicated to them by some poor sinner of a cook out of gratitude for spiritual help received. There was a magnificent sauce which Juanita used to make now and again for serving with fish. *Salsa Padre Guzman* it was called. If Father Guzman really invented that sauce he deserves to be canonized. A rich mayonnaise with a little finely chopped parsley in it and plenty of lobster coral. It was grand to watch it being made. Between her knees, Juanita held the bowl of darkish, watery-looking egg-yolks. Her left hand controlled the steady lazy trickle from the oil bottle while her right hand stirred the eggs into a frothy whirlpool, that soon quieted down to a thick primrosy cream. Lemon juice next, and then the coral which spread its pink over the sauce like a blush over a dusky cheek. When the sauce was finished, she always cut off a corner of *pan de cocina* and scooped up a taste of the sauce for me. It was lovely with this fresh crusty kitchen bread which was bought for the maids. The family ate Vienna bread. I thought the other nicer. Heavier, maybe, but when those big flat crusty loaves that looked like griddle cakes were eaten fresh there was nothing to beat them.

I could have lingered in the Basterra kitchen for ever. Indeed, I might be there to-day if Mr. Robertson had not caused that final row between the señora and myself.

Mr. Robertson and his little delicacy need a chapter to themselves.

CHAPTER THREE

THERE were two things I disliked about Sunday lunch in the big dining-room—angel's hair and Mr. Robertson. The angel's hair was a sweetmeat of candied cidras (a kind of vegetable marrow) thready and honey-sweet. It was always served with the cold ham which formed an integral part of Sunday's lunch. Señor Basterra had a passion for it, but to my Irish palate the combination of sweet and salt was repellent. Mr. Robertson, who was also an integral part of Sunday's lunch, I found just as difficult to stomach. He was a middle-aged business associate of the señor, and the family set great store by him. He had influence in England with the people who bought Basterra corks. I felt that some good reason would be necessary before one could make a welcome guest of Mr. Robertson.

It was his sloppiness I disliked. His mouth and his loose flesh and his pale eyes were all sloppy. He had sloppy little fins of hands with which he kept patting various parts of his person as he talked. He had a sloppy way of eating and a still sloppier way of smoking. Fascinated horror used to come over me as he smoked. Whenever he took the cigar out of his mouth, a rope of saliva still attached it to his lips. Even the man's feet were sloppy. By this I do not mean that there was anything about their natural structure which would have excited a chiropodist. It was his shoes. They were made by the best shoemaker in Madrid, but when Mr. Robertson sat with his toes turned in, his soft cushiony shoes with their floppy-bowed laces gave him the finishing touch.

All that sounds very hard and uncharitable. I think I would not have been so hard on Mr. Robertson if he had not been such a renegade. There is no forgiveness for the man who turns his back on his own country. Mr. Robertson had not a good word to say of Ireland. He was fond of boasting that he was Irish by birth and British by the grace of God, and he was for ever thanking Providence that his people had taken him to live in London when he was five. I felt that Dublin had just as much reason to be grateful.

Mr. Robertson was the hero of my first Spanish love-affair. It was Luisita's rowanberry dress that ignited the fuse of his passion. Until I wore it on the night of Señora Bas-

terra's party, his pale eyes had looked at me as coldly as if
I were a Dublin Bay herring.

On St. Stephen's Night, the señora gave her annual
Christmas party for her friends of the English colony.
When I had put the children to bed, she kindly invited me
to join the guests. I did myself up, and put on the red dress
and the high-heeled black suede shoes which Miss Carmody
had helped me to choose. My finery did not make much of
a general impression. With the exception of Mr. Robertson
the guests were all married couples who were very well
known to each other. It was "dear" and "darling" all over
the place. Feeling out of things, I sat down in a corner of
the window-seat. I thought no one was taking any notice
of me, but my red dress must have been playing like a
beacon-light on Mr. Robertson's lonely cruising heart, for
suddenly he was standing before me with a dish of sweets.
I took one—it was a big toffee, I remember. There must
have been something very endearing about the way that
chunk of toffee made my cheek stick out, for from that
moment Mr. Robertson remained at my side.

After supper the party went all Merrie England. They
played hunt-the-slipper and postman's knock and spin-the-
platter and twenty other different kissing games. I have
always thought these kissing games very overrated. Surely
if two people at a party have a notion to kiss, they will kiss
away without having to use a game as an excuse. And anyway, it is always the person you least want to kiss who falls
to your lot in these games. That, of course, is what happened to me. I was sent out to join Mr. Robertson in the
corridor. He went for me. The next minute those little fins
were flapping about me and he was blowing asthmatically
into my ear. It was an awkward situation. I dared not
offend such a valued friend of the family, but not for all the
gold in Ireland would I have let his mouth near my face.
By going rigid and keeping my head down I managed to
field the clammy kisses with the back of my neck. I cer-

tainly gave Mr. Robertson no reason to think I was enjoying his embrace, but he seemed to believe I was getting as much out of it as he was. He was all for keeping it up, but I felt I had already stood as much as was consistent with the duty of a girl to her employers as laid down by St. Paul. I wriggled myself free and was away down the corridor before Mr. Robertson could do anything about it.

Love is a queer thing. Often it goes contrarily with a woman if she is anyway natural and honest at all. Let her be fond of a man and show her fondness, and ten to one her openness will chase him away. Let her detest a man and show her detestation in every way and she will only make his wanting of her all the stronger. Though I gave him less than no encouragement, Mr. Robertson's ardour increased. I think his conceit may have had something to do with the way he insisted on interpreting my coolness as coyness. No one could blame him for being conceited. For twenty years he had been fêted and run after as one of the most eligible bachelors in the British colony. He thought my stand-offishness was merely my technique and he played up. I used nearly have to put my feet in my lap at lunchtime on Sundays to get out of the way of his questing shoes. I had many an invitation to tea in Sakuska and Bakanik and the other swanky tea-shops but not for a pension would I have risked being seen with him by the governesses.

What the señora saw of my rebuffs made her very impatient with me. To do her justice, it was not merely that she was concerned with keeping the influential business friend in good humour. She was genuinely regretful to see me jeopardizing the chance of a lifetime, and she had a hundred little sideways things to say about the stupidity of girls who did not know their own luck, and about governesses who did not appreciate being honoured. She took things into her own hands on the Sunday week before Shrove Tuesday. Pepita put the soup on the table. *Potage de aluvias rojas* it was, a spicy heart-warming potage of scarlet runners.

"Talking to Freddie Woods in the Club yesterday," Mr. Robertson said through a mouthful. "Wants to make up a party of four for the Carnival Dance in the Ritz. He's taking Miss Glennie, of course. I thought of going and of asking Miss Scully to come."

No delighted exclamations from me. With stolid ingratitude I went on eating my lovely chocolate-coloured soup. Señora Basterra made up for my lack of appreciation.

"Did you hear that, Miss Scully? Mr. Robertson is going to take you to a dance!" She said it in the mesmerized tone of one announcing that the Prince of Asturias himself was dying to take me.

I saw a diplomatic way out. "I'm very thankful," I said, "but sure I can't go. I haven't a stitch of an evening dress." Instinct told me that the blue satin I had brought from home might look out of place in the Ritz. That silenced them all for a minute. Mr. Robertson had a very healthy respect for the opinions of his friends. You could see that he was considering how they would react if he appeared escorting a girl without a stitch of an evening dress.

Señora Basterra wrinkled her forehead. "There's that silver brocade of mine," she said. "I haven't worn it for years—as a matter of fact I was thinking of cutting it up for cushion-covers. It could be made over." She looked critically at me. "I doubt if your hair is just the right shade for it, Miss Scully"—she was very proud of her fairness— "but I think it should do you all right."

"That's settled, then," Mr. Robertson said, beaming. "I'll 'phone Woods in the morning." They did not give me a chance to put in another word.

When I told Miss Carmody how I had been press-ganged, she made me view the matter in a more optimistic light.

"You'll find that you'll enjoy yourself when you get there," she said. "After all, a dance is a dance. Wait till you see, you'll have a great time."

As Shrove Tuesday approached I began to feel that maybe

she was right. A dance *was* a dance, whatever one's escort was like. My one experience of public dancing had been that dance at home in the barn we called the Temple. I had a notion that the Ritz dance would be conducted along the same lines. Everyone in the room would be laughing and talking and making jokes as they danced by each other. The girls would sit together on benches ranged around the walls, chatting friendlily while they waited for the men to come and ask them out. My hopes of enjoyment were based chiefly on the belief that a free and easy exchange of partners would be possible. Basely I planned to shed Mr. Robertson as soon as he should have had the first dance and to promise away the other dances quickly to all the exciting partners that would surely offer themselves.

My first hour in that Ritz ballroom was the most shocking disappointment of my life. From the moment I went in I was intimidated by those pillared acres of polished floor. It needed all the height of my shining new silver heels to prop up my courage as I followed Mr. Robertson and his friends to our table. That table was the sorest feature of the whole affair. There were no benches whereon to sit and chat and make friends. Instead there were the tables. The space that separated them was a cold isolating sea that turned each into an island chilling in its neutrality. I thought it the queerest thing that all those people should have paid good money to get together, and then refuse to enjoy each other's company. When I realized that I was to be marooned at our table for the whole night with no partners but Mr. Robertson or Mr. Woods and not even as much as "Good evening" to anyone else in the place, my cup was full. At least, I thought it was full, but I found it was capable of holding another sup when Mr. Robertson took me out to dance. One would have supposed that after twenty years in Spain the man would have learned to use his feet. In what way he had wasted those years I do not know, but the fact remains that he could not put a foot under him.

I, who was only fresh from the bog, made a better hand of it.

We came back to our table and Mr. Woods ordered drinks. When they asked me what I would have I did not like to make a show of myself by saying that I had never had a drink in my life, so I copied Miss Glennie and ordered sherry. When it came, something warned me to go easy on it, and I just took a hen's sip. Mr. Robertson was drinking whisky and soda. He drained it, and a second later excused himself and disappeared. That was the first of his excursions which were to have such an important effect on my career. If he went to powder his nose once that night, he went twenty times. I never saw anything like that unfortunate man's internal mechanism. It was hail and farewell to every drink with him. He no sooner had it swallowed than he was away and out.

This was hard on me. A bad partner at a dance is better than no partner at all. For the greater part of the ante-supper period I was sitting at that table by myself. Mr. Woods and Miss Glennie were not much addition to me. They were engaged to be married and I suppose it was only natural that they should have wanted to dance together all the time. They were in love, the creatures, though it was difficult to think of such a warm glowing emotion as love in connection with those two pale polite people. If I had not taken such an interest in the other dancers, there would have been no comfort for me at all, not in the grand band, for its invitation was a mockery, nor in the silver dress which had turned out so well. According to the fashion standards of those days it was lovely, a brief sheath of dull silver. It was a pale little column of smoke breaking into vivid flame at the shoulder where Miss Carmody's flower was pinned.

During the first of Mr. Robertson's disappearances after supper, something happened which altered the night for me.

Rafael danced with me.

Rafael danced with me and altered not only the night but

my whole world. He altered my heart too, though this did not happen until after I had danced with him many other times and in many other places. After knowing Rafael, never again was I to be completely trusting, never again to have complete faith in anyone.

Our table was on the right as you go into the Ritz, close to those french windows leading into the patio. There was a party a few tables away from ours, a party of boys and girls who seemed to be having the height of fun. The girls were much louder in their laughter and much more free-and-easy with the boys than is usually the way with Spanish girls in public. Their gaiety kept drawing my envious eyes.

Mr. Robertson noticed them too. "What is the Ritz coming to?" he said testily. "Imagine allowing women of that class in here among respectable people."

My interest quickened at once. So they were "women of that class"? The governesses in the Retiro had enlightened me about many things. I gave the girls increased attention, and I was disappointed not to be able to detect any mark of Jezebel on them. They looked exactly like the rest of us, except that they were more alive and had more friendliness in their eyes. There was nothing in their appearance to inspire the scandalized horror which, as a well-brought-up girl, I knew I should be feeling. Instead that little line of Yeats jumped into my head ". . . for the good are always the merry. . . ." If that was true, there was far more goodness at that table than at ours.

Shortly before supper my interest in the demi-monde was suddenly smothered by my interest in one of the boys of the party. A boy of twenty-two or twenty-three with hair no darker than my own, and with a funny little quirk to the left side of his mouth. I was looking at him idly with no more interest than one would give to any nice-looking stranger when his eyes trapped me. They held me for a long minute. Not until they had imparted a wordless exciting secret did they leave me free to flutter back to myself. After

that the dark eyes were waiting for me every time I looked
over. I tried not to look often. At least, I honestly think
tried. I know for a fact that I shifted my chair a little so as
not to be facing him directly. I told myself that I was highly
insulted with him for the brazen way he was staring at me,
and he in such company into the bargain. My clutchings
at respectability were all in vain, for I found those eyes
drawing me again and again.

Supper and the presence of the rest of my party netted
me for a while. When I looked again the others had gone—
gay girls, laughing men and calling eyes, they were all gone
and with them my only diversion of the evening. The band
broke into a tango as sudden as the wail of a child who
wakes up at night to find himself alone. Mr. Woods took
Miss Glennie out to dance and Mr. Robertson went off to
his retreat. I was left sitting there in my silver desolation,
wishing it was time to go home.

Someone came and leaned against the frame of the french
windows. I felt his eyes on me. Without looking up, I
knew who it was. I was afraid to face him. To have stayed
back after his friends had gone, to have come and stood
there, betokened a direct attack, and I was not prepared for
it. My cheeks flushed and my hands did not feel too steady.
I had to do something to hide the turmoil and embarrassment I was feeling. The glass of sherry was still before me,
almost untouched. I tossed it off with the air of one to whom
sherry means no more than well-water. I have always liked
to blame the sherry for what followed. I have always tried
to appease my conscience with the thought that I would
never have acted in such an undignified common way if I
had not been the worse for drink. Maybe I am fooling myself. Maybe the low drop had to come out in me sooner or
later, drunk or sober. At the same time, there is no denying
that the sherry did queer things to me. It gave me courage
to lift my head and to look Rafael straight in the face. It
translated for me the message of his eyes into little blood-

racings and heart-thumpings. It ousted all consideration for my escort and all fear of the señora. When he came over I stood up simply and got out on the floor with him.

I had never known that dancing could be like that. With Rafael guiding me I tangoed as well as any girl in the room. I, whose mother—and her mother before her—had never danced anything more languid or sensuous than a jig, found myself gliding and swaying and turning as if I had been born and bred in Buenos Aires. The wide floor that had been so unfriendly and frightening became a magic carpet. The orchestra fulfilled its promise, and the little Latiny things that Rafael was saying were part of the music. This was youth and joy: music in your ears, a good-looking boy holding you and ardent eyes looking into your own. This was life! "You're drunk, God help you," my conscience said sadly. "Mind your own business," my heart shouted back. "If I am itself, isn't it a lovely feeling?"

Mr. Robertson had not yet returned when we got back to the table. Miss Glennie and Mr. Woods had stopped at another table at the far end of the room to speak to some American people they knew. I sat down and Rafael sat opposite me. He started to speak in the extravagant flowery language that Spaniards have invented for the gratification of woman's vanity. Fluthered though I was, my common sense steadied itself and prompted that in offering his trouba-dour compliments he was only obeying convention and that he could not possibly mean a tenth of what he was saying. I did not want to hear conventional things from Rafael. Already I was more than half in love with him, and I wanted him to say only the things he meant. I brought the conver-sation to a more practical level by asking him about himself. He was a civil engineer. At any moment he expected to get a big commission. He had only just graduated and was very proud of being the youngest civil engineer in Spain. He told me his name, Rafael Moragas. I told him mine, and all about my job.

"When will we see each other, Delia?" he said suddenly.

I had not thought of taking our affair beyond the ball-room, but with Rafael's smoky eyes looking at me like that, and with the sherry and the tango still bubbling in my brain, I would have promised him anything in reason. "On Thursday next," I told him. "At five under the clock in the Puerta del Sol."

With this settled, he relaxed and began to tease me. "Do English girls always go dancing with their grandfathers?" he wanted to know, the little quirk at the side of his mouth making him look like a mischievous boy of ten.

I was becoming accustomed to the Spaniards' way of robbing the Irish of their nationality. We spoke English, therefore we were English. "Las inglesas," we were always called. It was no use insisting, "No! Inglesa, no—*irlandesa*." As often as not, our faulty accent and pronunciation made that "irlandesa" be interpreted as "holandesa," and it was silly to pursue the matter further. If you were going to be called out of your name, it did not make much difference whether they called you English or Dutch. One was as good as the other. You just shrugged your shoulders and let it be.

I did not try to put Rafael right when he denuded me of my ancestry of saints and scholars. But I could not let it go with him when he gave me Mr. Robertson for a blood relation.

"He is not my grandfather," I protested indignantly. Before I could explain the peculiar relationship that existed between Mr. Robertson and me, the orchestra was playing again and there was the man himself making straight towards us.

"*Bailarémos, guapa?*" Rafael dared me. I accepted the dare.

It was nothing sobbing or lonely they were playing this time, but a gay, blood-quickening paso-doble. The tango had made me feel sentimental and yearning. The paso-doble did other things to me. I am not saying that it did not get some help from Rafael's eyes and the still-active sherry. Whatever may have been the cause, my heart and my blood began to race to the rhythm and the rush of the music. Up and down the floor we went, round and round, in and out between the other couples while our feet and our arms and our whole bodies became one with the blood-quickening saxophones and the heart-calling violins. Rafael was saying things again, the same little warm, pleading, flattering things he had said when we had danced before. Then, his words had been blotted by the soft wail of the tango, but now the loud exciting drumming of the paso-doble caught them up and underlined them. I heard them all right, and I made no objection at all when, right in the middle of the dance, he led me to the french windows. Before we passed through I looked back. Mr. Woods and Miss Glennie had joined Mr. Robertson at our table. I caught a glimpse of their shocked faces but they were no more to me than the chairs they sat on. I went out into the patio with Rafael.

For a second we stood looking at each other, and in that second I thought to myself, "Why, this is last year's dance all over again. He is a Spaniard, but he has the very same look in his face that Frank Breslin had before he kissed me. And I myself am feeling the same as I did then, frightened and glad and sorry." The setting and the parts were the same, but Rafael, I found, was better rehearsed than my first love. Poor Frank had been tongue-tied and shy, but Rafael was word-perfect. While we still stood there looking at each other, he scorched me with a lava-flow of fiery phrases. It was my first intimation of the importance of speech in Spanish love-making. Indeed, after knowing Rafael, I often wondered how a Spaniard who is so unfortunate as to be born deaf and dumb can get any enjoyment at all out of life. What Rafael had to say would have made pleasant hearing for any girl, but there was so much of it that I was beginning to think maybe he did not mean to kiss me at all. I should not have doubted him. Just when I had given up all hope, I found myself being kissed. But Rafael did not get a chance to show me how Spain compared with Ballyderrig in the way of kisses. The kiss had barely started when I heard Miss Glennie's horrified voice behind me.

"Are you mad, Miss Scully?" she demanded. "Do you realize that this is a public function? Have you no decency? Be sure Señora Basterra shall hear about this."

That sobered me. It knocked all the romance out of me.

"On Thursday, niña," Rafael said. Shamed and humiliated, I nodded, and followed Miss Glennie back to the ballroom. Mr. Robertson's cold displeasure gave his face the look of a well-set blancmange. I was taken home at once. Not one of the three of them had a word to say to me on the way. With a frigid good night they saw me safely into the Basterra house.

I have never been one to let to-morrow's troubles interfere with to-night's peace. I knew what was coming to me in the morning but I put the knowledge away with the silver dress, and lay awake thinking of Rafael and love. I went back over my love-life and decided I had gained a lot of experience in the past twelve months. First there had been Frank Breslin. Four times in all Frank had kissed me. It had been very sweet and thrilling while it lasted. My next amorous experience was something I did not like to dwell on. Even now my mind veers away from the shame of it. It happened on the boat coming out. There was a fair-haired blue-eyed cadet, a Shropshire boy. I was attracted to him by the way his hair grew on the back of his neck and because he told me I looked much older than seventeen and a half. On the second evening out he held my hand in the shelter of the boat-deck and told me his people had sent him to sea because of some trouble over a farmer's daughter. The very next morning my Shropshire lad came upon me as I clung weakly to the rail of the rearing boat trying hard not to hear the way the sea was begging for my breakfast. The mildewed colour of my face should have told him that it was solitude I wanted and not romance. Shropshire people must have very little understanding in them. Instead of leaving me to cope with that nest of mad eels in my stomach, he lingered and took up where he had left off the night before. Twice I opened my mouth to ask him to go away and each time I had to shut it quickly. The third time the eels were too quick for me and the sea got all it had been calling for and more besides. No romance could have weathered a scene like that.

I put the shameful memory behind me and hurried on to the next erotic episode, my little *affaire* with Mr. Robertson. With the best will in the world, I could not say that Mr. Robertson had contributed anything to my knowledge of love.

My mind dropped him and I turned to Rafael. In the half-hour I had known him, my heart had taken twenty different photographs of him. I took the photographs out and examined them one by one, and I loved them all. There he was sitting with his friends, the nice-looking stranger who had first attracted me. And here was one taken in that moment when he had ceased being a stranger—when his eyes had spoken to me. There was a lovely one of Rafael dancing, and a very happy one of him sitting at the table with me, teasing me about Mr. Robertson.

I remembered how I had lain awake beside Gran after the dance in Ballyderrig, thinking and remembering like this. There was a difference, though. That time I was thinking only of this wonderful new business of kissing, and what a pleasant grateful thing it was that two people should be able to give each other such wonderful joy so easily and without any bother to either of them. Frank Breslin's face hardly came into my thoughts at all. Now it was all of Rafael I was thinking and the memory of his kiss did not mean half so much to me as that funny little quirk at the side of his mouth. It was queer, and the meaning of it did not come to me until months later when I was in Bilbao and kind Miss Myers who was trying to teach me French lent me a book. There was a little verse in it which went:

> Tu m'as dit: Je pense à toi tous les jours.
> Mais tu penses moins à moi qu'à l'amour.
> Tu m'as dit: Mes yeux brouillés ne peuvent pas
>   t'oublier lorsque je me couche.
> Mais tu penses plus au baiser qu'à la bouche.

That was how it had been with me after that dance at home. Frank's face had not remained with me because I had been in love with love and not with him. Rafael was another pair of shoes altogether.

$\bullet \qquad \bullet \qquad \bullet \qquad \bullet \qquad \bullet$

Miss Glennie called the next morning while I was away with the children getting the Blessed Ashes. The señora was waiting for me when I got in. I would be sorry for any unfortunate sinner who had to hear his character read out to him as Señora Basterra read mine. I was a disgrace to her house, to the nuns and to Ireland. I had acted as only an ill-bred loose creature would act. There was no forgiveness for me in this world or the next. I had insulted a respectable gentlemanly man for some cheap Spaniard who could not possibly think anything but the worst of me. Let me not think that that was the way to get a husband. It was not how she had got married. Señor Basterra had been introduced properly to her and he had gone all the way to Ireland to meet her family before proposing to her. How would she ever be able to look Mr. Robertson in the face again? Did I not know that he had brought me to the dance on one condition: that I should try to behave like a lady.

It was a pity she said that. I had listened to her abuse

with genuine humility, for morning had brought sanity and I knew I well deserved everything she said. But to be told that sloppy Mr. Robertson had made conditions about taking me out was more than I could stand. Indignation ousted contrition in me. "Well, the cheek of him!" I said stormily. "An old fellow like that to be putting conditions on a girl! Sure, I was the fool to have made so little of myself as to go with him at all! Mary Ann Burke at home wouldn't be seen dead at a dance with him, and she has the pension and a wooden leg." I saw a month's notice trembling on the señora's lips and I hurried to forestall it. "I'm not staying in this house another minute," I said. "You don't like me and you never liked me. Well, I don't like you either."

By the time I had the dress-basket packed I was in a panic of fright. The remaking of that silver dress and the shoes to go with it had left me with three pesetas and a few coppers in hand—not enough to keep me for one day. I ran to Miss Carmody for advice. What the señora had said was nothing to what my friend had to say when she heard the whole story—and I told it all, the sherry, the patio, the appointment for Thursday, everything. It was always that way between Miss Carmody and me. There was something about her grey eyes which always forced a full confession from me.

She made me see the real gravity of the situation. "You've been a reckless little fool, Miss Scully," she said bluntly. "If this story gets around you may go home, for you'll never be able to get another post in Spain. There is one thing no Spanish lady will tolerate and that is flightiness in a governess. If the boy concerned had been English or American it would not have been so bad. That he was Spanish makes the thing a million times worse. These ladies know their own men. They know what a girl can expect when she makes herself cheap with a Spaniard."

"What am I going to do, Miss Carmody?" My lips were

trembling and I had to fight hard to keep back the tears. I saw my sin written in scarlet all over Spain.

"You're coming straight with me to Señora Basterra, and you're going to apologize and ask her to take you back."

That was unthinkable. "I couldn't do it, Miss Carmody," I burst out. "I don't like the place. I like the children, and the maids are grand, but I don't like her. And I hate that old man! I couldn't stay there after what happened."

"I'm not asking you to stay," Miss Carmody said calmly. "Indeed, I'm quite sure Señora Basterra wouldn't wish to keep you on. But you must have somewhere to live until you find another post. There is a chance I may be able to get you in with the Marquesa de la Rojas. Miss Leaming is going home at the end of the month."

"Won't she have heard about me?" I asked shamefacedly and with the humility of the sinner who stands in danger of being exposed.

"It is not very likely. The Basterras move in a very different circle, thank goodness. Anyway I'll do my best. Luisita is very friendly there and I'll ask her to put in a word for you." She cut short my thanks. "You'll have to promise me two things," she said. "First, that as long as you remain in Spain you will never again take sherry or any other drink."

That was easy. I gave the promise. What is more I kept it, and very glad I am that I did. If I was capable of my many later foolishnesses while in my cold sober senses, what might I not have done if I had taken to drink?

"What else do you want me to promise you, Miss Carmody?"

"That you won't meet this boy on Thursday or on any other day." This was not so easy. The abuse and scoldings had cheapened me in my own eyes and had made me feel common and ashamed, but they had done nothing to belittle my liking for Rafael. That was sheltered inside me, out of reach of them all. Miss Carmody saw my hesitation. "For Heaven's sake, don't be a fool, Miss Scully," she said sternly. "That kind of thing will only lead to your ruin. He may be very fascinating and fill you up with romantic talk but believe me, he is not going to do you any good. You don't know these Spanish boys. He probably likes you —he may even fancy himself in love with you. But he has no serious intentions towards you. When a boy of his type marries he always takes a girl whose family and background are known and acceptable to his own people."

Still, I could not promise. I did not care if Rafael did not want to marry me. I had no wish to marry him or anyone else for years and years. All I wanted was to meet him again and to dance with him and talk to him. And maybe have him kiss me a few times. And Miss Carmody was only talking foolishness when she said he would be my ruin. Didn't I know and didn't everyone know that so long as a girl was good and remembered the things she had been taught, there was no fear of her coming to any harm?

Miss Carmody lost patience and stood up. "Make up your mind, Miss Scully," she said coldly. "Either you promise me to have nothing more to do with this Spaniard or I wash my hands of you altogether. I cannot possibly recommend you to the Marquesa if you continue to associate with this man. Instead, I shall go to Señora Basterra and ask her to see the Consul with a view to getting you sent home."

After that I had no option. I felt she was hard and prejudiced, but I gave her my promise. I kept it for a year.

CHAPTER FOUR

IF, as I have often been warned is likely to happen, I should have to end my days in the poorhouse, there will be great comfort for me in the memory of my seven months with the Marquesa de las Rojas. No hardship will ever rob me of the satisfaction of that one taste of real luxury. I had thought the Basterra ménage was luxurious, but it was only a County Council cottage to the de las Rojas mansion in the Calle Quénco. The marble entrance hall, the lift, the warren of bathrooms, the army of servants, the furniture, the silver, the food, the paintings—I had not dreamed there was the like in the world. The linen on my bed was changed three times a week; I was given a pile of towels that would have done a boarding-school. When my stockings went to the wash, they were darned for me before they were left back in my room. My shoes were polished for me every night, and the way the laundress ironed a hundred little fancy pleats into my underclothing made me feel it was a shame to change my clothes.

There were five children, all girls. A staff was kept for them alone. Miss Madden had the two big girls, Angeles and Maria Dolores. I looked after the two little ones, Rosita and Concepcion. There was a baby of five months who was in the charge of Tomasina, a wet-nurse from the mountains. The girls did not have to rely entirely on Miss Madden and myself for their education. A whole university of professors called at odd times during the day to give them every class of instruction.

The Marquesa was an exquisite delicate creature with a still, cold, contemptuous face and enormous cinnamon-velvet eyes. When I had come for my first interview my heart failed me after one minute with her. The contemptuous look, the untouchable air, the chill withdrawnness of the clear even voice—what did all this mean if not that she had heard about my misbehaviour in the Ritz? But the Marquesa's contempt was not for me. It was for life, and, if I could believe the governesses, life deserved it from her. According to the girls in the Retiro, and they knew the scandals of every family in Madrid, the Marquesa's husband had another home in Cuatro Caminos where he had three sons, one of them younger than the Marquesa's baby girl. I found that hard to believe. The rare glimpses I got of the Marqués showed me a tall spare grey-haired man with a grave spiritual face. Surely that story could not be true of someone who was the living image of St. Ignatius of Loyola?

There were drawbacks to the luxury. Those exciting walks down the Calle Mayor were finished. Rosita and Concepcion refused to be taken anywhere but to the Retiro where they liked to play sedately with their little friends. And a stop was put to my lessons in Spanish cooking. It would have seemed less forward to have dropped into the Marquesa's boudoir for a friendly gossip than to have intruded on the chef and his acolytes in that catacomb of a kitchen. However, it was not nearly so lonely here when the children were in bed, for now I had Miss Madden to talk to. Not that she was a lively or entertaining companion, but at least she was Irish.

She was a bony, dried-up woman with easily shocked eyes, a prim mouth and very ladylike ways. She wore her greying hair in two straight side-pieces and shingled tightly at the back. Her long thin neck always looked as aggressively clean as if she had used a nail-brush on it. She had three good tailor-made costumes: My Best, My Second-best, My Everyday. Everyday came out in the mornings, Second-best went on in the afternoons and Best made an appearance only on Sundays. Such changing of coats and skirts implies an effect of variety, an effect that was lacking in Miss Madden's case for the reason that the costumes, though of different vintage, were all three of navy blue serge cut to exactly the same pattern. She had been in Spain only a year and was very homesick in a queer fidgety furious kind of way.

I felt sorry for the creature when I heard her story. I did not come by the story through any full easy bestowal of confidence on Miss Madden's part, for she never made a friend or confidante of me. I lost all chance of intimacy with her on my first evening in the house when her ladylike probings discovered a complete lack of priests, bank clerks and doctors in my family. I had to piece the story together from her pathetic little boastings at mealtimes and from the little half-confidences that homesickness sometimes forced from her as we sat together in the evenings.

It was easy to see the comfortable old house she came from in the small town in Westmeath where her brother was a bank manager. Her mother had died when she was eighteen. The daughter came confidently into her heritage of linen-presses and account books and keys and recipes, and for thirty contented efficient years she looked after that home, feeding and caring her brother, giving little parties for his friends, making strawberry jam in July and apple jelly in October. Her fowl were the best layers in the town, and the parish priest himself had nothing in his garden to compare with her larkspur. She lived for her brother and the house and the little treasures her mother had bequeathed them—the half-set of Crown Derby, and the walnut bureau in the drawing-room and the afternoon tea-cloth of fine Irish lace.

How she cared for those treasures!—"I always say servants cannot be trusted with good china. I never allowed our maid to put a finger near our Crown Derby. I always washed it myself." It was easy to see those bony capable hands become gentle and caressing as they glided a piece of soft old linen over the bureau, or pressed the Irish lace tea-cloth with a careful lukewarm iron. But her gentleness was all for things. She had no softness at all for people. Maybe this was because for thirty years she had lived like a snail inside her shell of dusters and jam-pots and weekly accounts, stretching forth cautious horns towards such refinements as tea with a visiting bank inspector or a shopping trip into Mullingar or an exchange of genteelly girlish letters with her old school friend who was a governess in Spain, shrinking back into her shell in a hurry when any of life's more real aspects threatened to approach.

A serpent came into her Eden in the shape of a young pretty school-teacher. Mr. Madden knew the girl only two months when he married her and brought her into the quiet spinsterish house.

I could understand what a sore heartbreak it must have been on poor Miss Madden to have a usurper elected to her kingdom, and such a flighty, scatterbrained, unhousewifely usurper into the bargain. Just the same, I had to make certain mental reservations on those few occasions when resentment forced the prim-lipped woman to let off steam about young Mrs. Madden. I would not have been in that girl's shoes for all the bank-managing husbands in Ireland. Certainly not when, in her eagerness to do her share of the housekeeping and win approval from her sister-in-law, she used the ordinary common floor-polish on the walnut bureau. Not for the world when she scorched the lace teacloth with a miscalculated iron. And I would sooner have died than have been in her place on the day she broke one of the Crown Derby cups. Miss Madden's voice trembled when that scene was squirted from her—"And there was the cup smashed to pieces on the floor and she just standing there looking at it without a word of excuse or apology." Some of my sympathy had to go to Miss Madden over the breaking of the precious cup, but more went out to the unfortunate terrified dumb-stricken wretch who had broken it. I was given to understand that after this piece of vandalism the girl gave up all interference with the housekeeping and left it to Those Who Knew Something About It. This would have made things run more smoothly if only the bride, who came of a family that bred greyhounds, had not imported a pair of dogs from home. Her husband soon became as interested in the dogs as she, and bitches and mating were discussed at every meal. This was too much for Miss Madden's untried virginity. The ruining of the bureau, the scorching of the tea-cloth, the breaking of the Crown Derby, these were fleabites compared with the way such shockingly coarse talk made her suffer. She wrote to her friend in Spain begging her to find her an asylum from the low vulgarity that had vitiated her home. The post with the de las Rojas was the result and Miss Madden went out into the world for the first time in her forty-eight years, without, I gathered, any very strong protests from her relatives.

Poor innocent creature. In coming to Spain to escape life she had come to the wrong shop. The very vehemence of the country must have been hurtful to her watery soul. The postcard blue of the sky, the emphatic light and shade, the over-coloured landscape with its red-tiled houses and harsh red-brown earth—these things had a loud demanding quality that must have jarred on one accustomed to the grey half-light of an ultra-refined existence. Here the crudest manifestations of life assailed her at every turn, in the way the men in the streets sometimes deflowered the women with their hot hungry glances, in the prohibiting notices painted on every gateway—constant reminders of the labourers' habit of using the public daylit streets as a lavatory. The very toys in the shop windows were symbols of the crudeness she abhorred, dolls seated on miniature china vessels, celluloid boys astride little dishes of bon-bons, a silvery wire issuing from them to simulate a jet of water, papier mâché models of dung which were guaranteed to win roars of laughter if put on a plate and left on the dinner table.

It is likely that Miss Madden managed to ignore the things that would have outraged her most sorely. After all, most of these things belonged outside the house and it was always possible for her when out walking to retire so deeply within herself as to escape them. But there was one strident manifestation of life from which she had no escape, for it was under the very roof with her in the person of Tomasina, the ama. The wet-nurse was voluptuousness incarnate. Miss Madden represented the cold negation of the flesh, Tomasina its warm brazen championing. They hated each other.

There was life-relish in every move of Tomasina. She could turn the taking of a sip of cold water into an act of carnal gratification. She was a magnificent woman, a strapping big creature with massive hips and breasts and limbs. She was handsome too, with a broad face surmounted by coil upon elaborate coil of oiled black hair. Bold full eyes smouldered under heavy brows, and she had a fine proud nose. The shortness of her curved upper lip gave her a rather forbidding look, but I found her amiable enough. I certainly could not agree that she was the rude surly creature Miss Madden made her out to be. She was always ready to look after the two little girls for me if I wanted to run out for some message, and on two occasions when I had a bad headache she offered to bath them and put them to bed.

To see the big woman when she was taking the baby for an airing was a sight to remember. Like most of the amas, she dressed for the street in her regional costume. Tomasina's was a splendid affair: a full-skirted ankle-length dress of thick purple silk with long tight sleeves and a fitted bodice that strained over the heavy shoulders and breasts. Over this went a black satin apron covered with bright embroidery. She had white cotton stockings and black shoes with silver buckles, and, finally, the silver jewellery belonging to the costume—hairpins with knobs as big as apples and huge filigree ear-rings that dangled to her shoulders. As she walked proudly along with the infant in arms, head boldly high, hips swaying, colours flashing, she was a barbaric symphony in purple and black and silver.

Part of Miss Madden's dislike of Tomasina sprang from her resentment of the ama's position in the house. She thought it disgraceful that an ignorant mountain woman should receive more consideration than the governesses. Miss Madden was unreasonable in this. Tomasina was only getting the privileges which were accorded to every ama as her right. It was held that the infant's physical well-being depended on the ama's contentment. If Tomasina were upset her milk would not agree with the child, so every care was taken to keep her in good humour. She was fed like a fighting-cock. The car was hers when she expressed a wish for an airing. The maids had instructions not to cross her under pain of dismissal and even the Marquesa thawed and became less contemptuous when speaking to Tomasina.

It was a pity Miss Madden showed her dislike so openly. She was subtly rude to the woman, and this of course only spurred the ama to taunt her with a hundred mockeries. My little girls loved to see their baby sister and Tomasina brought her to the nursery every day. She often timed her visit so as to be with us when Miss Madden came to give them their needlework lesson. Then, with a jeer in her dark eyes for the older woman's barren prudishness, she would lay the baby on her wide lap and unbutton her bodice. With an expression of shocked distaste, Miss Madden would immediately shift her chair so as not to see. To one so desiccated as the bank manager's sister, the sight of Tomasina baring her breasts to the baby must have been disturbing. Those big dusky reservoirs of nourishment were such an overpowering epitome of fecundity. As she bent over the child, it was not maternity the picture suggested. Motherhood owns a tenderness and gentleness that had no association with Tomasina's fierce intentness and pride as the child sucked. She gave the impression that there was nothing passive about her nursing, that the milk was not being drawn from her, but that she herself by some primitive inner force was pouring it down the hungry little throat in a warm vitalizing stream. You felt that an infant suckled in this way could not fail to receive some of the strength of the foster-mother.

Miss Madden could not see that it was an essentially innocent thing for Tomasina to perform her duties in front of us. She thought the ama positively indecent—and this although she had been living twelve months in a country where *la madre* is so sexless and sacred that a woman may nurse her baby in the tram without drawing any but reverent eyes. She developed a loathing of the big natural creature and, through her, of Spain. Tomasina came to embody everything in the country that shocked her. Its generosity, its warm-heartedness, its kindness to children, its decent good-living common people, its saints, its painters and its poets—these and all other aspects of the country that were noble and lovable and good were hidden from Miss Madden by Tomasina's broad shoulders. If her pride had not been so stubborn, hatred of the ama would have sent her scurrying home to Ireland where the most outspoken kennel talk would surely have seemed refined after what she had to endure here.

Those who are at war are so taken up with adding to the enemy's wounds and licking their own that they have no time to pity the unfortunate neutral who is sandwiched between them. There was I, asking nothing at all but a peaceable life, and all day long I had to listen to the noise of battle that rolled around my unfortunate head, terrified to budge in case by a glance or whisper I might incur the rage of one or other of the belligerents. It was anything but a salubrious atmosphere and I was always glad when Thursday came and I could escape for a few hours to Miss Carmody and the Molinero. When all is said and done, I have reason to be grateful for that war between Miss Madden and the ama. If they had not hated each other I might still be a governess.

As I left the house each Thursday my heart would always quicken a little and I would tell myself, "To-day, surely. You'll surely walk into him to-day. You'll be walking along looking straight ahead the way Miss Carmody told you a girl should always walk in Madrid. You'll be taking no notice of anyone and then suddenly someone will step right in front of you, and there he will be. 'Delia, *mi vida*,' he will be saying, the very same lovely whispered way he said it in the patio." What would I do then, I wondered. Would my promise to Miss Carmody bind me when we should meet like that, by chance, and without either of us arranging it? Ah, surely not. Surely no oath or promise would ask me to walk on without speaking to him, without standing for just five minutes—even one minute, then—to be warmed by the liking his eyes showed for me and to hear him saying, "*Te quiero mucho*, Delia." Even if, as Miss Carmody said, he only meant that for the moment he said it, I would have to stand and hear it before I told him I could never go out with him, and that I must rush away now, for my friend was waiting for me in the Molinero.

My promise was quite safe, if I had but known it. There was no danger at all of my being tempted to break it, for Rafael was hundreds of miles away, building a bridge in Jaen. Within a week of the Ritz dance he had got the big commission he had been expecting.

.   .   .   .   .

In April the household was transplanted to the de las Rojas summer villa in Neguri, a lovely seaside village outside Bilbao. The migration did not usually take place until May, but Rosita and Concepcion were delicate that spring so the doctor ordered the early move. Rosita had stomach trouble of some kind and her diet was watched carefully. Concepcion had a weak spine and had to lie down for two hours after lunch each day. The villa stood with its back to the sea and facing the Zugazarte, the long narrow patch of shaded green that ran between Neguri and its neighbour village, Las Arenas. While Concepcion took her daily rest on a couch in the front garden, I sat beside her and Rosita with me. I was supposed to read to them during those two hours, but since my chair commanded a good view of the people passing along the Zugazarte I am afraid my eyes often strayed from the book and the poor children got the story in bits and scraps.

I liked watching the peasants who came in from the country to do their shopping in Las Arenas. In the appearance of these people—the Indian-brown men in their grey smocks and red boinas, the sun-dried women in their cotton dresses and white rope-soled alpargatas, there was little enough to put me in mind of my own light-skinned heavy-suited friends who at that very moment were making ready to save the turf and earth the potatoes. Just the same, there was a similarity between them. It expressed itself in the peaceful easy-going walk. All people whose appointments are with the soil acquire that unhurried way of walking, for the earth is not like a factory or a shop whose little span is so short. Half an hour one way or another makes no difference to the earth. The sight of the Basque peasants wakened little stirrings in me, and a hundred times a day I found myself thinking of how the gorse would be scattering its golden sovereigns at home, and how the banks along the Monasterevan road would be cream-splashed with primroses. At the thought of the primroses my fingers would feel the sweet coolness of delving deep in the moss and leaves for the little darning-wool stems of downy pink. The stirrings increased in me so that by the end of April I had a restlessness that had no way of easing itself except in a poem. I had written many a poem since coming to Spain, but I had torn them all up because I had no one to read them to. I felt shy of letting on to Miss Carmody that I wrote poems. I did not tear up the poem I wrote that spring in Neguri. When I had it written I liked it, and I sent it home to a paper in Dublin that had given me a prize for a poem when I was fourteen. I called it "The Vision of the Travelling Woman." This is the poem:

As I walked over blue Dunmurry Hill
 Knee-deep in young things growing,
I came upon a Lady dressed in white
 On the hillside, sewing.
White dress, gold gorse, and blue and purple heather,
And a glad Lady stitching in the April weather.

"God save you, Lady," were the words I said.
 "What might that be you're making?"
Her voice came softer than the small soft waves
 On pebbles breaking.
"A small shirt, a warm shirt, for a King to be wearing,
And the great King, O woman, is the Child I am bearing."

As I walked through the froghan-sweetened bog,
 Warm in the summer's glowing,
I came upon the Lady dressed in blue
 On a turf-bank, sewing.
Blue dress, brown turf, and silver leaves of willow,
And a proud Lady stitching on a heather pillow.

"And who'll be wearing that fine cloak," said I,
 "You've stitched so neatly?"
The Lady smiled. My heart leaped up in joy,
 She smiled so sweetly.
"My tall Son, my fair Son in this cloak will be dressing,"
And her kind hands the folds of the cloak were caressing.

I walked along the river's reedy edge,
 Chilled by the winter's blowing,
And there I met the Lady dressed in black,
 In the pale light, sewing.

Black dress, dun sky on the ragged branches leaning,
And a sad Lady stitching in the cold wind's keening.

"What work is that?" I asked, and when she spoke
    Her voice was full of sorrow,
"A shroud to wrap the body of a King.
    He dies to-morrow.
A high cross, a rough cross, is the throne of His choosing,
For the White Lamb of Love is the Son I am losing."

Maybe that poem would not satisfy T. S. Eliot, but I will
never belittle it. It did not win me the ten and sixpence, but
when it was published among the highly commendeds with
my name, age and address at the end of it it won me my
first letter from Michael.

I remember well the day the letter came. It was an early
afternoon in May, a few days after my eighteenth birthday.
I was in the garden with the children as usual. There was
more diversion now in looking through the gates, for during
the past few weeks every governess in Spain seemed to have
come to Neguri, and they crowded the benches along the
Zugazarte in the afternoon. The gate suddenly opened and
Joaquin, the fat postman, came slopping towards me in his
canvas slippers and raggedy suit of faded blue. The only
contribution which the Spanish Ministry of Posts and Tele-
graphs made to the postman's uniform was a cap. Even his
salary was not paid entirely by them—the public paid him a
halfpenny for every letter he brought. God knows, and I
say this truly, the de las Rojas fortune, if it were mine to
give, would be little to pay Joaquin for what he brought me
in bringing me Michael's letter that day.

First I looked at the signature. It was as unfamiliar as
the handwriting and the address. I read the letter, I have
it before me as I write. Here it is, word for word:

Windgap,
The Curragh,
Co. Kildare.

Dear Delia Scully,

In your little poem you make your Travelling Woman a lonesome sort of creature. I suppose all who must travel are lonesome at heart. If this is the case with you, maybe you would welcome a letter now and again from someone who knows and loves the bog as well as you do yourself. But I am not offering the letters for nothing. If I undertake to keep you informed on such important matters as the way the turf is coming on and the prospects for this year's Johnny M'Gorey crop, and the birthrate among the curlews, you must promise to send me a regular bulletin on bullfighters and orange groves and ladies with high combs and embroidered shawls.

What are you doing in Spain, anyway?

I am wondering if you could possibly be the Delia Scully who became so excited during the weight-throwing competition at a Sports in Robertstown a few years ago? I'll be surprised if you're not, for she seemed the kind of odd little girl who would grow up into an odd big girl.

And now I have written enough to introduce
Your Bog of Allen Correspondent,

MICHAEL WALSH.

Sure, of course I remembered. Not the man himself, for he was only a blurred memory of someone slight and sandy-haired and kind. But I remembered the incident well, and I thought it was not too nice of him to remind me of it, either. Why wouldn't I be excited during the weight-throwing? Wasn't my friend Mike Brophy in for it? And wasn't Judy Ryan, the girl Mike was engaged to, standing there beside me? At least she should have been standing there. In my excitement I did not notice that Judy in *her* excitement had strained away from me towards the competitors. With my eyes hopping on Mike, I thumped her back and tugged her sleeve and hung out of her arm, and it was not until Mike had won and I turned around to hug her that I discovered I had been committing assault and battery on a black stranger. Tell the truth, he was very nice about it and never said a word, although his anger would not have been so hard on me as that amused way he kept smiling down at me. When he saw how ashamed I was, he took me over to the refreshment stand and bought me cakes and lemonade. We talked for a good while and I did not feel at all shy of him, although he was a grown-up man years older than myself—at least as old as Mike Brophy and Mike was twenty-five.

I was delighted with the offer of letters and I wrote at once to seal the bargain. I was just a little annoyed with him, though, for insinuating that I was odd. "Odd" was a word you used of people who were a bit daft in their ways. Miss Madden was odd that time she hid my stockings in the bottom of her workbasket and tried to make me believe that Tomasina had stolen them. I was ready to admit that it had been odd of me to have tried to tear the coat off his back that day in Robertstown, but girls of fifteen do many an odd thing. What was odd or queer about me now that I had grown up? If it was my poem he was hinting at, plenty of people wrote poems and nobody thought the worse of them for it. I forgave him when his next letter arrived. It brought me just the kind of news I had been dying for and which none of my other friends thought worth the ink and paper.

Each sentence was a little carrier pigeon that nestled in my heart all day and fluttered out to deliver its message when I went to bed that night. "*A cow belonging to a woman in Brackna has had a calf with five legs.*" There would be queer exc tment over that! The roads would be alive with people coming to see the calf—rattling traps and jogging carts and whirring bcycles, a long line of them moving between the foaming hedges. It would be as good as a fair. "*There talk of a new road being made between Robertstown and Lully-more.*" That was great news to hear. The Lullymore people had got it hard enough in their time, and they trying to live out of the turf alone. Their little boggy holdings wouldn't graze a goat. Starting off in the dead of the night to walk the thirty-seven miles to Dublin with an ass-creel of turf. No rest for them the next day but tramp tramp from door to door trying to sell it. "Would you be wanting any turf, ma'am? Twopence a dozen. It is good and dry." "No turf for us, thanks. The smell of it would kill you and it covers the place with ashes. We use the coal." Tramp again with you, man, and the devil damn the one of them cares that the legs are breaking under you and the heart falling out of you and yours with the hunger. Ah, well, the new road would give them a different story. There would be drainage now, and a living for man and beast on the little farms. Plenty of ready money too—the making of the new road would give work to every man in Lullymore. Make no mistake about it, many a frying-pan that had rusted for years would soon be greasy again. "*The weather is keeping up grand—no rain for the past three weeks.*" That was what you wanted at this time of the year, plenty of sun and wind. At this rate, every sod in the bog would be heaped by Peter and Paul's Day. That was what you wanted for the froghans too. If the weather only kept up another week or two, the froghans would be so plentiful that the heather would look as if it had rained ink.

That letter, and every other letter Michael wrote me while I was in Spain, was as good as a pair of seven-leagued boots to me.

I was not the only one in the house to get excitement by post. Miss Madden had a letter from her brother announcing the birth of a little daughter. Her sallow face was flushed when she came out to the garden to tell me the good news. "Seven and a half pounds," she said, trying to sound off-hand. "They're calling it Mary after my mother." Her voice was almost soft as she added, "My name is Mary too. My brother and his wife are very anxious that I should go home." Remembered wrongs killed the softness, and the words came hard and bitter. "A good housekeeper is very useful in a house where there are children. Well, I always say that if people cannot show gratitude and consideration they must put up with the consequences. I am not at all likely to give up my good comfortable post just because Certain People have discovered my value."

You could see that the creature was dying to go home and that it was costing her dearly to pay the mortgage on her pride. She became as fidgety as a hen on a hot griddle. Cantankerous was no name for the way she carried on. She took it all out on Tomasina, and insulted and belittled her at every hand's turn. Any other ama would have taken advantage of her privileged position to complain to the Marquesa. The reason Tomasina did not do this was simple. She had too great a contempt for Miss Madden to be upset by her. She sat there in her heavy strength, following the older woman's peevish mosquito-dartings with her smouldering jeering eye, and waiting until Miss Madden's venom should carry her close enough for a lazy well-aimed swipe.

Her chance came one baking hot day in July. The children and myself were almost speechless from the heat when we got in from the beach. The dim nursery with its lowered *persianas* and electric fan was as welcoming as a green glade after the glare outside, and the white and crystal and silver of the table which was set for our lunch added to its cool pleasantness. The ama joined us. Even her swarthy endurance had yielded to the fierce noon, and she looked pale and a little harassed.

"*Madre de Dios*, what heat!" she said sinking carefully into the window seat with her whimpering, beautifully robed foster-child. "This is the only cool room in the house. With your permission, mees, I will feed my baby here."

"*Darle de mamar a mi preciosin*" was the phrase she always used—"give suck to my little precious one."

"*Con mucho gusto, ama,*" I replied, hoping fervently that the child would not make a long meal of it. Miss Madden always ate with the younger children and myself, and I was expecting to see her walk into the room at any moment. It was too hot a day for strife.

The baby finished in record time and there was still no sign of Miss Madden. I was just congratulating myself that all danger had passed when the Father of Trouble put it into Rosita's little polished black head to ask Tomasina to do her trick. After feeding the baby, she sometimes amused the children by squeezing one of those great inexhaustible breasts and squirting a jet of milk across the room. To be quite honest I was always a little repelled when she did this. It was a dignified thing for her to use her breasts, even publicly, for the purpose for which nature intended them, but to use them to entertain Rosita and Concepcion was, I thought, nothing but low comedy. Once or twice I thought of saying this to the little girls but I could not find the words to convey what was in my mind. Like all Spanish children, they had a lovely natural innocence. To them the ama's trick was only a funny bit of clowning. I was afraid that my interference might harm their innocence. I left them alone.

Tomasina did as Rosita had asked. The children laughed their bubbling clear laughs, "Now do it for me, ama," begged Concepcion. "Very very high for me."

Miss Madden arrived in that moment. My heart thumped. This was something she had never seen before. Pretending not to have seen the governess though the sly amusement which crept over her face gave her the lie, Tomasina squeezed her breast and sent an arc of milk ceiling-high.

"What indecency!" Horror made Miss Madden whisper the words. The children moved closer to me. The ama sat on unseeingly. My colleague turned on me. "So this is what you allow in the nursery, Miss Scully? This is the way you are training the children? Why, you are no better than the woman herself."

"But the children see no harm in it, Miss Madden," I stammered. "And Tomasina does not mean any harm."

"No harm? Why it's—it's downright immodesty."

"Not for Tomasina, Miss Madden. She doesn't look at these things the way we do. If I did it, now, or if you did it——"

"*I*, Miss Scully?" Her voice was a shriek of outraged modesty. "How dare you suggest I might ever be capable of such vile indecency?" That biological reasons alone forbade it did not occur to either of us.

The poor distraught homesick creature was beside herself. She took a liberty which until now had been refused to her by discretion and cowardice: she opened a direct attack on the ama.

"You are a low indecent woman!" Each word was stabbed home with a shaking forefinger. "You are a shameless coarse creature!"

The mosquito had buzzed too near. The ama's eyes narrowed, and that curved upper lip drew back. Quick as a cat, she made her swipe. She whispered an ugly word and the next minute the front of Miss Madden's grey silk blouse was splattered with Tomasina's milk.

She left for Westmeath the following morning. The Marquesa decided not to engage another senior governess until we should return to Madrid. Elena, the nursery-maid, was given charge of Rosita and Concepcion and I got promoted temporarily to Miss Madden's place. It was this promotion which catapulted me into freedom. If I had been left with the two little girls I should never have got myself into disgrace over Art McBain.

CHAPTER FIVE

THAT summer in Neguri was a pleasant time for me. The gold of sun and the sapphire of sea and sky would in themselves have been nearly sufficient to keep me happy. But life held plenty of other pleasant things as well. There were Michael's fortnightly letters to give me my flying trips home. There were the occasional evenings in the Hotel Inglés. There were the new friends I made among the governesses, and there was my old friend, Miss Carmody, who had arrived in Neguri with the Juanes family early in June.

From the time she came our weekly outings were resumed. Every Thursday we took the train into Bilbao for tea at the Suizo, a dark spice-smelling little teashop in the Calle Correos. Sometimes we were joined by Helen Quinn, a girl Miss Carmody had known for years. Helen was in her late twenties. She had eyes of a hard bluey-grey set a little too closely together over a small thin nose and her teeth were frankly prominent. Still, she was attractive in a carefully groomed, neat-legged, well-made kind of way. I had a feeling that in spite of the long friendship between them Miss Carmody did not have a great *gradh* for her. I remember one evening when the two of us were sitting in the Suizo. Helen came in. She made straight for us in that firm self-assured way of hers, her bag clamped between arm and side, her smallish eyes fixed steadfastly on the goal of our table, the prominence of her upper teeth giving her mouth its habitual look of wearing a little mirthless smile. As Miss Carmody watched her approach, she said, more to herself than to me, "Here comes a girl who will never be guilty of an indiscretion," the tone of her voice suggesting that she liked Helen the less for her steadiness. She was right abou Helen's safe way of living. I was to know Helen Quinn through many ups and downs. I never knew her to put a penny astray or give way to an impulse.

The friendship that grew between Helen Quinn and myself was surprising. She despised my idiocy and improvi-
dent ways. I, while envying her thrift and discretion, was
repelled by them. Maybe it was these very differences that
drew us together. We supplemented each other at twenty
points. I have noticed that a dovetailing of qualities will
often join two people more neatly than the glue of liking.

Miss Carmody was glad to see me becoming friendly with
Helen. I think she felt Helen would be a good influence for
me. She was glad about Michael's letters too. I could see
she had a notion I was still pining for Rafael and that she
thought the letters were bringing consolation to a lovesick
heart. She need not have worried. My heart was never in a
healthier condition. The change of air and scenery had done
it a world of good. I rarely thought of Rafael, and then only
in the pleasantly regretful way one remembers a book that
promised to be interesting but which had to be returned to
the library before it was finished. In any case, I was becoming resigned to the idea of a celibate life. From what
I had seen since coming to the de las Rojas I realized that I
would have to be a nun in word, act and look until I should
be old enough to make a bid for freedom. Miss Carmody
put the minimum age for emancipation at twenty-five. I
determined not to let it go a day beyond twenty-one. It
frightened me sometimes to think of spending even three
years more in this atmosphere of chilling propriety. I had
visualized Spain as a laughing bare-shouldered girl with a
rose in her hair. She had turned out to be a bleak-eyed forbidding wardress, with a bunch of keys in one hand, a penal
code in the other. A governess must wear her skirts well
below her knees. A governess must not use cosmetics. A
governess must never be seen in male company. A governess must not smoke. A governess may eat, sleep and
breathe and go sedately about her lawful occasions but she
must give no other evidence of being a normal living creature. The better the family you worked for, the more strict

the code. After the comparative liberty of Señora Basterra's house the Marquesa's rules and regulations made me feel at times that I was in the Curragh internment camp. Her contemptuous all-seeing eye even followed me into the sea. Before leaving Madrid I had bought a grand little scarlet swim-suit in the English Shop in the Calle Serrano. I wore it for my first bathe in Neguri. "You may say good-bye to that bit of style," the other girls told me. They were right. I had no sooner returned from the beach than I was summoned to the Presence and told I must give up sea-water unless I provided myself with a *traje de baño* more suited to my calling. I was given a thumbnail sketch of the sea-going uniform of a governess. From the sound of it, it was identical with the creation which my poor mother had preserved from her Tramore honeymoon—a bloomer-legged, long-sleeved, befrilled garment of navy serge and white braid. We used to dress up in it when playing circuses. That was my first taste of the sea. It meant more to me than my appearance, so I put away my scarlet immodesty in the bottom of the dress-basket and bought myself a regulation garment. If I had had any hope of bewitching one of the wealthy bronzed idlers who sported themselves on the beach in the mornings, I said good-bye to romance after that. I was a sight going into the sea in that suit, but I was a beauty entirely coming out. The water used to make the cottony stuff stretch to twice its size, bringing the floppy legs well down below my knees and giving me weird pouchy effects where they were least becoming.

We Irish Catholic internees had a great envy of the English girls who were governesses with some of the British colony. Those girls were as free as if they had been living at home. They could dress to please themselves. They belonged to the Colony tennis club and they were invited to all the dances at the British-American Club. They were better propaganda for the temporal advantages of Protestantism than the soup kitchens which the proselytizers set up amongst us during the Famine. In the glory of their liberty they kept themselves to themselves, and did not mix with us poor serfs outside the Pale, but by virtue of the mysterious grapevine system which always exists in a community like ours, we knew of all their activities. We knew that Miss Colling, a tall dark good-looking girl with a supercilious face, was taking Bile Beans to make her slim. We knew that Miss Thorne, a plump little bustling article with a consequential walk, was mad about Mr. Woods of the Anglo-South American Bank who was engaged to her employer's sister. And we knew that the Greenes' governess, who had lank fair hair, a long nose, weak blue eyes and the extremely anaemic general appearance which only English girls suffering from anaemia manage to achieve, was "carrying-on" with her boss. Something which I myself saw in the Suizo gave support to this bit of scandal. I was having tea there one evening with Helen Quinn. The Greenes' governess was there too, a few tables away from us. Presently Mr. Greene came in. He gave the governess a casual uncaring nod and sat down at another table. He was a horrible little man with a bald head, a heavy snout of a nose and a mouth which, though small to meanness, was thick-lipped. He had nearly driven me mad one evening on my way home from Bilbao in the train. He had sat on the seat opposite me and for the full half-hour of the journey he had picked his nose with morbid concentration. Helen Quinn nudged me when Mr. Greene sat down and we prepared to enjoy the playlet. It was mean and scandalous of us, I suppose, but sure, Heaven help us, observing other people's loves was as near as we could get to romance. After a minute or two Mr. Greene took out his notebook and scribbled something. He tore out the page, folded it small and then got up and went towards the *caballeros*. As he passed the girl's table, he dropped the note into her lap. When she had read it she went out at once, and when he came back he collected his bill, and went after her.

"Now, isn't that disgusting?" Helen said, when they had gone. I thought about it. It *was* rather disgusting. But why? Not because of the sin. Not even the most strait-laced of the governesses felt disgusted with Miss O'Dwyer's mistress, the lovely Condesa de Villa Hermosa, although we all knew she was madly in love with the handsome young doctor who was treating her gouty husband. Some of the greatest lovers in history and literature had loved out of their turn and, though no one could say that they had been right, it was sympathy they aroused, and not disgust. I stumbled on the truth. The Greene affair was disgusting because neither of them looked the part. Their hearts might be palpitating with as grand and as poetic a passion as ever inspired star-crossed lovers, but because Mr. Greene was a grubby unpleasant little man and the girl a plain unsavoury poor creature, their love was disgusting. It was hard lines, but there you were. The world did not like its actors miscast. It condemned you in a part unless your natural attributes fitted you to play it convincingly.

I did not impart any of this profound philosophy to Helen. I could have said it to Miss Carmody, but not to Helen. She would have said I was trying to find excuses for Mr. Greene and the girl. "You know," she said seriously, "that's a situation that could never arise between an Irish governess and her Spanish employer. There is certainly a lot to be said for being a Catholic." She was right in saying the situation could never arise, but she was wrong in attributing its impossibility to Catholicism. Only a fool would claim unyielding purity for Irish girls, or admit it for Spanish men. The cause went deeper than religion or morals. It was racial. It was due to the Spaniard's regard for *el hogar*, the home. A Spaniard may have his love affairs but he keeps them outside his home. His family and his home belong on a plane of their own, and his female servants are as neutral to him as his furniture. Even the governesses who were most derogatory about the ways of Spanish men could not say that any one of them had ever been molested by the man of the house. And, now that I have said all that let me add that I am fully aware of another and perhaps even weightier reason why the sanctity of the Spanish home stood in no danger from us governesses. Our appearance afforded the best possible protection to *el hogar* and to ourselves. Take me in that bathing costume, for instance.

In July, Luisita Juanes threw a bombshell into my world by deciding to study art. She was going first to Italy and from there to Paris. She would be gone more than a year and Miss Carmody was going with her. Before my friend left she lectured me for an hour on the way I was to behave in her absence. I was a little hurt and offended that she should consider the lecture necessary. "If you conduct yourself properly and don't do anything foolish," she wound up, "the Marquesa will probably be paying you two hundred pesetas a month before we meet again." Before we should meet again, the Marquesa's two hundred pesetas were to seem very small potatoes to me, for I would have flown to a height of independence never before reached by an Irish governess in Spain, and I would have wounded myself badly on the way.

I found it difficult to imagine a whole twelvemonth without my friend, without her kind-eyed sympathy and sound advice, and the generous readiness with which she listened whenever I wanted to think out loud. It was her going away that was the start of my long letters to Michael. When I tried to write to Miss Carmody as fully as I had spoken to her, I found I could not do it. When she was away from me, the softer side of her became blurred somehow, and I kept seeing her as the reserved middle-aged woman who was separated from me by a lifetime of wisdom. I needed her actual presence, I had to see the kindness in her eyes, before I could speak my thoughts without feeling foolish and self-conscious. The fact that she was such a poor letter-writer may have had something to do with it too.

The first letter I had from her after her arrival in Rome was so stilted and conventional that I felt it would have been impertinent to write anything less stilted in return.

But I had to have somebody to talk to. I turned to Michael. Before, I had given him only little brush-strokes of the colour of the country—Tomasina walking along the Zugazarte with the baby in her arms, the crippled lottery vendor outside the Café Bilbaino who had been a bull-fighter in his time, the boys and the girls dancing under the fairy lights in the market square in Portugalete. Now I showed him the whole splashed untidy canvas of my mind. Fifteen and sixteen pages I sometimes wrote to him. A thought would occur to me and I would file it away for him. "I must tell that to Michael," I would say to myself. He responded with letters which not only brought the bog and my home to me, but brought the man himself with all his gentleness and niceness and quietly amused way of look-ing at life. He told me about his ramshackle old house that was falling to the ground for the want of money to keep it in repair. He told me about his work—he had something to do with the training of horses. He loved horses, and could write about them in a way that made me feel the Curragh wind on my face as the springy track unspooled itself under the smooth lovely satiny creatures.

Shortly after Miss Carmody's departure, Helen Quinn decided to make a move which she had been planning for a long time. At the end of August she would quit governess-ing and go to Madrid as a *profesora*. A love of money rather than a love of freedom was responsible for this decision. The family she worked for could not afford to pay her more than one hundred and fifty pesetas a month. As a *profesora* she could earn five hundred. There were plenty of decent *pensiones* in Madrid where a girl could live for seven pesetas a day. She was already in correspondence with a Mrs. Han-sen who ran a boarding-house for English people in Nuñez de Balbao, a quiet street near the Retiro. With even moderate luck she would be able to save well. I envied Helen the ten years' advantage she had of me, and my twenty-first birthday seemed further away than ever.

The de las Rojas were not returning to Madrid until the end of October, but Helen's departure would not leave me lonely. I had made plenty of new friends. Miss Myers was one of the nicest of them. She was a stout, black-satined old lady with very grand ways and a pile of white hair above her broad pink face. She had been governessing for forty years. The other girls called her the Maid of Athens because she had spent a couple of years in Greece before coming to Spain, and was always talking lovingly about that country. The greater part of her life had been spent in St. Petersburg as governess to the children of a prince. She did not talk much about her Russian experiences, and small wonder. Russia was a sore subject with the unfortunate woman. She had earned plenty of money there, for her employers were generous in their wealth. On the advice of the Prince, she had invested everything in Russian securities. She would have been able to retire in comfort at fifty if the revolutionaries had not used stocks and shares to light the torch of freedom, leaving her to begin life all over again at a time when she had grown bone-weary of coping with children. She was a brave dignified woman, with never a complaint out of her, though she had plenty of reason for whingeing. Her age and appearance were against her, condemning her to posts no other governess would take. When I knew her, she had charge of the Jausoro boy, a spoiled impossible brat who would have broken the heart in a stone wall. Poor Miss Myers's feet and legs were not the best, and it was crucifixion on her to use them much. That young demon had no mercy. He would not content himself with playing in one spot like the rest of the children and give the old woman a chance to take her ease on one of the benches. That would have been too Christianlike for young Jausoro. It was up and down the full length of the Zuga-

zarte with him on his infernal tricycle, with poor Miss Myers
trotting painfully and puffily after him. I am glad to place
on record that I managed to trip over that tricycle one day
and put it out of action for three weeks. I prophesied that
the boy would grow up to be a curse on mankind. I was
right. During the Spanish Civil War I learned that he was
responsible for many an atrocity before a socialist bullet sent
him before his Maker to answer for what he did to poor Miss
Myers's feet.

Miss Myers was kind to me. She spoke French beautifully
and undertook to teach me the language so that I might be
able to better myself. We met on the beach in the mornings
and on the Zugazarte in the afternoons.

When I went to the Zugazarte and watched the children,
I always had a feeling that they were playing at grown-ups.
The little girls were so bedizened in their smocked dresses
of apricot and lemon and white crêpe de Chine, every one
of them with little gold rings in her ears, a tiny pearl-set ring
on her finger and a thick halter of amber beads around her
neck. The little boys in their long-trousered sailor suits of
white linen were as grave-eyed and as self-contained as
ecclesiastical students. It was funny to hear those scions of
the Spanish nobility deliver their English in a thick Irish
brogue. The heir of Sus Excelencias Los Condes de Villa
Hermosa would come running up to his Antrim governess
with "Mees, thon boy's after tekken ma wee ball." When
the sun was too much for the eight-year-old Marqués de
Rio Tinto he would give his little sweater to Miss Barry of
Cork with, "Mees, will oo keep an eyes on dis? I'm dead
out wid de heat." I had no qualms about the accent of my
own charges. Was it not known the world over that Kildare
people had no queer ways of speaking, and that you would
never guess they were Irish at all unless you were told?

After Tomasina frightened Miss Madden home to Westmeath, I rarely got a chance of going to the Zugazarte in the
afternoons. Now I had to chaperon the two big girls to the

tennis club, or to the dentist or to tea in their friends' houses. When the Marquesa was very sure of the company they would be in, I had instructions to leave them at their destination and to call for them later. This gave me a couple of hours of freedom. Even if I took no more advantage of it than to come back to my room and write to Michael, it was a grand respite from playing reluctant gooseberry while the girls and their friends giggled and whispered and wished me miles away.

I still brought the two little ones to the beach every morning. It was friendly and bright and pleasant down by the sea. Before us the restless Bay of Biscay tossed its sail-specked blueness. The beach was alive with sun-soaked people whose well-cared bodies, even when clad only in bathing suits, bespoke wealth and good living. Spaniards have a good sense of proportion about many things. When they become elderly and paunchy they do not display themselves, and so there were only youth and grace to gladden the eye as the bronzed figures ran down over the warm pale sand to meet the waves. In little mushroom groups, the white-hatted children squatted over their play. Behind us rose the Balneario, the beach restaurant, a gay backdrop of red and white and green. The ground floor was honeycombed with bathing boxes that opened onto the beach like the doors in a dovecot. Projecting over the beach was a tabled veranda, its wooden pillars planted like strong brown legs in the sand. From the Balneario music came dropping on us, music and the tinkle of glasses and the cymbal-chime of gay talk and laughter. There were cymbals on the beach too, and out at the rocky Punta a muffled drumming.

We governesses did not use the bathing-boxes. Every family had its own tent which was brought down in the back of the car every morning. When we and our charges had had our bathe, we dressed and, having seen the children settle down to their play within watchable distance, we went to the Echevarria tent, where Miss Moore, the doyenne of the governesses, held court. She had been longer in the country than any of us, and had governessed two generations of Echevarrias. There the contented little woman would be sitting, knitting happily away at a winter sweater for one of the Echevarria boys, the older governesses sitting at her feet in the inner circle, we younger ones on the outskirts. It was said that Miss Moore had not always been so contented. Many of the older women could remember a time when she had done nothing but grouse and grumble about her exile, and talk longingly of the day when she should have enough saved to go home to Ireland and set up a little business. That day had seemed to be very remote, for Miss Moore was no Helen Quinn. She was only a normal Irishwoman and most of her few pounds flew as soon as she got it into her hands each month. An incredible wonderful thing happened. She won sixty thousand pesetas in the Christmas Lottery. Now her dreams could come true. With two thousand pounds she could start any kind of business she liked. She said good-bye to Spain and went home to Ireland. In six weeks she was back again with the Echevarrias. She had been in the cage too long and had forgotten how to use her wings. That trip home cured her nostalgia for ever.

We talked about many a thing there on the beach. That summer our talk was mostly of Miss Donnelly's marriage. Miss Donnelly was a gentle faded woman of forty, an emancipated governess. She lived in lodgings in Portugalete, a village on the other side of the river, and she earned her bread by giving English lessons. She had electrified us early in the summer with the announcement that she was going to marry Herr Schmidt, a thin elderly professor. Our man-bereft way of living made us very excited about the wedding. We were all extremely vague about the realities of sex. This was understandable. We had come straight out here from school and had never had a chance of acquiring knowledge. We retained our Victorian idea of the marriage bed as a place where men might love but women must weep.

"Be subject to him" was a command to endure unguessable things with meek submission. We were devoured with curiosity as to What Actually Happened. We speculated privately and in public on the ordeal that awaited Miss Donnelly at the hands of her bespectacled professor. When the bride-to-be joined us one morning, curiosity got the better of some of the bolder spirits, and they made her promise to come down on the morning after the wedding and tell everything. She was the kind of timid soul who can be bullied into promising anything. When she had gone away, Miss Moore said it was all wrong. She could quote you chapter and verse of the Bible on every subject and she said that the relations between man and wife were what St. Paul was referring to when he said there were things that should not be even mentioned among Christian people.

Wrong or right, we were waiting in full force when Frau Schmidt came down to us on the morning after the nuptials. She looked a wreck. Her pale unslept face and red-rimmed eyes told their own story. Our hearts beat quickly in anticipation of her fearful revelations. What she had to tell was a sore disappointment. Nothing at all had happened. At the last moment she had let us down by giving way to stage fright. In her fear of the Great Unknown she had flatly refused to be subject. The unfortunate professor had had to spend the night in armchair while the bride turned her face to the wall and wept nervous tears. Though we had to admit she had proved herself refined and nice, we were all raging with her.

It was through Miss Donnelly that I met Art McBain. In return for a set of china which we gave her she invited a crowd of us to tea in the Hotel Inglés in Portugalete. To get to the hotel, you had to cross the river from Las Arenas in the ferry-bridge. The little town was sprawled on the side of the hill as if it had dropped in exhaustion while trying to climb it, and had lain ever since where it had fallen. The hotel was run by a Mr. and Mrs. Ortiz. Their clientele was mostly British clerks who were working in the Babcock and

Wilcox factory. Mr. Ortiz was a pale scrap of a man with big anxious eyes and a harassed manner. The hotel had a drab unsuccessful look about it which accounted for his anxiety. His wife was Liverpool Irish. He had met her while working as a waiter in a Liverpool hotel. She was not the best wife in the world for an enterprising hotel-keeper, poor soul—a big soft slob of a woman with beige hair, an ineffectual manner and an apologetic smile. I never met Mrs. Ortiz without being reminded of the field at the back of Gran's house at home. When you lay there with the long June grass rising like a forest around you, there were a hundred interesting things to watch. Most interesting of all was a dusty-looking globe-shaped thing that came lumbering carefully towards you. When it came close enough, you saw that it was a mother-spider with her babies clustered all over her body. Poor Mrs. Ortiz was as thickly barnacled with children as the spider. She had them in her arms and under her arms and hanging in their dozens out of her skirts. And in spite of the way she was assailed, she always managed to be pleasant.

After that first evening in the hotel, several of us got into the clandestine habit of crossing over on Thursday evenings for our tea. When the clerks came in we played games or sang songs, and sometimes we danced while Helen Quinn played the ghostly piano. The boys were right enough but Art McBain was the only one of them I liked. The others were full of lordly condescension. Something queer happens to a certain type of Englishman as soon as he sets foot in a country where English is not spoken. Here were boys who at home would have known their place. Since arriving in Spain they had come to consider themselves better than the Duque de Alba. They had the greatest contempt for Spanish boys of their own class. "Dirty dagoes," they called them. I think the colonizing tradition may have something to do with this little peculiarity on the part of the British. It does something to their brain, making them imagine every foreign country is Darkest Africa and that all foreigners are bushmen.

Art McBain was different. He was a nice simple Scots lad, small and quick-tongued and as dark as a Spaniard. We took to each other at once and became very friendly. There was nothing romantic about my feeling for him, although I am not saying that there might not have been if, two minutes after we first met, he had not explained with native caution that he was engaged to a girl at home.

One evening in late August he invited me to go bathing with him the next day and to have tea afterwards in the Balneario. A prudent refusal was on the tip of my tongue Then I remembered that the girls would be having tea with their aunt and that I would have a couple of hours free. I told myself that it was not at all likely that I would be seen by the Marquesa's friends, since in the afternoon the quality always left the sea to the workers who came out from Bilbao in droves. Dare I take the chance? I did. I dared more. I dared to smuggle out with me the forbidden scarlet swim-suit. Not for all the world would I have let myself be seen in the other garment by any man in whom I had the remotest interest.

We had our swim, and afterwards we sat on the sand and let the sun bake the sea-water into us. It was lovely there in the sun. I ceased to be a repressed creature of neuter gender and uncertain age. For the first time since my birthday in May I knew the joy of being eighteen. I forgot I was a governess, and became a happy girl in a becoming swim-suit who was out for the evening with a nice boy. The joy of it went to my head like that glass of sherry at the Ritz dance, and when Art borrowed a beach-ball from some children who were playing near us, I played with him as daftly as if there were never a Marquesa in the world. By the time we were dressed and running up the steps of the Balneario we were ravenous for tea. I must have been a little sunstruck, for though I had never smoked a cigarette in my life I accepted one from Art as we went in the door. I sauntered out onto the veranda with him, puffing away with the air of one who was born with a cigarette in her mouth.

That is how the Marquesa and her sister and her two daughters saw the de las Rojas senior governess when they looked up from the table where they were having tea with their friends. From the look on their faces I knew they had seen all that had gone before—the scarlet swim-suit, the sun-bathing in company with a man, the disgraceful exhibition I had made of myself by running around in front of a beachful of people in an indecent costume—every detail of my evening's debauch had been seen from the veranda. Without returning my frightened conciliatory salute, they gathered up their belongings and went.

I did not enjoy my tea. Thoughts of what the Marquesa would have to say came between me and the cream cakes.

There was no lecture—only two months' salary and an eviction order. I sat on the side of my bed and reviewed the position. By to-morrow, every governess-employing family in Bilbao would have the story—the Marquesa and her relatives would see to that. I had no chance in the wide world of getting a post in any Spanish house. There was no Miss Carmody to turn to now. I was eighteen. I had ruined my career, and I had ten pounds between me and the workhouse. The situation was worrying. There was just one post I might get. Madame Rouget, the Frenchwoman who drank, who had five unmanageable children and who changed governesses every six weeks, was looking for a girl again. She would probably be glad to get me, besmirched though I was. I started to pack the dress-basket. As I folded my things, another alternative kept occurring to me. But, no— that would be madness. It was safe enough for Helen Quinn. She had introductions to plenty of people who would get her lessons. But I knew nobody in Madrid. I would never be able to keep myself in lodgings there. Better go to Madame Rouget and put up with it. But what a life it would be with those five children and Madame in her tantrums. Wouldn't any risk be better than that? Maybe— at the same time there was a lot to be said for being sure of a roof over one's head and three meals a day. Besides, Miss Carmody would eat me if I broke loose.

I had until the morning to make up my mind. I decided to settle it in this way: when I should go out in the morning I would put it to the first governess I met. Whatever she advised, I would do. The first I met was poor fat Miss Myers toddling painfully home from Mass in her black satin. She had already heard of my disgrace, and she shook her white head over me.

"I advise you to go to Madrid," she said. "Any girl who could act so foolishly as you did yesterday evening is not fit to be a governess. Go to Madrid, child. You'll probably find it hard enough at first, but you'll be all right. Providence looks after fools."

I thanked her for everything and took her advice. On the 1st of September I went to Madrid. After paying my fare and buying myself a garnet brooch and a hat I never wore, I had enough left to keep me for two weeks. The moment I put my foot on the train all fears and doubts left me. In the first grand moments of freedom a newly escaped prisoner does not insult his swelling heart with petty mundane anxieties.

I am glad to say that somebody profited by my misfortune. The Marquesa had to have a chaperon for her girls. She reviewed the governesses with a view to selecting the one least likely to don a scarlet swim-suit and go playing beach-ball with men outside the Balneario. Her choice fell on Miss Myers.

CHAPTER SIX

NOT for a minute did I begrudge it, but the price I had to pay for my first few months of freedom put Shylock's demand in the ha'penny place. All he wanted was sixteen ounces. Twenty-three pounds were taken off me. I could well afford to lose them. The ease and high living in the Marquesa's house had given me a chest like a nursing mother and embonpoint to match. After four months in Mrs. Hansen's pension I had a pair of hip-bones that would have chopped cabbage in a bottle. This was no reflection on the fare provided by Mrs. Hansen. The food was grand, and I would have been as fat as butter on it if I could have afforded the usual number of meals. But I had only three regular pupils that winter. What I earned from them paid only for bed, breakfast and a light supper, leaving me with a modest balance of fifteen pesetas a week to cover stamps, fares, dinners and other incidentals. Dinner days were red-letter days with me. I nearly died with the hunger.

Helen Quinn soon had every hour of her day filled up. She had come armed with letters of introduction, but she could have done without them. One look at her and the most anxious of mamás was willing to entrust her daughters to her care.

Pupils who really wanted English lessons were difficult to find. I answered scores of advertisements which appealed for an English-speaking duenna, only to find that Spanish mothers liked their daughters to be chaperoned by someone who looked at least as old as the girls themselves. I answered other advertisements which read, "Serious gentleman wishes to practise the English." I soon gave up answering these. The first lesson always went off very well, but at the second I invariably found that the gentleman was not serious and that it was not the English he wanted to practice. I got one real job through an advertisement—teaching English in a language-school which was run by a Frenchman in the Calle Geronimo. I had to teach only three evenings a week and the pay was good, a hundred pesetas a month. At the end of the first week I walked out in a temper after a row with my employer which he started by asking me if it was true that the Irish kept pigs under their beds. Helen Quinn ate me for leaving that job. She said I deserved all that was coming to me and that it would be plenty.

I got my first pupil by chance. Mr. Yamada, the commercial attaché at the Japanese Legation, had stayed with Mrs. Hansen before he and his wife found a flat for themselves. One night he called back to the pension to inquire about a book he had left behind. Mrs. Hansen was out. I happened to be in the hall when the little melon-faced man was trying to explain himself to Maruja, the younger of the maids. He knew little English and less Spanish, and he and Maruja became so mixed up in each other that I had to extricate them. The upshot was that he engaged me to come to his house for a half-hour each evening to teach him English and Spanish. His Spanish was unbelievably poor. I remember he gave me his address as " Calle de Jorge Juan, 16, *Asegurado contra incendios.*" In his innocence he thought that notice over the front door, "Insured against fire," was part of the address. He paid me the equivalent of seven shillings a week. The pay was bad, but the value the poor man got for his money was worse. If he had been content with ordinary conversation lessons, he would have been all right, but some involved oriental reasoning in him made him believe that the longer and more unusual the words he learned, the better value would he be getting. To achieve his object, he decided to translate a highly technical English handbook of electricity into equally technical Spanish. That English book contained words I have never seen before or since. I had to guess at their meaning. My Spanish pocket dictionary was no help. But Mr. Yamada wanted the Spanish equivalents of those words and I could not let him down. I made up words that would have made Cervantes turn in his grave, good long words with no scarcity of syllables. With great satisfaction, my pupil wrote them into his notebook. I often wondered what would happen should he ever try out his knowledge on a Spanish electrical engineer.

My second pupil was Pepe Blanco, a blocky hedgehog-haired assistant in the grocery store around the corner. He was an earnest simple-minded likeable chap with an uncle who had a shop in London. The uncle had promised to make him his heir. That promise gave Pepe many an hour's anxiety. He took a poor view of the integrity of English lawyers and was convinced they would try to rob him of his inheritance when the time should come. He confided the whole story to me one day when I was buying a sausage sandwich for my midday meal. I agreed that it was more than likely the lawyers would cheat him. I warned him that his ignorance of the English language would leave him completely at their mercy. This bit of sales talk told, and Pepe engaged me to give him a lesson three times a week for fifty pesetas a month. I am filled with shame when I think of how hunger made me trade on the good nature of that boy and of his sweetheart, a pretty little waitress in the Café Hernani. Pepe took his lessons in the shop during the slack early afternoon hours. When the lesson was over, I would sometimes tender my couple of coppers and ask for a quarter kilo of the cheapest biscuits which were priced at one peseta a kilo, knowing well that Pepe would give me a big bag of the five-peseta kind. Whenever I felt I was in danger of over-doing this stunt, I would switch over to Micaela in the Café Hernani, where for fifty cents you could get a glass of coffee and an *ensaimada*, a big fresh spongy bun. Micaela always gave me half a dozen *ensaimadas* and as much coffee as I wanted for my fifty cents. Shame prevented me from trying on these mean devices as often as I would have liked, but I think now that I was not being nearly so ingenious as I

thought myself, and that both Pepe and Micaela knew well
how things were with me.

That is one reason why you will always find your best
friends among the poor when you are badly off. The poor
have an intuition about these things, and will give you the
kind of help you most need. What is more, they will give
the help in such a sensitive understanding way that you will
not have to shame yourself with a single admission of
poverty. The rich are thoughtless. To them, hunger is an
obscure disease to which only beggars and slum-dwellers
are subject. It never occurs to them that those they admit
into their homes might relish more a square meal than a glass
of sherry. It was a thought that struck me several times
that winter when I went to 58 Calle Barquillo to give Carola
Valiente her lesson.

I got Carola through the kindness of Miss Carmody.
When I wrote to her confessing the ignominy of my departure from the Marquesa's house, I had a letter by return
which made my ears burn. However, there was salve in the
six letters of introduction which she enclosed. Only one of
them brought results. It was addressed to Señora Valiente,
the wife of a well-known lawyer, who had mentioned to
Luisita that she would like an English chaperon for her
daughter, Carola. It was lucky for me that the señora was
in bed with a cold on the afternoon I called. She told me
afterwards that she would never have engaged me if she had
seen how young I was. It was Carola herself who inter-
viewed me, a sixteen-year-old girl as lovely as a poem, fair-
haired and brown-skinned and with amber eyes that seemed
to take up half her face. She had a little throaty voice and
the friendliest kindliest smile. The drawback of my age did
not weigh with Carola. She was delighted I was young, for
she had been expecting a dragon of sixty. The two of us
got on like a house on fire. She kept running from the
drawing-room to her mother's bed to enlarge on my good
qualities, and when I left the house I had my third pupil.

Her fee brought my total earnings to about six pounds a month.

That house in the Calle Barquillo showed me a new side of Spanish life. It was a grave cultured orderly home. After the luxury of the de las Rojas mansion it was austere to the point of bleakness. The Valientes were not society people. They came of the self-denying, coldly thinking stock that gave Spain its greatness. You could imagine Señor Valiente enduring the rack or inflicting it. He would do either unemotionally if it brought him nearer his ideals. He was a spade-bearded man with stern eyes who was Mr. Barrett to the life—indulgent to his wife, son and daughter so long as they gave him implicit obedience. Carola told me that he refused to let Señora Valiente visit her elder daughter who was married and who had displeased him by giving her baby son a name he disliked. The señora was not likely to incur his displeasure. She was as submissive as Mrs. Quilp.

Señor Valiente was in partnership with Gil Robles whose articles in *El Debate* were even then making a stir. Carola's elder brother, José Valiente, was also serving his political apprenticeship. I often met them and their friends, serious-faced young men who looked almost too much like conspirators to be convincing. Spanish history was being made in that house in the Calle Barquillo, but I was too young and ignorant to be interested. All my interest was for the songs which Carola tried out, songs from *El Huesped del Sevillano* with which Miguel Fléta was delighting Madrid, and for the new clothes Carola was getting made, and for her romantic passion for a young man who was at that time studying agriculture out in the Parque del Oeste—an ill-fated young man who was later to be stricken with paralysis, but who from his couch in an office in *El Debate* was to dictate articles that would overthrow a régime.

I went to Carola's house for two hours every afternoon for a whole year. I doubt if the child learned more than a dozen words of English in that time. I honestly tried to teach her, but she refused to be taught. Every time I came she had so many new things to talk about, so many confidences to make. In that bleak austere house she was as lost as a sunflower in an igloo. She was delighted to have someone to whom her dresses and songs and romances were not inanities, but matters of even greater importance than *caciques* and *camarillas*. I liked those two hours, although they had a couple of features which were not so pleasant. It was a terrible hardship on me to accompany Carola up the stairs to the top of the house and out onto the roof where she sometimes went to take photographs. On our way out, she always stopped to visit the top attic where their pensioned janitor lived with his wife and sister-in-law. I said "lived" but those three unfortunate old people were dead to everything but their own terrible misery. They were stricken with some kind of leprosy which was eating them away finger by finger, limb by limb. The old man and his wife had lost both their legs, and the sister was dragging herself around on a crutch and one leg trying to look after them. Though fear twisted my stomach every time I went up those stairs it was not fear for myself I felt—if the thing had been contagious, the señora would never have allowed Carola near them. My fear was of the unguessed horrors that are in the world.

There was another hardship which in its own way was just as distressing. It was to look on while Carola ate her *merienda* of chocolate and toast sippets. Often when I arrived I found her in the middle of it. That would be at five o'clock, and many a time that hour would find me fasting since my early morning coffee and rolls in Mrs. Hansen's. It was agony to smell the spicy chocolate, torture to see her dip those golden fingers of crisp toast into the heavy creamy smoothness, hell to watch her moving them around and around so as to take up a good coating. As she took each bite, I used nearly go down her neck after it. I was never invited to have some. To be sure, she always tendered me the conventional invitation of Spaniards when disturbed at a meal: "*Usted gusta?*—Would you like some?" But this meant nothing. It was intended to elicit only the formal answer which I always gave: "Thank you. May it do you good." She would have been shocked to death if I had taken her invitation as anything but a polite formality. It was not that Carola was mean. She was rich, and hunger was a state she could not imagine. She was probably convinced that I had come to her straight from a good tea that had been preceded by an even better dinner. And, in any case, hospitality is not one of the Spanish virtues. With all due respect to Spain I felt Ireland could teach them something here. No Irish person would run the risk of letting a friend out of the house with an empty stomach. My people would pay no attention to polite refusals. It would be, "Sit down there with you and not another word. Sure you're not going to go out with the curse of the house on you."

From twelve to five was always the worst time with me. For the benefit of Helen Quinn and Mrs. Hansen, I invented a pupil in whose house I had lunch every day. The lie saved my pride but it added to my hardship for it meant that hail, rain or snow I had to get out of the pension every day at twelve. Sometimes I went to the Prado, sometimes to the National Library. More often than not I sat on a bench in the Castellana in the cold sunny dryness and read, or just looked at the people passing. Mondays, Wednesdays and Fridays were not too hard. At three o'clock I could go and give Pepe Blanco his lesson and fill up on biscuits. When I had no money in my pocket the other days were bad for me. A famine era stretched between one and my eight o'clock supper. Hunger does queer things to you. The emptiness under my suspender belt filled my head with wicked thoughts. When overpainted befurred women passed, I wondered if they were the kind that the girls in the Retiro had told me about and, if so, was it through hunger they had fallen. I felt that if this was the case there was every excuse to be made for them. Sometimes I even went so far as to wonder how my virtue would stand the test if a rich man should stop in front of me and offer me a fur coat and diamonds and a flat with a maid. Temptation never assailed me. No rich man ever approached me with glittering offers. The only ones who stopped in front of me were ragged lottery-vendors and peanut-sellers. Now and then a venturesome student would stop, but he had nothing with which to tempt me except flowery phrases. In other circumstances I might not have turned such a deaf ear to these same blandishments, but it is difficult to respond to romance when your highest yearnings are for a plate of floury potatoes and a good lump of butter. Occasionally I wondered what would happen if Rafael should stop before me, but I doubt if even he could have created a tremor in one whose stomach clamoured more loudly than her heart.

If all this gives the impression that I was miserable that winter, it is far from the truth. Hardship is easy to bear when you know you can end it at any moment. I knew I had only to write a truthful letter home and I would be helped at once. Pride prevented the writing of the letter, pride and the fear that I would be ordered to pack my bag and to return at once to a home that was not the home which inspired my nostalgia. I wanted to develop in my own way, to discover life for myself, and if going without meals was the price of freedom, I would pay it and welcome. Miss Carmody would have helped me too, I knew, but here again pride demanded that I should write highly exaggerated accounts of the money I was earning. There was no fear of Helen Quinn betraying me to her, for Helen never took a pen in her hand except to make entries in her savings book. I had hardship that winter but no unhappiness. I was less homesick than I had been since coming to Spain. Michael's letters continued to be a delight—I warmed to him in a special way because he was the only one who had a good word to say for my decision to leave governessing. Life was

D

good. I was free and eighteen, and even if I was making no money I was making plenty of friends. Two of these were in the boarding-house with me, La Serena and Miss Wilson.

I loved La Serena from the minute I laid eyes on her. She was the older of the two maids. She could have been the grandmother of rawboned Maruja, the second maid. She was even older than Mrs. Hansen herself, and that is saying much, for Mrs. Hansen was as old as the hills and looked like one, a big rolling comfortable hill. It would be difficult to imagine anything more dried or sapless than La Serena. She was like a scrap of crumpled chamois leather that has been shut away in a drawer and forgotten for years. Eyes as bright and as big and as black as the Our Fathers on a nun's rosary beads looked on life with such a childish wonder that you felt her wrinkles and thin white hair were only make-believe. This impression of youth was heightened when you saw La Serena working. She swept and dusted and cooked and ironed with the energy of a woman quarter her age. The amount of work she got through was astounding in view of how little of her there was in it and the length of time that little had been in use. She did far more of the work than Maruja, and there was plenty to be done in a pension where in addition to Helen Quinn, Miss Wilson and myself there were four men—three English clerks and an American student. That old woman was the most gentle, most humble soul I have ever known. There was nothing craven about her humility. She had the lowliness of a great saint. She was so humble she never used the first person. A knock as timid as a child's first steps would fall on the door of the room I shared with Helen Quinn. "Who is there?" I would ask, just for the pleasure of hearing the withered-leaf rustle of her little voice as she answered, "*Es la Serena.*" Never "It is I, Serena," but always, "*Es la Serena*—It is the Serena one." I would open the door and there she would be with a pleasant surprise—something she had taken from my room to wash and iron for me, or a buttered roll and milk, or a little bunch of grapes, or some other scrap of food which in her own jackdaw fashion she would have filched when Mrs. Hansen's back was turned and have hidden away for me. The sight of her standing there, so small and good and kind, always did something melting to me, and I would have to thank her quickly and close the door. If I looked too long at La Serena when her rosary-bead eyes told their kind affection, another face, nearly as old and far more loving, would be there before me, filling every vein of me with lonesomeness and longing. At other times, when La Serena was not tearing down my defences with the kindness of her eyes, when she let my heart be, and became just a deft housewifely little body—at such times the way she put me in mind of Gran did not hurt at all. It was a delight. I used to get great enjoyment out of watching her in the kitchen at night preparing her tisanes. It was then she was in her element. She had a tisane for every ailment under the sun, and as Mrs. Hansen imagined she had all of them, La Serena had plenty of scope for her skill. She would mix and stir and brew in happy absorption, all the time looking like a child letting on to be a witch, all the time murmuring her prescriptions in a way that made them sound like beneficent incantations. I could set up as a doctor myself on what I learned from watching and listening to La Serena.

"To calm the nerves, the root of valerian is indicated, the which is prepared by throwing a good handful into boiling water and letting it simmer a long time."

"Against the indigestions is prescribed the tisane of manzanilla. Four heads of manzanilla are required for each cup of infusion."

"Very refreshing, soothing and stimulating for the appetite is the tisane of wild chicory. Prepare it like the tea. Throw the leaves into a pot of boiling water and sweeten. This is best taken fasting."

She rarely got a chance to make her concoctions in peace. In the middle of them would come an imperative screech

from Mrs. Hansen: "*Serena! Venga usted enseguida!*" and
away La Serena would have to dart to whatever new task
her mistress had invented for her. Twenty times an hour
that summons would pierce the house. The landlady abused
La Serena's good nature unmercifully. She gave the creature
neither ease nor rest. Mrs. Hansen is dead and buried this
many a day, and far be it from me to speak ill of the dead,
but this much I must say or choke: she was a cruel selfish
bully of the first water. She never raised her voice to the
other maid, Maruja, for Maruja was young and independent,
and could have walked out of the house and into another
job at a moment's notice. But La Serena's age placed her in
a different position entirely, and Mrs. Hansen knew this and
took full advantage of it. She bullied and ballyragged and
browbeat that submissive little handful in a way that was
past forgiveness. La Serena never once answered back. At
Mrs. Hansen's most choleric outbursts, La Serena would
only plead with genuine anxiety. "*Por el amor de Dios*,
señora, remember your heart! You will injure your heart,
señora," and in next to no time after the row she would be
at Mrs. Hansen's elbow with a cup of tisane. You would
need to know La Serena's complete freedom from malice
to understand that there was no sly impertinence in this.
For all I know, that wrinkled little Spanish woman may still
be cooking and ironing and brewing tisanes, but if her bones
are at rest, she is surely wearing a martyr's crown in Heaven
this minute for what she suffered from Mrs. Hansen.

The landlady never did a hand's turn herself. Her
cushions of fat gave her a slowness of movement that was
compensated for by her quickness of eye. She had eyes in
the back of her head and though she sat in an arm-chair at
the window all day, little escaped her of what went on in
the house. Next to persecuting La Serena, her greatest interest in life was watching the funerals which passed the
house. She would watch for them and count them and be
highly delighted when they were numerous. Her first greet-

ing when we came in each evening would be to tell us how many corpses she had seen borne past that day. "Seventeen!" she would say gloatingly. "Just think of it—seventeen." I used to think this daft of her until the reason for it dawned on me. The poor old thing was puffed up with pride in being still alive while so many others were dead. She gave herself a pat of congratulation every time the Gardener's hand missed her as he did his thinning-out.

It was pleasant enough in Mrs. Hansen's that winter. I liked my fellow-lodgers with the exception of Mr. Huxton, and only the mother who reared him could have liked him. He was a Yorkshire man of twenty-five or so. An Irish Republican would give ten years of his life for the gratification of meeting him and of knowing that such an Englishman as Huxton really existed. In Ireland, those of us who do not love England play a kind of jigsaw game which we find very enjoyable. Possibly English people play the same game using Germans as the pieces. This is how the game has been played by Irish Diehards since the time of Strongbow. You gather together every mean, contemptible, lowdown, despicable trait that has ever earned a man the scorn of his fellows. You pick out all the ill-favoured, ungainly odious physical attributes that have ever hurt the human eye. Then you assemble all this repulsiveness into one design and you call the result a Typical Englishman. That Huxton was the only Typical Englishman I have ever known may or may not be accounted for by the fact that I have known very few English people. But here is a queer thing: I have met a baker's dozen of men who I would have sworn were Typical Englishmen if I had not known for a fact that they were bred and born in Ireland.

I have no wish to cast aspersions on Huxton's mother. She may have been a decent woman who, since misfortune can fall on the best of us, should not be blamed for her son. But there is no denying that his eyes and his mouth and his complexion would lead the most charitably minded to sus-

pect that a ferret and a rabbit and a fox had a hand in the
making of him. Only a donkey strain could account for his
bray of a laugh, and his nasty little habits hinted at blood-
relationship with slimy crawling things that were never seen
on land or in water. It was Purgatory to see him eating.
Ravenous though I always was for my supper, I think I
would have been put off my food if the clean kindly bulk of
Mr. Newman, one of the other clerks, had not intervened
between Huxton and me at the table. He used to crouch over
his food, elbows spread protectingly as if he was afraid someone would snatch it before he was filled, and when his hand
went out for salt or bread it looked like the paw of an animal
grabbing for its share of the kill.

Huxton never lost an opportunity of getting a dig at me.
He said Irish people were noted blasphemers. The poor
deluded ignoramus thought we were taking the name of the
Lord in vain when we said "God bless us" or "God save
us," or "God save the mark." He jeered my accent too,
as if the speech of Ireland's kings were not as Greek is to
a pig's grunting compared with his Ilky-moor-bar-dat. He
tried to cap it all by christening me "Paddy," but with a few
well-chosen words I put a stop to that.

La Serena did not like him either. I often heard her warning Maruja against him and advising her to use her nails if
he did not give up his habit of pawing her when they met
in the passage. Poor unfortunate Maruja did not take advice
kindly, and more is the pity. She would only toss her
coarse-braided head at La Serena and say she did not need
any old woman to tell her how to take care of herself.

Miss Wilson detested Huxton as much as I did. He had
tried to make up to her at first, but she soon put him in his
place. It would have been the greatest waste in life if she
had taken any notice of him. She was far too sweet and
good for the like of Huxton. Even if I were not so deeply
indebted to her—I owe the complete independence which
later came to me to Miss Wilson's kindness—I would still

say she was a darling girl. She was in her early twenties, a little Staffordshire girl with no claim to beauty beyond a lovely pair of hazel eyes and a cloud of fine dark hair. She was what the Spaniards call *muy poca mujer*, a scrawny little flat-chested thing with colourless clothes that gave the impression that she had lost weight since buying them. I have always been attracted to people who have known hardship. They are nearly always interesting, for trouble is a swift-moving river and will carry you to countries undreamed of by those who dip lazy paddles in the placid waters of easy living. I was attracted to Miss Wilson from the first night I sat down to supper opposite her, and we soon became friendly. She had known want all right. Not the want of physical things, for her father was a fairly well-to-do man and she an only child. The want she had known was the kind that is sorest to bear, the want of love. Before she was old enough to walk, her mother had run away and left her. She showed me the wedding photograph of her father and mother—a hard, cold-looking man who might have been the disapproving father of that dainty laughing-eyed girl in the long white wedding-dress. When Miss Wilson was twenty she had a letter from her mother giving an address in London. The letter explained that the writer was short of money owing to some investments having failed and asked for a loan. The girl gathered together and sent off whatever she could lay her hands on. It was not much, for she dared not let on to her father about the letter. But from that moment she lived with the thought of visiting her mother and of being able to put her arms around all the soft daintiness and warm sweetness which the photograph had always been promising. She started work on a present for her. It sounded lovely. An afternoon tea-cloth of fine linen with a big bunch of cut-work snowdrops in each corner, and a foot-wide border of hand-made lace. The cloth was sent at Christmas with all her love. The summer holidays brought an opportunity for the surprise visit. Only someone made of granite could have remained dry-eyed when Miss Wilson told of that visit. It was no dainty laughing little mother she found in the dirty lodging, but a poor frowsy drink-fuddled wreck with a greasy dressing-gown pulled around her. What broke Miss Wilson's heart entirely was to see the beautiful tea-cloth, and it with the lace torn and beer stains and cigarette-burns all over it. She offered to look for a job in London and to take the unfortunate creature to live with her. But Mrs. Wilson was not so drink-fuddled as to agree to that. She sent the girl away and told her not to come again.

Miss Wilson sent money to her mother regularly from Madrid. She could well afford to spare it, for she earned seven pounds a week in the Anglo-Spanish Engineering Corporation. At that time English shorthand-typists were at a premium in Spain. They could pick and choose their jobs, for there were hundreds of firms with agencies for English engineering and electrical equipment. How I envied Miss Wilson her independence, and how I regretted not having taken advantage of the commercial course provided in the Wicklow convent. I knew I had as much brains as the next, and it seemed hard lines to me that I should be doomed to the humiliating insecurity of lesson-hunting just because I had never learned to make little squiggles on paper nor to play the piano on a machine. I envied the girl's moral freedom even more than I did her financial security. She could dress as she liked and go where she liked without a by-your-leave to anyone. Such freedom would never be mine. The scarcity of genuine pupils like Mr. Yamada and Pepe Blanco made me realize that only by chaperoning would I be able to earn a reasonable wage. The best I could hope for was that time would bring me the steady appearance of Helen Quinn and that this in turn would bring me a half-dozen señoritas to chaperon. When this day should come I would have almost as little freedom as I had had as a governess. Every stitch I would wear, every wave in my

hair, every step I would take would all have to be sanctioned
by the women who employed me. It was a terrible thought.
I wrote to Michael about it.

Michael's reply gave me a lantern for the road. "You are
quite right," he wrote. "Delia Scully should have perfect
liberty to dress like a Zulu lady should she feel so disposed.
If the notion should take her to wear her hair like a banshee,
she should be free to do so without let or hindrance. Should
she be denied these rights, then our seven hundred years'
fight has been in vain. Seriously, Delia, I cannot understand
why you are making no effort to escape a life which you
obviously hate. What is wrong with you, girl? I'll tell you:
you think your couple of terms in a boarding-school gave
you all the learning any human brain is capable of assimilat-
ing. You believe that when you left Wicklow you said
good-bye to school. Don't be a fool—you are eighteen, and
you may take it from me that people have been known to
acquire knowledge even after that advanced age. For God's
sake, stop whining like a chained pup and go and teach yourself enough to get a real job. The little girl I met at Robertstown Sports would have had more guts than to let herself
be dragged along a road she didn't want to follow. Stop
whining and strike out for yourself. By this I don't mean
that you're not to whine if you should ever find yourself in
a tight corner. If this should ever happen, I'd never forgive
you if you didn't whine to me—and loudly. By the way,
how are you for money? This is a question I've asked you
before and you never give me an answer. Don't forget that
what I have is yours, up to and including my overdraft."

It was good of him to have made that offer, though he
should have known that I could never bring myself to take
advantage of it. Most of us—even those to whom money is
something to be thrown away before the ink on a cheque
is dry—have a queer way of putting great moral value on the
ability to earn it. It is easier to confess to a friend that you
have broken the Ten Commandments of God and the Six

Commandments of the Church than to admit to him that you cannot make enough money to keep you.

I took the remainder of his letter to heart. Never again would he be able to call me a whining pup. That very night I went to Miss Wilson and asked her how she had fitted herself for her job. Her answer was not very encouraging. She had spent two years in a commercial college where in addition to shorthand and typing she had been initiated into the mysteries of such things as invoicing and bookkeeping and double entry. Even if there were such a college in Madrid, I had no way of paying my fees there. Miss Wilson told me not to despair. She said there were plenty of jobs going where all one needed was a fair speed at shorthand and typing and a knowledge of business routine. Then the girl from Staffordshire made me an offer which, in so far as I personally am concerned, wiped out Ireland's grudge against England. "If you feel you'd like to try it," she said, "I'll lend you my Pitman, and a book on business routine."

That was how I started. I remember well it was All Saints' Day, and feeling that the better the day, the better the deed, I commenced that very night. Miss Wilson was better than her word. She asked the American student, Mr. Owsley (inevitably, Huxton called him "Uncle Sam") for the loan of his typewriter for me to practise on. I have not mentioned this boy before, because he was so pale and thin and quiet that he played only a wraith's part in the life of the pension, but he is very real in my grateful memory for the ready generosity with which he lent me that typewriter.

From then on it was studying day and night with me. Helen Quinn thought the whole idea just another daft notion of mine, and she poured cold water on it. Miss Carmody did not think anything would come of it, either. "Do not be too hopeful," she wrote. "Remember that all those English girls came to Madrid with good recommendations from previous employers and after years of study." Both Helen and Miss Carmody were inclined to base their beliefs on precedent. No Irish governess had ever worked her way into an office in Spain, therefore it was ridiculous of me to attempt it. I let them have their say. I was convinced I would succeed and I had Michael's belief in me for backing. "More power!" he wrote when I told him what I was doing. "Here's believing that this time next year you will be an emancipated woman." I worked like a demon, for neither then nor since did I ever know the meaning of moderation when I put my heart into the doing of a thing. I would have worked all night but that Helen Quinn shared the room with me and she insisted on the light being put out the minute she had finished entering in her notebook every penny she had spent during the day.

With all this work to occupy me, Christmas was on us like a shout. It brought a lovely jumper from Miss Carmody and ten pounds with which to buy myself a Christmas box from Michael. He had had a good win on a horse. That ten pounds solved many a problem. It enabled me to give presents to La Serena and Miss Wilson and others who deserved the world from me.

We had good fun in the pension that Christmas. Mr. Newman and Mr. Blair, the two nice clerks from the Anglo-American Bank, brought in sweets and crackers. Mr. Owsley contributed a cake that was sent to him from his home in Minnesota, and Helen and Miss Wilson and myself made a plum pudding. There were only the six of us at the party. Huxton and the landlady were in bed with colds. It was a grand Christmas.

CHAPTER SEVEN

I WILL always have a good word to say for the advantages of culture and higher education. They deserve it of me, for it was through my interest in Comparative

Mythology that I won the friendship of Luis Sotelo, three square meals a day and an engagement ring from Siemen Kronz.

Early in the New Year I had a letter from Michael advising me to give myself a break from the shorthand and business routine. "You will go stale on it if you stick to it all the time," he wrote. "Why not give a few hours a week to something entirely different—Comparative Mythology, for instance? Anyone so fond of pishogues as yourself should have a great time finding out if Spain has anything to equal the Children of Lir and the Gobán Saor."

Comparative Mythology. I was not rightly sure of the exact meaning of the words, but they had a good look to them and they sounded even better. No one could fail to admire the serious-mindedness of a girl who would be studying Comparative Mythology. The following Sunday I tried it on my fellow-lodgers after breakfast. "Don't expect me back after Mass," I said, addressing the table in general and Helen Quinn in particular. "Why not?" she wanted to know. "I have to go to the library," I said casually. "I am studying Comparative Mythology." You could have heard a pin drop. They were all impressed.

When I arrived at the National Library in Recoletos I found a stumbling-stone on the path of learning. I had no notion of what books I should ask for. An antique librarian was bent over a *Blanco y Negro*. He was huddled inside several layers of dusty black overcoat, and the way his little bald head and thin wrinkled neck protruded from that collection of coat-collars gave him the look of a knowledgeable turtle. He did not look up when I approached. "I wish to study Comparative Mythology," I confided to the back of his head. "Does your mercy wish to have the goodness to tell me how one begins?" His mercy was as deaf as a doorpost and paid no attention to me. I tried again. In that hushed atmosphere I had to keep my voice low, and, anyway, Comparative Mythology is not the kind of thing one cares to shout at the top of one's voice. The librarian went on reading. I looked around for help. A thin brown-faced man who was sitting at a nearby desk glanced up and saw my lost look. He came over to me. "The señorita is a foreigner? If she is in difficulties and will pardon the liberty, perhaps I can help. Our poor librarian may be reached only by the written word." In next to no time I was deep in the adventures of the Cid Campeador, a Spanish hero who might have been own brother to Fionn McCool himself.

When I left the library the nice brown man walked with me as far as the pension. By the time we said *Hasta la vista* I had made as good a friend as any girl could hope for.

That at my very first meeting with Luis Sotelo I should receive a kindness from him, was only in keeping with what I was later to know of him. There was no end to his kindness. It was not on me alone he showered it, but on everyone he met. He was the makings of a saint, and one had only to look at him to know it. The gentle mouth, the nice open forehead and the good eyes: these said, "Here is a man who is all virtue." His eyes especially were good. When they looked straight into mine I always felt the need of going to the nearest church and of making a general confession. Not that there was anything censorious in Luis's eyes. They were as merciful as they were good. If Luis were a priest and had to hear the confession of the worst sinner breathing, he would let him off with three Hail Marys. But there was no likelihood that he would ever become a priest, for he was an ardent theosophist.

After that first meeting we had a regular appointment in the Castellana on Sunday mornings. Sometimes we met on week evenings as well. Helen Quinn and I had a quarrel over this new friendship. She insisted on calling it a flirtation with a man I had picked up. That sounded like sacrilege to me. I would as soon have thought of trying to flirt with a priest on the altar as with Luis. In any case it would

have been no use. Had I been Deirdre of the Sorrows,
Grainne of the Ships and Niamh of the Golden Hair all
rolled into one, Luis would still have seen me only as he
saw all women: as his sister. Fifteen years before he had
loved a girl. She died of consumption. After her death he
turned to theosophy for comfort. It gave him more than
comfort. It gave a spiritual fulfilment which he had never
found elsewhere. Mysticism proved the right soil for the
soul of Luis. Under that eastern sun, his soul grew strong
and shapely and beautiful. It outgrew worldly things as a
daffodil bud outgrows the sheath. When I knew him he
was wearing his body as a quaker woman wears her clothes,
fastidiously, but only as a compromise. I was interested in
this least common multiple of religions out of which Luis
was getting so much, and he lent me *A los pieds del Maes-
tro* and other books by Mrs. Besant and Krishnamurti. I
read them, but they did not seem to offer anything that was
not offered by the Penny Catechism. I decided that the religion in which I had been born and reared would do me to
be going on with, and I returned his books to Luis. He did
not make a theosophist of me, but he almost converted me
to vegetarianism. After listening to his views on the iniquity
of eating one's fellow-creatures, I often made up my mind
never to touch another morsel of meat. Unfortunately these
good resolutions were always wrecked on a flood of saliva
when supper-time came, bringing the smell of La Serena's
lamb-stew—browned cubes of lean lamb simmered with
artichokes and green peas and new potatoes in a rich winy
gravy, or her gorgeous *cocido*, a mixture of greens and potatoes and chick peas and tender beef and spicy sausage all
bedded down together in a casserole on top of the stove to
win succulence from each other before being served in big
heartening helpings.

Mrs. Besant was not the only writer to whom Luis introduced me. He read English well, and he had hundreds of
Tauchnitz books. Queerly enough, it was through this

Spaniard in Madrid that I first learned of an Irish playwright called Synge.

I had known my new friend a month or so when he invited me to supper in his flat off the Plaza Colon where he lived with his sister, Romana. When Romana came out to the hall to meet me that first evening, I felt she was the ideal person to be looking after Luis. Her square-built practical efficiency was just the right ballast to keep him from floating off the earth altogether. Although ten years younger than he, she cared for him like a mother. She did not share his religious beliefs, but she respected them. The inevitable Spanish loveliness of hair and eyes and teeth were hers, but she had a stolidity which prevented these gifts from adding up to beauty. The stolidity left her on a few occasions during the evening. Whenever the name of their great friend, Siemen Kronz, was mentioned, Romana's eyes became shyly uncertain and her strong mouth gentle. I learned that this Siemen was a Hungarian, a purchasing agent for a big engineering firm and that he was in Andalusia on a business trip.

"You would like Siemen, Delia," Luis said. "He is a very good fellow. He speaks good English too. When will he be back, Romana?"

Romana stood up to take away our plates. It was the maid's day out. Luis had eaten a salad, Romana and I had had breaded veal cutlets with endive and fried potatoes. She turned to the sideboard for a dish of oranges, and her back was to us when she spoke. "In to-day's letter he said he hoped to be back this day fortnight." There was a little secret lilt in her voice.

"I'll tell you what we'll do." Through Luis's uncurtained face shone the joy of planning a treat for others. "We'll welcome him with a supper party. Delia will come, and Juan and Consuelo. Just the six of us. Afterwards we'll go to the Café Asturias and listen to their new tzigane orchestra. What do you say?"

Romana said it would be lovely. So did I. I was delighted to be drawn into Spanish life in this way. It was something I had been wanting for a year and a half. "Who is Juan?" I wanted to know. "And who is Consuelo?"

My mind was on the question but my eyes were on Luis's thin brown hands and they peeling the orange. He used the little silver fruit knife as neatly as if it were a pen. A quick cut right around the crown of the orange. Another around the base. Then four downward nicks to connect these two lines. A gentle rolling of the orange between his palms to loosen the peel, and the bright sheath was stripped off in six clean pieces. "Juan Negrin is as good as bread," he said, using a Spanish phrase which, next to our Irish *macánta* is the best way I know of describing real goodness and wholesomeness. "He draws cartoons for a living."

Sure, of course I knew his work. With a single pencil-stroke Juan Negrin could tell you more about his subject than a writer would convey in ten pages.

"He calls himself an anarco-sindicalista," Romana said. "But whatever he might choose to call himself he would always remain Juan. Consuelo is his wife and she is as generous as he is. They have no children and perhaps it is better so. They give so much to the poor that the children might fare badly."

"*No lo créas*, Romana. Gifts to the poor are investments that pay good dividends." There was truth in everything Luis said.

"I'll be looking forward to this day fortnight," I told Romana when I was saying good-bye.

"I shall have much pleasure in seeing you," she said. "Go with God until then." Though her tone was cordial I knew well she had not warmed to me. All the evening she had been a perfect hostess, but, in the unspoken language which women use to reach an understanding with each other, she had conveyed her feelings to me from the start: she was willing, since Luis wished it, to admit me to her friendship, but I must not expect entry to her heart. Before we were finished with each other she had good cause to shut me out.

During the following week Luis solved my financial problems for me. He got me a post as part-time governess to the daughter of his friend, Dr. José Martinez. I looked after little Catalina from nine to one every day. In return I received my lunch and sixty pesetas a month. I was in clover.

There had been plenty of excitement in the pension all this time. The colds which kept Mrs. Hansen and Huxton in bed over Christmas developed into influenza. Mrs. Hansen did not get out of bed until the middle of February. At the end of January, Huxton was better. Maruja waited on him hand and foot during his illness. Even when he was convalescent and well able to wait on himself, she still coddled him. She was in and out of his room all day long. I heard La Serena scolding her for this, though scolding is hardly the word for the gentle old creature's mild-voiced reproof.

"Have a care, Maruja," she said. "To attend the sick is a good thing, but when a man is well it is not right that a girl should be in his room at all hours. That one will not bring you luck."

"Leave me in peace, old woman," Maruja retorted rudely. "Am I your granddaughter that you should wish to command me?"

"La Serena does not command you—she only counsels you. When our señora is well again and able to take notice of what is happening in this house she will have something to say."

Maruja expressed her opinion of the señora in words for which I have never learned the English equivalents, and walked down the passage towards Huxton's room with her hips swinging defiance. La Serena shook her head forebodingly and went on with her work. She had little time to spare these days. As if the two invalids were not giving her enough extra work, another boarder had arrived soon after Christmas to add to her labours. He was a commercial agent from Aragon, a small long-nosed bespectacled man called Rico Cortes. I had heard that the people of Aragon were the Scots of Spain. They had a great name for thrift. Rico bore this out. He had chosen our pension because, having several agencies for English goods, he wanted to learn English cheaply. I had had a notion that Helen Quinn was the only person in the world who entered pennies and ha'pennies in a little black book at night as religiously as a monk sings vespers. She could not hold a candle to our new lodger. Helen at least performed her evening devotions in the privacy of her room, but Rico could hardly wait for the supper table to be cleared before taking out notebook and pencil, and setting to with a look of holy concentration on his narrow sallow face. His solemn preparations for the nightly long-tot were like the incensing of an altar before a ceremony. Out of one pocket would come all his loose change and this he would arrange in its separate piles on the table, the small mean carefulness of his fingers making every penny seem as big and as heavy as a crown piece. Out of another pocket he would take every tram and tube ticket, every neatly folded receipt that he had accumulated during the day. Then the adding and the balancing and the checking would commence. If the total fell short by one five-cent piece of the amount with which he had started the day, he would puzzle and worry and cross-check until the missing ha'penny had been run to earth.

He mesmerized me. When I got to know him, I could not resist asking him why he wasted so much time every night in adding and subtracting. "You know that you have to spend a certain amount of money every day," I said. "Once it's spent, it's spent, and all the sums in an arithmetic book can't bring it back to you."

I spoke in Spanish, for the little man aggravated me and

I would not please him by speaking English. It might have been double Dutch I had spoken for the astonishment with which Rico looked at me through his big round spectacles. "Putting one's affairs in order is not a waste of time," he explained patiently. "You are studying business routine. Have you learned yet that in business it is necessary to keep books?"

I quoted glibly, "It is of the utmost importance to check and balance the petty cash regularly." By the satisfied way Rico nodded to the tune of that, he might have been John McCormack listening to one of his own records. "There. You see," he said. "Are one's personal affairs of less importance than those of a business concern? And, since each day we spend so much time and effort in the earning of money, is it not logical that we should spend fifteen minutes each night in caring for it? Believe me, señorita, the nightly quarter of an hour is the most important period of the twenty-four." Put like that it sounded logical. Still . . .

It was only natural that Rico and Helen should have been attracted to each other. He was full of steadiness, the quality she most admired in men, and she was *una mujer seria*, the only kind of feminine creature for which he had a good word. They had not known each other a fortnight when they were getting the height of enjoyment out of doing their nightly accounts in unison at the dining-room table. At the other end sat Miss Wilson and myself doing shorthand. "Bet you he asks her out one of these fine days," Miss Wilson scribbled on the margin of Pitman one evening. "Bet you it will be Dutch treat," I scribbled back. We were both right. In next to no time it was a regular thing for the two of them to go out together when their incomings and outgoings had been checked satisfactorily. They went to a little café around the corner where there was no risk of Helen being seen by any of her employers and where a bedtime glass of coffee could be had for twopence ha'penny. Mr. Blair and Mr. Newman sometimes took Miss Wilson and myself there. Other nights they took us to one of the cafés in the Puerta del Sol and bought us chocolate and mojicones. These were fourpenny sponge cakes as big as a three-quart can and lighter than bog-cotton. They were grand for a fancy snack but useless if you were hungry, for there was no substance at all to them and they melted like snow in your mouth.

One night when I was in the Café Madrid with my three fellow-lodgers I saw a queer frightening thing happen. I was watching the door idly and taking no part in the conversation, for my friends were discussing some revue which all three had seen in London. The revolving door flickered like the leaves of a book and into the café came an old woman, and a young girl behind her. They sat at a table near ours. The girl was waved and painted and powdered to the last, but her little immature figure and her scared eyes made me put her age at no more than sixteen. It was terrible to see such young timorous eyes looking through that mask of make-up. She sat in a shrinking hunched-up attitude as if trying to hide inside her cheap coat. Every now and then the old woman would nudge her and whisper something and the little girl would sit up straight for a moment. The old woman wore a shabby black coat fastened right up to her throat, and under the black mantilla her white hair was combed neatly back from her forehead. Her face was fresh-skinned and her features were small and handsome. She should have looked a nice old woman, a good old woman, but she stank of evil. It was her mouth, principally, that was bad. The withered lips were parted in a knowing little leer as if she were remembering some dirty story told to her by Satan himself. It was horrible to see that leer on the mouth of one so old and grey. Horrible too to see the busy alertness with which her eyes communicated with any man whose glance she succeeded in catching. She seemed to be trying to conduct a wordless higgling with him. I could not inter-pret it, but her nods and winkings told me it had some frightening connection with the shrinking girl at her side, and I felt horror gushing up in me like a hæmorrhage. Most of the men ignored the old woman and went on with their coffee-drinking and dice-throwing, but presently she succeeded in winning an answer from one of them. He came over and sat at her table, a thick-lipped heavy man with hot bullet eyes. He talked to the old woman but he kept his eyes on the girl, and his podgy hand kept straying to where her little fingers clutched the edge of the table.

"Are you not well, Miss Scully?" I heard Miss Wilson ask. I mumbled something about a slight headache, so Mr. Blair paid the bill and we went home. When we got in, Miss Wilson made me come into her room for an aspirin. "Here," she said, giving me the tablet with a glass of water. "You've been studying too hard lately. Take a rest for a week or two. When I looked at you in the café just now I thought you were going to faint. You were as white as chalk."

I told her what had upset me. She was silent for a minute and then she explained the incident to me. She had lived for almost a year in Paris before coming to Madrid and she had seen the horrible things that are part of life in a big city. "It is no use shutting your eyes to the fact that life can be pretty beastly," she said. "If you remain here long enough you won't be able to avoid seeing plenty of ugly things. They won't upset you so much if you know about them beforehand and are prepared for them." Her reasoning was right, I suppose. But, though knowledge may prevent sudden shock, I have never found it an anodyne for the hurt which comes from having to look on helpless while life singles out victims for its cruelties.

Miss Wilson changed the subject. "I love the grey in that jumper of yours," she said. Glad to avail of the door she opened I rushed through it into the world of little safe ordinary things. "It is a nice grey," I said quickly, looking down at my jumper. It was the jumper Miss Carmody had sent me for Christmas, a lovely neat-fitting jumper in angora wool. My eyes never fell on the bluey-grey of it without remembering the dabchicks that had been hatched out on the pond near our house one spring. I had watched the hatching of those little creatures with such attention that I was almost a third parent to them. First the father and mother had come to build the nest, the father a handsome fellow in fine black and brown and white feathers, the mother an elegant palely feathered creature, the black band around her slender neck giving her a strong resemblance to the minister's wife who always encircled her throat with a black velvet ribbon. The dabchicks built the queerest nest in life, just a platform of mud among the rushes, as smooth and as rounded as the top of a mushroom. Here the two eggs were laid and here a pair of fluffy bluey-grey babies presently appeared. It was fun to watch the babies being taken for an outing—once around the pond and home again, the whole family looking as sedate and respectable and well-behaved as a group in a Victorian photograph.

"I wonder if your friend would get me a jumper of the same shade," Miss Wilson said, pulling me back to Madrid. "I don't know when I've seen such a becoming shade of grey."

"Can't you take this one?" I said. "I don't care for it much. It doesn't really suit me." I was delighted to get a chance of paying off a little of the debt I owed the girl. I had the greatest difficulty in the world in making her accept it. That is a thing I have noticed about English people: they are very generous in giving, but ungenerous in accepting. Miss Wilson thought nothing at all of spending hours coaching me in shorthand and typing, and yet she acted as though I was giving her a mink coat when I offered her the jumper. She would not give me the pleasure of accepting it for nothing. She made me take in exchange a length of woollen stuff as red as sealing-wax which, in a moment of temporary bedazzlement, she had bought at a London sale and which she had carted around ever since without finding courage to make it up and wear it. She said it was too loud for the street and that maybe I could make a dressing-gown out of it. I had no intention of wasting its gay warmth in such a fashion. With the help of La Serena I made myself a new dress to wear at Luis's supper-party. La Serena had a little more time to spare these days, for early in March Huxton had had himself transferred to his firm's Italian branch. Since his going, Maruja had become strangely sullen in her manner. La Serena did the plain stitching and the pressing of the pleated skirt. I made the top part which I fashioned like a tight-fitting jerkin after a design of my own. There was not a single ordinary seam in that jerkin. Instead, wherever there was a joining, I got a grand effect with the use of a darning-needle and crochet-hook. First I turned in all the edges and blanket-stitched them in black wool. Then I drew the edges together—down the sides and along the sleeves and across the shoulders—with a crochet stitch in white wool. I used the same black-and-white finish for the neck and for the edges of the two patch pockets which I covered with crochet flowers made from odds and ends of white and blue and green wools. Maybe that sounds terrible, but the effect was very happy. La Serena thought the dress good enough for a fiesta.

Before going to the party I went in to Miss Wilson's room to show myself.

"Ye-es," she said, but doubtfully. "I must say it looks nice on you. But it isn't the kind of thing I'd wear myself." Helen Quinn had said practically the same but in stronger words. "Not ladylike," had been her verdict. I didn't care. I liked the dress myself. I felt well in it. As it turned out, Siemen Kronz was to justify my liking of it, and Siemen prided himself on knowing what was correct in clothes. After we became engaged I often asked him what I should wear when we would be going somewhere together. Always he said, "Wear the red dress with the flowery pockets."

I was the first guest to arrive. Luis gave me a kindly

welcome. "Have you come to take possession of your house?" he said, putting such warmth into the conventional greeting that he really seemed to mean it. We went into the living-room where Romana was putting the last touches to the table. She looked up and smiled. "Your dress suits you," she said. "Well wear." Under the low-hung shaded light, I hardly recognized her for the girl who had kept me at arm's length during my last visit. There was no stolidity in her this evening. A faint colour warmed her creamy skin, and she had taken pains with her hair. Her dress was nice too—a plain dress of the black georgette so beloved of Spanish women. The doorbell rang as we stood admiring each other. "That will be Siemen," Romana said quickly. "I'll let him in." Her small high-heeled shoes beat a happy urgent rhythm along the tiled hall.

"I have a book here that will please you, Delia," Luis said in his quiet way. "It is *The New Moon*, by Tagore, the Indian poet. No one understands children as Tagore does." He took the book from its shelf and came and sat beside me on the couch. "Listen to this passage." He had barely started to read when Romana ushered the guest of honour into the room. Luis rose to greet him. As if wishing to retain this moment, Romana remained in the doorway with her glance resting happily on her brother and Siemen Kronz.

I was interested in this Hungarian whom Luis had praised so highly and for whom Romana seemed to have such a warm regard. I studied him as he stood talking to Luis. He seemed about thirty, ruddy-blond, a big broad man, but graceful and quick. He put me in mind of a huge tortoise-shell cat. This likeness was furthered by the shortness of his face, so wide and flat at the cheek bones, and by the greenish colour of his eyes. Those eyes caught mine over Luis's thin shoulder and held me privately for a second until Luis turned to introduce us. In that second I had the queer feeling which sometimes comes at a first meeting, a feeling which says: This is no ordinary introduction. This handshake is going to make a difference in your life. It made me uncomfortable that I should have this feeling about Siemen Kronz for, though he was good-looking in his own Slavonic way and had a kindness to his mouth, I did not take to him. His foreignness disconcerted me. Spanish people had never had this effect on me. I had always felt a kinship with them. We differed in speech, looks and habits, but these differences went no deeper than the varicoloured dyes which are used to tint the shells of eggs at Easter time. Siemen's foreignness went right to the speck of the egg.

Juan and Consuelo arrived immediately afterwards. I found both of them as likeable as Luis had promised. Consuelo was beautiful—black satin hair, blossomy skin and heavily fringed eyes set at a Chinese slant below a wide brow. She was the sister of the girl to whom Luis had been engaged and who had died of consumption. Consuelo was delicate too, but vivid and intense as a flame. Her voice was an E-string tremolo that gave a singing suspense to her words, and she had a rapid grace that made every movement exciting. Her little fine-drawn body seemed too fragile a vial for the fiery elixir of her spirit. She adored her husband. She let all of us share in the delight of her voice and smile and gestures, but the way she kept directing herself to Juan put me in mind of a gipsy violinist whose music is enjoyed by a café of people, but who stands by one chair, playing his soul out to one person alone. At first sight it seemed strange that Juan Negrin should have such an enraptured and exquisite wife, for in his outlines he was like the cruellest of his own cartoons, a duck-egg with little quick limbs, and a plasticine face topped by a few fronds of seaweed hair. I thought him a calamity until he smiled and spoke, and then I realized that the finest of letters may come in the queerest of envelopes. His voice fitted him to play the Angel Gabriel in a nativity play, and he had the clear innocent eyes of a child. It was lovely to see his smile rise to the surface of his eyes, hesitate there a second and then send sudden beauty over every feature of him. Juan Negrin was one of the most talented men in Spain, loved by the revolutionaries, feared by the Rightists. It may seem impertinent that I, an ignorant little Irish girl, should have pitied such a one. But pity him I did, and right well he merited my pity. Behind his stockade of culture and talent and laughing pleasant ways, the man lived in terror. The terror reared itself twenty times during the evening. There were moments when Consuelo allowed one or other of us to hold her attention. In those moments Juan's eyes had a chance to rest on her unobserved, and an agony of fear came into them. Not knowing then how quickly the gay lovely flame of Consuelo was burning away, I did not realize the cause of his agony. But I saw that it was tearing and real and born of love, and it would have wrung me even if my heart had been hewn out of the marble quarries of Connemara. Those two people would have been saddening if there had not been such glory in their love. Not long ago I heard a famous preacher describe human affections as being "clammy with the clamminess of earth." I thought of Juan and Consuelo, and the Jesuit's discourse lost all meaning for me.

It was a grand supper party. We talked about everything under the sun. The entrée of batter-coated sweetbreads lost its savour when Siemen told us of the poverty he had seen among the Andalusian peasants.

"Your Spanish romances picture the Andalusians as lean and dry," he said. "No wonder they are lean. I never knew people could live and work and love on so little food. Often I saw a family sitting down to a midday meal of lentils and bread in a hovel not fit for cattle. I was told that they rarely eat meat. Bread and black coffee morning and evening, lentils at midday. And I noticed that all the family ate their lentils from the one dish."

"That is usual among the peasants," Consuelo told him. "They have a saying for it: 'bathing in the same bath.'"

Juan laid down his fork and his mouth became bitter.

"Two pesetas a day is what an Andalusian agricultural labourer is paid by his master. Two pesetas a day on which to support a wife and to rear plenty of children for the greater honour and glory of Mother Church."

I put in a word. "The ama in the de las Rojas house told me that the Marqués spends twenty-five pesetas every day of his life on cigars alone. The *puros* he smokes cost five pesetas each."

Juan turned his clear eyes on me. "Don't worry, señorita," he said quietly. "These things will be put right."

Romana rang the little handbell for the next course, a lovely little bell of Toledo work, steel inlaid with gold. "Revolutions will never abolish poverty, Juan." Her voice was full of practical common sense. "We will always have the poor. It is the will of God." Luis was taking no part at all in this conversation. I never knew him to join in when politics or religion were being discussed. He had a modesty which is unusual in very religious people. He did not consider himself especially singled out by Heaven to act as a missionary, and he made no effort to impose his religious beliefs on others. "It is the will of God that some should know hardship and poverty," Romana went on. "It is useless to try to go against the will of God."

This made Juan impatient. "For an intelligent woman you say very stupid things, Romana."

Romana was not perturbed. "Do I?" she asked calmly. She was so firmly entrenched in her own convictions that no criticism could rile her.

"You do," Juan told her. "And the funniest thing about you people who believe in God is the way you malign the Being you worship. You make God a scapegoat for the rottenness of the world. A child develops twisted bones through starvation. It is the will of God, says the craven father, and he continues to starve for the people who crippled his child. A factory worker loses his arm in an unprotected machine. It is the will of God, his wife says, and goes on the streets. You religious people make me laugh. You make me cry too. You are not to be blamed, I suppose. The priests have been lulling you to sleep so long with these parrot-cries that you have forgotten that human dignity has a voice of its own."

"Eat, Juan," Consuelo counselled. "Your chicken will be cold."

"And it's cooked in your favourite way with tomatoes and olives." Romana's voice held no rancour. Juan might have been praising her instead of belittling her.

"There is something in what Juan says," Siemen said slowly. "I think we are too ready to act as interpreters of the Divine Will. Of this I am certain: the things I saw in Andalusia could not have been the will of the beneficent Being we call God."

Romana looked a little put out. Juan might rage at her but he could not disturb her. For Siemen to criticize, however mildly or indirectly, was another matter entirely. Luis must have sensed his sister's discomfort for he turned the conversation by starting a discussion on the great public demonstration in honour of Primo de Rivera which the Dictator himself was organizing so as to prove to the people of Spain how popular he was with them. I was relieved that religion was dropped. It gave me an uneasy feeling to hear Juan criticize the priests. I felt that such talk was neither good nor lucky, particularly as I found myself agreeing with it.

I was not able to take much part in the conversation, but I got great pleasure from listening and watching, and it was as interesting to watch the hands as the faces. Since coming to Spain I had developed a great interest in hands. This was because I was self-conscious about my own. At home in Ballyderrig my hands had seemed no bigger than the rest and as good a shape as most. Here, by contrast with the fine small hands of the Latins, they looked what they were: a legacy from the generations of my foremothers who had heaped turf and thinned turnips, and baked and scrubbed and washed. Such a contrast in hands as we had at the table that night. Mine, the big spawgs of an Irish peasant, but, though I say it who shouldn't, not mean-looking, and saved from ugliness by the length of the fingers. Consuelo's were blue-veined and narrow. She used them all the time when talking. The little tapering fingers were a *corps de ballet* that danced joyously to the music of her voice. Romana's hands were smooth-skinned and white. They moved deliberately and surely. It was impossible to imagine them letting a cup fall or bungling a task. Good-looking hands, well-kept hands, but in their plumpness a negation of sensibility. That was a queer thing: Juan Negrin's hands were cushioned with fat, and yet there was feeling in every move of them. He drew his finger-tips along the table-cloth and the damask became twice as smooth and satiny. He gently fingered a peach before peeling it, and you enjoyed with him the caress of rose-and-green plush. He crumbled a bit of his roll and your appetite quickened for brittle-crusted fresh bread. To watch Juan's hands savouring everything they contacted was to have your own sense of touch heightened a hundredfold. He had an exciting way of sketching in air with his thumb the people of whom he spoke, and he spoke so well that the outlines of his aerial cartoons stayed there before your eyes. There is little to be said of the thin brown fingers of Luis except that they were a true and full expression of the man's character, gentle when they rested slack on the table, kind when they twined themselves loosely together. Though so deft in use they never gripped anything tightly—a symbol of Luis's indifference to every material thing. Siemen Kronz had interesting hands too. When we had been introduced, I was grateful to him for the decent-sized hand that shook mine. So often in Spain, a handshake brought me embarrassment. At supper I was startled to see that the felinity of his face and movements extended even to his hands. Not that they were stealthy or sinuous. They were good honest hands, quiet and strong-looking. It was his nails that were catlike. Though he kept them short, the tops of them curved in slightly over his finger-tips. I was a little repelled. On the third finger of his right hand he wore a heavy twist of gold. Little did I think that before twelve months would pass I would be wearing that ring on my engagement finger.

When supper was over Juan said it was time for Consuelo to go to bed and he took her home. The rest of us went to the Café Asturias for coffee and to hear the music of Siemen's homeland. That music was an intoxication and a distress to me. An intoxication because no one could listen to the tzigane orchestra playing the czardases and marches which inspired Liszt and Brahms without becoming a little drunk, a distress because my ignorance of music kept me all the time on the brink of a great satisfaction that I knew would never be mine. The lack of a musical education is a great hardship. I find listening to music a bitter pleasure. My ears are delighted, but my heart and soul are thwarted. The same used to happen to me as a child when I read Shakespeare at school. The sound of the words was a delight but it gave me an aching dissatisfaction not to be able to reach the meaning behind the words. There is so much meaning behind the sound of music, and I have never been able to reach it.

Since Romana spoke no English, our talk was all in Spanish. The conversation was not general. Romana's tone put a screen around Siemen and herself. I had a feeling that he would have been just as happy without the screen, for though he talked and laughed with her in great friendship, his manner towards her had none of the intimacy in which hers was soaked. At twelve o'clock the orchestra left and so did we. Siemen lived in Claudio Coello, much nearer to me than Luis and Romana, so we split at the Plaza Cibeles, Romana and Luis getting into a tram, Siemen and I walking on past the Retiro. It was a mild night for March. The breeze was soft enough for a May evening in Ireland. To the left of us the Retiro trees fluttered behind their railings like birds in a cage, and the tram-lines on the lamp-yellowed road were a gridiron on a pale fire.

We talked a little as we went. Siemen's English was good, but some words he pronounced in a funny way. Sword was "so-woard" with him, and once when he disagreed with me about something and I was silent for a minute, he asked apologetically, "Have you ainjer with me?" After we became great with each other, I told him a hundred times how to pronounce "anger," but he preferred it his own way. When we came to the little café at the corner of my street he suggested we should go in for another glass of coffee. "It is early yet," he said. It *was* early for Madrid. The cinemas would not be emptying for another hour, and the cafés would be full until three and later. We went into the café and we sat there and talked until two o'clock. Or, rather, Siemen talked and I listened, throwing in an odd word here and there. He was not so old as he looked—only twenty-six. He had been in Spain two years. Before that he had lived a year in Milan and two years in Paris. His people owned a business in Budapest and wanted him to come home to help to run it. He expected to do so one day, but first he wanted to see the world. From the way he spoke of his home I could see that he and his two brothers had been brought up in great comfort. He was well educated too, and spoke five languages besides his own. I liked him for the way he talked about his mother. He thought the sun rose and set in her. He showed me her photograph—a stout white-haired woman with the same broad flat cheek-bones and short well-shaped nose as himself, but with less kindness to her mouth. Her eyes were hard. "What do you think of her?" Siemen asked. "She is a lovely woman," I said, though I did not mean a word of it.

There were things that irritated me about him during that first chat. For one thing, I thought he was inclined to boast. "I had my first sweetheart when I was fourteen. My first dress-suit when I was fifteen." "We must go out to the mountains one day and take some photographs. I have three cameras—one of them the best German make obtainable." "There are five doctors in my family, my two brothers, two uncles and a first cousin." He had little dandified ways that annoyed me. That gold rope on his finger, the whiff of eau-de-cologne when he took out his handkerchief, and the way he refolded that handkerchief into a neat square before returning it to his pocket. If all this makes him sound unlikeable I have libelled him. He owned plenty of likeable qualities and he had already shown one of them in being sorry for those poor people in Andalusia. Cardinal virtues aside, we had not been half an hour in that café until I discovered him to possess a virtue which would have made me willing to overlook graver faults than his foreign dandyism and childish bragging. I discovered that he liked me. He did not say it in so many words, but his eyes and his smile said it. I have never been able to dislike anyone, man or woman, whose heart holds a soft corner for me. If Siemen had been the greatest rogue unhung, instead of the pleasant well-reared man he was, I would have had to warm to him in gratitude for his liking of me.

"Will you come out to dinner with me one evening?" he asked when we were saying good night. "Just the two of us." He clapped his hands for the night watchman to come and open the door. "I come!" came the man's answering shout from down the street.

I did not like him well enough to risk incurring Romana's enmity over him. "Maybe later on," I told him. "I'm studying hard to get myself a job in an office, so I can't go out much. Anyway, aren't we all meeting this night week in the Café Asturias?" Just then the caped watchman came running up with his lantern and bunch of keys, so we left it at that. Siemen bowed and clicked his heels like a Prussian officer.

I went up the stairs congratulating myself on the way life had improved for me. Supper-parties with grand people who could talk better than a book, music and chatting and coffee-drinking to my heart's content, invitations to dinner from men who could speak six languages and who had strings of doctors in the family—was it Delia Scully who was in it at all? By the time I had reached our pension on the third floor I had composed a letter to Michael telling him all the grand things that were happening to me as a result of his suggestion about the Comparative Mythology. Some of the elation fizzled away as I opened the door quietly and tiptoed down the passage. Helen Quinn would be waiting to read the Riot Act to me for having stayed out so late. The house smelt like a herbalist's shop—La Serena must have been brewing tisanes.

Helen was not in our room. There was a note on my pillow and a letter beside it. "Have gone to the pictures with Rico," the note said. "Expect to be in late. This letter came after you went out."

The letter was from *Our Boys*, a magazine run by the Christian Brothers at home in Dublin. The editor wrote accepting twelve translations of Spanish legends and enclosing a cheque for nine pounds. I nearly went out of my mind with delight. It was Michael I had to thank for this joy too. It was he who had suggested that I make use of my mythology by trying some of the stories on *Our Boys*. Twelve stories at fifteen shillings each, six shillings a thousand words—not trades union pay, maybe, but as I sat on the side of the bed that night and gloated over my beautiful cheque, I was so proud and rich and thrilled that a Nobel prize winner would have been very small potatoes beside me. It took me a long time to undress. Half-way through the shedding of each garment I had to stop and examine the cheque and read the accompanying note all over again. By the time I was in my pyjamas and dressing-gown and had collected my toothbrush, I knew so well every stroke of the handwriting on the cheque that I could have forged the signature blindfolded.

The kitchen was at the end of the passage, opposite the bathroom. I was turning the handle of the bathroom door when I heard the sound of a spoon cautiously scraping the side of a saucepan. La Serena must be up! I was dying to tell her my good news. Without waiting to wonder what she would be doing out of her bed at this hour, I opened the kitchen door. In that confined space the herbal smell was breath-catching. La Serena was standing at the stove, intent on whatever it was she was stirring. Maruja sat on a chair with her feet in a basin of steaming water. The girl's face was puffy from crying and her eyes were fixed on La Serena as if the old woman were her only hope of salvation. That helpless terror on the face of one so strong and independent as Maruja was frightening to see. I wondered what was wrong.

"Have you *la gripe*, Maruja?" I asked. They had not heard me open the door, had not seen me during those few seconds I had stood there. When I spoke they looked around quickly. There was such scared secretiveness in their faces that I felt a sudden embarrassment.

"What does the señorita want?" For the first and only time in my knowledge of her, La Serena's voice was curt and cold. I had sense enough to know that talk of cheques and good news would have been out of place in that kitchen just then. "It's nothing—it doesn't matter—it will do to-morrow," I said confusedly, and left them.

Maruja did not get up the next day. Mrs. Hansen asked for her several times; and not content with La Serena's explanation that the girl had a cold, she went into her room to investigate for herself. She stayed there a long time. When she came out her face was very angry. "The idea!" she kept muttering to herself. "The idea! In my house!" At the end of the week Maruja got up and packed her bag. She left without a word to any of us. The following day we had a new maid in her place, a middle-aged, sour-faced woman. I never liked Paca. She hated foreigners. Rico Cortes was the only one in the house with whom she condescended to pass the time of day. Towards the rest of us, Mrs. Hansen included, she was as aggressively rude as if each of us was personally responsible for the occupation of Gibraltar.

I continued to meet my new friends. We did not sit in cafés all the time. Sometimes we took the tram and went away out to the Paseo de las Delicias or to the Parque del Oeste. One evening when Luis, Romana, Siemen and myself were leaving the Metro in the Puerta del Sol, Luis stopped before a lurid advertisement for somebody's sausages which was set into the white-tiled wall at the turn of the stairway leading from the tube. "Look at that," he said with loathing in his voice. "I get sick with disgust every time I pass it. It would disgrace a land of cannibals." The advertisement showed a butcher astride a pig. He was plunging a knife into the animal's neck, and big gouts of blood were spurting from the wound. The artist had managed to achieve a very realistic beastliness. Several of Madrid's tube stations were disfigured with that advertisement.

"Why not get rid of it?" I suggested. "If we could prise out one of the tiles it would be easy enough to pull down the rest."

They were delighted with my suggestion. Siemen took out his pocket-knife and in two minutes the butcher's head and shoulders were in Romana's handbag. We worked like furies in between interruptions. When people passed we dissembled our lawlessness by huddling together in front of the defaced advertisement and talked loudly in English. The Madrid people were willing to accept any madness as the normal behaviour of foreigners, even the madness of choosing the stuffy stairway of a tube station in which to hold a conversazione. When we finished our work in the Puerta del Sol we went on to the next station for more vandalism.

The following morning there was not a single gory pig in the metros of Madrid.

I found Siemen growing on me as I got to know him. Several times he repeated his invitation to come out alone with him and each time I was finding it more difficult to make an excuse for refusing. One evening in April he asked me again. He was seeing me home along Alcala. As we turned into Nuñez de Balboa we almost collided with a boy who was standing outside the grille of a ground-floor window. Inside a girl was sitting. She had her hand through the grille and the boy was covering it with kisses. The scene made me feel lonely, somehow. I felt it would be nice to have a sweetheart. I thought of Rafael and the dance in the Ritz and I wished it were he who was with me instead of Siemen.

"I wish you would come," Siemen was saying. "I feel we could be good friends, but friendship gets no chance to grow when there are other people around us all the time. I should like to take you to Ult Heidelberg, the German restaurant. They serve the kind of food that is eaten in my own home. Good marrow soup—you fish out the marrow and spread it on little triangles of toast. And then *Wiener schnitzel*, and afterwards *apfeltorten* and *strudel*. You'd like it, Delia."

"It sounds nice," I said.

"Why won't you let me take you, then? It can't be that you want to study all the time. But, perhaps it is——" his voice took on a note of childish hurt that sounded strange in a man who had had his first sweetheart at fourteen and who spoke six languages—"perhaps it is that you dislike me."

"It isn't," I assured him. "Sure I have a great liking for you."

"What is it, then?" he persisted.

He forced the truth from me. "It is Romana," I told him. "What about Romana?"

"Oh, so that is it?" He gave a little affectionate laugh. "Poor Romana. She's a dear."

That put an end to my scruples. No man could have a romantic feeling for any woman of whom he spoke with that affectionate pity. If I accepted Siemen's overtures, I would not be taking from Romana anything that belonged to her. "I'll come," I said. "Wednesday of next week would be grand for me."

"I'll call for you at seven," he promised.

He called all right, but I was not there. I was out with Rafael. On the Tuesday I came face to face with Rafael in the Castellana, and from then until the day we parted I forgot there was any other man in the world.

CHAPTER EIGHT

A DIET of bread and lentils fills you with wind. There was a loud noise as a million half-starved Spaniards relieved their flatulence. The noise was heard in the royal palace in Madrid. It sent the heart of King Alfonso into his mouth. "Is it the legs of my throne I hear cracking?" he asked. "No fear of that, your Majesty," Primo de Rivera assured him. "Didn't I put grand new legs under your throne with my own two hands? The noise you're after hearing was only your loyal friend and subject the Marqués de las Rojas and he clipping the end off his cigar."

"*Está bien,*" said the King, and he relaxed. But he knew, and Primo de Rivera knew, that the noise had a threat in it.

"*Está bien,*" said the Queen. "I'll take the little sports watch at two thousand pesetas." She was in the pavilion of the Industrial Exhibition that was being held in the Retiro. Carola Valiente and myself were standing right beside that nice dignified unfortunate woman when she bought her little toy for more money than would buy a labourer's sweat for three long years. She had the two Infantas with her that day, English-complexioned, Habsburg-featured girls. You might look for ever at the cold gracious face of the Queen without seeing a sign of the sorrow she had supped since the day she married Alfonso. Little did she guess, and she buying her watch, that at that very moment Juan Negrin and his friends were packing her trunk for her.

"*Está bien*," said the tenant-farmers of the south. "We'll pay the usury you demand," and they signed their agreements with the Catholic Agrarian Confederation with never a tremble of the hand to betray the resentment that burned in them.

Don Angel Herrera Orio, the Jesuit editor of *El Debate*, read over the latest article by his henchman, Gil Robles. "*Está bien*," he said with satisfaction. "The dignity of the Church must be upheld." The article would be read by thousands and thousands of poor little secular priests, hard-working, badly fed men who found it no easy matter to be dignified on twenty-five pounds a year and the charity of people poorer than themselves.

Outwardly everything went on as usual that May and June, but under the crust of custom there was a yeasting and a bubbling of change, and we were all caught up in it.

Miss Wilson continued to work in the Anglo-Spanish. She gave her employers the same quiet efficiency as always, and they never guessed that she had grown tired of Madrid and was exchanging letters with the firm for which she had worked in Paris.

Helen Quinn walked behind her señoritas with a sedateness that hid the way her brain was worrying at a big problem. "I have sixty thousand pesetas," Rico had told her. "If you had thirty thousand to put with that we could marry. It would not be judicious to marry on less." One thousand pounds. Not an unreasonable dowry for a steady

industrious man to ask, especially if, like Rico, he earned
ten pounds a week. Not impossible to gather together,
either. That tenement at home in Dublin which her uncle
had left her was surely worth five hundred, and with what
she had in the bank. . . . Would it be wise to sell, though?
Were Rico's prospects of getting that new agency as good
as they seemed? Better not do anything in a hurry. She
would wait and see.

In the pension La Serena—the little active handful—continued to scour and polish and slave, while Mrs. Hansen
ballyragged and bullied her more than ever. None of us
guessed that the cold which had laid the landlady low at
Christmas had pulled the cornerstone from that edifice of
fat, and that Mrs. Hansen's increased shouting was the
rumbling and cracking of a house about to fall.

I too went on in much the same outward way as before.
I gave my mornings to little Catalina, the doctor's child,
and my afternoons to Pepe Blanco and Carola Valiente and
Mr. Yamada. I must have managed to speak and look and
act as usual, for not one of these people passed any remark
on me. They did not once say, "What is after happening to
you?" or "Is it sleepwalking you are?" or "Are you sure
you're right in the head?" It remains a mystery to me how
they never suspected that during those two months they
were holding converse with a few clothes and an English
dictionary, and that Delia Scully was not in it at all. For
eight solid weeks Delia Scully was in her body only whenever Rafael was sitting beside her in a café, or dancing with
her in the Alcazar or walking with her in Moncloa. When
he left her at the door each night, he took away with him
anything that was vital and feeling and loving in her.

Not for diamonds would I wish to be nineteen and go
through that again. I do not know how it affects other
people, but I had it very bad. It was a delirious seesawing
from mad jealousy to blind faith, from high ecstasy to bitter
hurt and from wild joy to black sorrow. I suppose all young

people have to go through it. They have my heart's sympathy, and so has that unfortunate wretch who went out of her mind about Rafael Moragas. There is impatience mixed up with my pity, for now that I am nearly twice her age and have learned what real love is, I could shake her for not knowing that the queerest thing about the queer affliction that came over her is the way it burns itself out. My impatience goes when I remember that one of the most painful symptoms of the affliction is the way the sufferer believes she will never get over it. Poor Delia Scully was convinced that she was past praying for. With pity and impatience I look back on her, but with envy too. If a mature, firmly planted tree could feel, it would know the same kind of nostalgia for the exhilaration with which the pliant sapling bowed and strained and danced to the wind.

．　　　　．　　　　．　　　　．　　　　．

The minute I wakened that morning I had known that it was going to be what I have always called a Limbo day, the kind of day when you cease being earthbound and your flesh is so light on you that you might as well be disembodied. It is well such days come seldom for, though lovely, they are very wearing. Familiarity with everyday joys and sorrows, sights and sounds, puts a leather jerkin on the heart. On Limbo days you leave the jerkin lying on the bed and walk about with every nerve exposed and reacting to the smallest, most commonplace things in a way that is hardly bearable. The conductor of the tram that takes you to the corner of Carrera de San Geronimo where Catalina lives—he is no thinner than he was yesterday, and only a day older. Yesterday, if you noticed him at all, you only thought with lukewarm pity: "It's a sin to have the like of him working and he with one foot in the grave," but to-day the tired boniness of the poor old hand that gives you your change twists the heart in your body. The fountain in the Plaza Cibeles has undergone no structural change during the night and yet what was yesterday only a jet of water in a stone basin is to-day a miser gone splendidly mad and pelting the sun with diamonds. At ordinary times you do not let yourself be upset by the surliness of the girl who opens the door of Catalina's house, but to-day her unfriendliness cuts you to the soul. On Limbo days the heart is an aeolian harp amplifying every breath of feeling into a storm of passionate music.

It was blue and gold afternoon when I left Catalina. There were two hours to spare before the time for the Calle Barquillo and Carola Valiente. Should I go into the Prado and let El Greco improve my mind, or should I sit on a bench in the Castellana and let the sun improve my complexion. My complexion won, and without any prolonged struggle.

It was lovely there under the heavy-thatched plane trees. There was a little breeze and it brought the leaf-shadows playing in ripples about my feet. I thought over the letter which had come from Michael that morning. "St. Patrick brought the summer with him this year," he wrote. "Spring was left out entirely. If the year keeps galloping at this rate we'll be having Christmas on St. Swithin's Day. You never saw anything like the epidemic of lambs we've had. The Curragh is like a mushroom field with them. I was over in your direction yesterday to look at a mare. I was up to my knees in cowslips." I wished I could have been there with him, and I had a sudden longing for a dodge, one of the cowslip balls which every child in Ballyderrig makes in May. I always took one to school with me. It was like taking the fields and the sunshine into the chalk-smelling dusty schoolroom. The knowledge that it was waiting there in my bag helped me to endure the chief exports of England and the conditional of *beir*. Every time the nun's back was turned my head went into the bag like a horse's into a bucket of oats and I took a good long soul-satisfying sniff. The smell of cowslips in the fields was wine, but taken out of the school bag it became a heady cocktail to which leather and india-rubber and bread and books all contributed something. Until well on in the winter I would be coming on the remains of dodges around the house, withered shrunken things lying loose and skeleton-dry within a circle of string, but, if I shut my eyes and sniffed hard enough, still with a ghostly fragrance of May on them.

I was sitting on a bench in the Castellana in Madrid, but I was looking across four years and hundreds of miles, and watching myself at fifteen and I making a dodge at home in the kitchen in Derrymore, I holding the string, and Gran straddling the cowslips on it. "Hold it steady now, alanna. Don't let it shake. Steady now, steady——" I am holding it steady but suddenly someone comes right up beside me and speaks my name. The cowslips fall and Gran is gone and the whole world breaks in a million shining pieces around me. Rafael is sitting beside me, and talking to me, telling me where he has been ever since, and how the eyes are outside his head with watching for me since he came back from Jaen, and how much he has been thinking of me. I hardly hear him, for my ears are still ringing with the music of that first "Delia, *mi vida*," and the glad surprised way he said it. Was it yesterday, or a year ago or a century ago that I dreamed of meeting him just like this and of hearing him speak my name in just this way? And now, when I had begun to believe that it would not cost me a thought if I never heard him say it, here he was with the same likeable quirk to his mouth and the same dark eyes that had first kindled me. Within two minutes of our reunion I was in love—head, neck and heels into it.

There is little of those two months that I remember clearly. The everyday people of my world were only shadowy supernumeraries, walking on now and then to speak their little unimportant lines. I remember Miss Wilson asking me if I no longer wanted to get a job in an office and if I had given up shorthand and typing. I remember Helen Quinn threatening to go to the Reparadoras nuns about me if I did not come in earlier at night. "Rico says that no man could respect a girl who lets herself be taken to cabarets. Rico says you're a fool if you think he is serious. Rico says a Spaniard never marries a flighty woman." And, when I answered her back, she said, "Rico's father is coming to Madrid soon to meet me. Has Rafael introduced you to his family yet?"

Since I no longer went to the library on Sunday mornings, it was a while until I saw Luis, and then I met him by accident in the Puerta del Sol. When he chided me gently for not coming to see them, I started a stammered explanation. He said, "You have fallen in love. When I first met you, your aura was yellow and blue, the yellow of joy and the blue of contentment. Now I see you surrounded by a disturbed red aura of passion." I got away from him quickly. A clairvoyant is the last person in the world a girl wants near her and she having a love-affair with a Spaniard.

Even Michael ceased to have meaning for me. His letters still came regularly, but they meant no more to me than the sight of her home to Yeats's Stolen Child after the fairies had bewitched her. I read the letters in the way a man suffering from loss of memory will read the papers, and I left them unanswered. Miss Carmody wrote too, and since the sight of her handwriting was an uncomfortable reminder of the way I was breaking my promise, I did not reply to her either.

La Serena is the only one of the extras that I can evoke with any clarity. She stopped me in the passage one night when I was on my way out to meet Rafael.

"*Cuidado que es guapa la señorita!*" the kind old creature said admiringly. It was no lie for her. I *was* looking nice those days. My worst enemy would have had to admit it. Heaven knows I have never had any illusions about my face. I would need to be blind not to realize that I was passed over when the good looks were being given out. I have not a feature that matches. Even my eyes are odd on account of that tea-leaf in the left one. Even so, even though my nose is queer and my mouth is of the size that kind people describe as generous, I can say without lie or deceit that for two months of my life I was good-looking. My skin would need to have been a blackout curtain to have prevented the lovely light in my heart from shining through.

I accepted La Serena's compliment. "*Gracias*, Serena," I said, "you see me with kind eyes."

I made to pass on, but she put a little quiet hand on my arm and looked up at me shyly. "There are two occasions in a woman's life when she becomes as *bellota* as the señorita has become during these past few weeks. One is after the midwife has gone and she is left lying so contented with her firstborn in her arms. The other is when she falls in love for the first time. The señorita is in love, no?" I nodded, pleased with her teasing. Suddenly she lost the teasing expression and became anxious. "Take care, *hija*," she warned urgently. "Men are *embusteros, engañadores, mentirosos*—pretenders, deceivers, liars. The men are bad."

"My *novio* is not like that," I assured her happily.

She shook her head. "In the village where la Serena was born they have a saying: The wise woman kisses but does not love, she listens but does not believe, and she leaves before she is left. If the señorita will remember that, nothing bad will happen to her." How pitiable, I thought, to be so old and blind and cynical. How sad not to know that if the world had its Huxtons, it had men like Rafael with enough goodness in them to atone for a million Huxtons.

Vague I am about most of the things that happened during that time, but many a scene with Rafael remains photographed on my memory. Two in particular. One is the night in the Alcazar Cabaret when Rafael said something that rocketed me into the seventh heaven and made me convince myself I had the perfect answer for Helen and Rico and La Serena. That same night two other memorable things happened.

We went to the Alcazar nearly every night. It was supposed to be the best night-club in Madrid. The floor was wonderful. If you had two sods of turf for feet you would have danced well on that floor. The cover-charge was enormous. There were two orchestras, a negro jazz band imported from the States and a tango orchestra from the Argentine. Everything was *de lujo*, which is the Spanish translation for "the height of style." Even the cloakroom attendant was expensive. She was dressed so well that I used to feel ashamed not to be offering her paper money. The clientele was *de lujo* too. The array of gorgeous wraps with furry collars used to frighten the life out of my poor little linen jacket. Still, it was true for Helen. Stylish and all though it was, no decent woman would have been seen dead in the Alcazar nor in any other Madrid cabaret. No decent Spanish woman, that is. English and American women sometimes came with tourist parties, and now and again foreign office-workers came with their boys. But nearly all the other women were *cocotas*. These girls were so correct in their ways that I would never have guessed their way of living if Rafael had not told me. I was surprised at myself for not feeling harrowed, but with their prettiness and nice clothes and light-heartedness it was impossible to imagine anything sordid or saddening in connection with them. And, anyway, my imagination could not follow them outside the doors of the cabaret.

I was enchanted with the shaded lights and the music and the atmosphere of gaiety and luxury. If there was an underlying tawdriness it escaped me. When you are young and in love there is nothing shoddy in the world. If, now and then, I caught a look or a gesture that gave me a sudden uneasiness, I turned quickly to Rafael and his eyes assured me that there was nothing in life but what was happy and beautiful.

The music was heavenly. The negroes set your feet tingling with rhythm, but the South Americans set your heart on fire.

On the particular night that I am talking about they started to play a new tango. "*Todo a Media Luz*," it was called, "All in the Twilight." Maybe the words were as mushy as tapioca—to me they seemed the height of lyrical inspiration—but even Austin Clarke would have had to admit that the tune was grand, particularly when played as those gauchos played it. We waited to let the bailarin and his partner be first on the floor. The bailarin was employed by the Alcazar to teach the girls all the new steps and to lead the dancing. He was a tall weedy Austrian, a die-away, unpleasant-looking poor lad with a long ugly face. His hair was so pale and sleek that his head seemed to be covered with satin-stitch done in lemon embroidery floss. There was a rumour that he belonged to titled people in Vienna. To watch him dancing was something that delighted and re-pelled. The narrow feet and long legs had a grace and rhythm so excitingly perfect that they were part of the orchestra. The music flowed through the bailarin on its way to the rest of us. There was poetry in his dancing, but there was something else that I could not put a name to. I did not like him. His partner was a negress who sang the jazz numbers, a magnificent girl with shoulders as broad as a man and flat unfeminine hips. She always wore a scarlet carnation in her short-clipped wool and a thin white dress embroidered all over with sequins.

It was lovely dancing with Rafael. When the tango had carried us a few times around the floor, one of the gauchos started to sing the refrain. I remember the words well. The gaucho half-whispered, half-sang of velvety evening in a little flat hidden away by itself at the top of a house, with the whole world shut out. Inside there is happiness, all the small kind of things of home grouping themselves in the shadows, an old song coming from the softly playing gramophone, on the mantelpiece a porcelain cat watching with friendly eyes two people who are lost in the still en-chantment of their love.

That kind of song is as good as a glass of John Jameson
to you when you are nineteen and having what you believe
to be the big romance of your life. It finished me entirely.
It affected Rafael too. A queer strained silence came over
him and he brought me back to our table. For a minute or
two after we sat down he kept looking at me in a way that
told me he was trying to say something.

"*Qué te pasa*, Rafael?" I said. "What's on you, Rafael?"

If Shakespeare could have heard the lovely things Rafael
said then he would have sat up in his grave and have called
for a pen to rewrite the poor tonguetied lines he gave to
Romeo. It was a rhapsody on the theme of the tango we had
been hearing. To come down to plain English, his biggest
wish in life was to be living with me in a home like the one
in the song.

La Serena had warned me against the way men deceive
women. She would have been better employed in warning
me against the way women deceive themselves. I can see
now that it was my own wishful thinking that was the black-
eyed deceiver of the piece, and not Rafael. Never once did
he say straight out: Will you marry me? But with Helen's
taunt in my ears, and my respectable upbringing goading
me, and my fool of a heart putting its own interpretation on
every word and look, I found it the easiest thing in the world
to believe that he was offering me marriage.

"It would be Heaven, Delia," Rafael was saying. "In the
autumn I shall inherit my grandfather's money. Do you
love me enough? Will we take the little house?"

"*Qué más quisiera yo!*" I said. "What more would I
ask!" I succeeded so well in deceiving myself that by the
time the orchestra started playing again, I had decided to ask
Helen to be bridesmaid.

This time it was a waltz—something from *La Casta
Susana*. As we danced, my mind ran joyfully ahead to the
marvellous curtains I would make for the living-room. Suddenly a face thrust itself onto the bright background of my

happy plannings. A disturbing face, pale and set, and with
the eyes hurt and jealous above those broad flat cheek-
bones. It was as unwelcome to me just then as the discovery
of a small dark cloud on a sky that has promised blue
serenity. It reminded me of the broken dinner date.

"What is it, *querida?*" Rafael wanted to know.

"It is a friend of mine—he has just come in. He is standing there at the *entrada* with those Germans. I think I
should stop and talk to him for a minute. I owe him an
apology about something." I had no chance to apologize,
for the next minute Siemen turned abruptly and went out.

After we left the Alcazar a third thing happened to fix
that night in my memory. So as to push a little further away
the loneliness of good night, we decided to walk home instead
of taking a taxi. Day was waking, not yawny and heavy-
eyed, but fresh and sweet-smelling. In the opal light,
familiar things became illustrations from a child's storybook.
The big modernistic Bellas Artes building was not the pile
of cubes it was at ordinary times. It was a heap of luggage
belonging to the old maid aunt of all the giants: first the
trunk with the portmanteau on top of it, the hatbox on top
of that again and, crowning all, the domed cage for her
parrot. A boy of a waiter came to the door of the Apolo
Café, napkin over his arm. Wilted, he leaned against the
door-post and wiped his forehead with the napkin. Then he
looked up at the sky and the light caught the listlessness of
his face and emphasized its tired vacuity until it seemed that
poor dull young Philip the Fourth had strayed here from
where Velasquez had put him on his canvas in El Prado.

Four men came out of the café past the dreaming waiter.
They wished each other good sleep. Three of them went
back together up the Gran Via. The fourth went on down
Alcala before us. As he came level with the big doorway
of the Banco de Bilbao near the corner of Barquillo, the
shadows stirred and a street girl stepped out in front of him.
There was no mistaking the raw strong cut of her. It was

Maruja, the maid from Mrs. Hansen's. With a rough impatient exclamation the man made to push her away. She moved out of his path but she turned and walked on beside him over the crossing and for a few yards beside the high wall of the Ministerio de la Guerra. Her high-heeled shoes seemed too small and she hobbled in a painful way trying to keep up with him. She was looking up at him as she went and all the time she was making horrible little coaxing gestures. She did not let him be until he turned and cursed her in a voice so loud and angry that it reached and bruised myself as well. Maruja shrugged her shoulders. She backed to the wall and stood there tapping her heel in time to a little tune she was humming. That humming was a terrible thing to hear. It had a thin layer of defiance on top but, underneath, it was solid loneliness and fright. It had the pitiful sound of a song a child would sing to himself for courage and company and he alone in the dark in the dead of the night.

. . . . .

"H'mm," Helen said when I told her the news. "When is the wedding coming off?"

"We haven't fixed the day yet." I remembered how Rafael had said, "*Me muero por ti! No puedo aguantar más*," and I added with assurance, "It will probably be sometime before Christmas."

Helen gave me a look I resented. "Just the same," she said, "I won't be in a hurry ordering my bridesmaid's dress until I hear something more definite." She was getting some of her things packed, for she was leaving in a few days for San Juan de Luz where she would spend the summer chaperoning one of her pupils. All the *profesoras* made sure of summer board and lodging by going back to governessing for the three months. Everyone seemed to be going away. Mr. Owsley was going back to America, Miss Wilson had finally decided to return to her job in Paris, and Luis wrote me from El Escorial to say that he was spending a couple of

weeks in meditation in that grand gloomy place so as to prepare himself for a big rally of theosophists which was due
to take place in Holland, or somewhere: the Star Convention, he called it. Two of my pupils would also be leaving
Madrid at the end of the month. Little Catalina was going
with her mother to San Sebastian, and Carola Valiente was
looking forward to a summer in Bilbao.

Helen looked up from her packing. "What are you going
to do for the summer?" she wanted to know. "With Carola
and Catalina gone, you'll only have the Jap and the grocer's
assistant. What they pay won't keep you. Are you making
any arrangements? You will want to hurry up or all the
summer posts will be filled. As it is, only the worst ones are
vacant."

I had not given much thought to it, though now that
Helen brought the matter up I realized its urgency. On one
thing I was determined. I would not go away from Madrid.
I could not leave Rafael. "Maybe," I said hopefully, "Miss
Wilson would recommend me for her job in the Anglo-
Spanish."

"Maybe," Helen said briefly and sceptically, inserting
layers of tissue-paper between the folds of her frock. The
neatness and care with which she was packing her clothes
made them seem twice as expensive and attractive as they had
ever looked on her. "I wouldn't count too much on it if I
were you. I don't imagine a little smattering of shorthand
and typing would be much use to a firm like that. It's a girl
with experience they'll be looking for."

She was right, of course. Miss Wilson put in a good word
for me, though she warned me that it would not be of much
use. The Anglo-Spanish did not want me when they discovered I had no experience. I took to answering the advertisements for *una taquimecanografa inglesa* which appeared fairly frequently in *El Debate* and *A.B.C.* and *La
Tarde*, but I failed to get myself a job. Any kind of recom-
mendation from a previous employer would have got me

into one of those offices flying, but none of them wanted a girl without experience even if she held the world's championship in shorthand and typing. I was not much good at either, but I knew well I would be able to hold down a post if I could once get my nose in.

It was worrying, but I pushed the worry to the back of my mind. I have always been a believer in the saying that the worst never happens. "Something will turn up," I assured myself, and I proceeded to live for the moment. That was easy enough with a *continental* ten pages long waiting for me from Rafael every afternoon, and an outing with him in the evenings and sometimes an hour or two with him in the Retiro when I left Catalina.

I went with him to bull-fights too, though I did not like them. Luis had taught me to see them as they really were— a brutal sadism masquerading in king's robes of colour and music, and undeservedly crowned with the courage and skill of the matador. It was impossible not to want to retch with pity for animals and disgust for humans in the awful moment when the reaping-hook horn entered the belly of a poor broken-down hack of a blindfolded horse, lifting him high and sending the picador sprawling before ripping the horse open. It was Houyhnhnm-land gone topsy-turvy. The Yahoos were in the ascendant and were venting their brutishness on their gentle masters. Among the Yahoos who sat on the terraced seats were some who roared with laughter to see the unfortunate creature's entrails come tumbling through that terrible wound into the sand. The horse stood on petrified legs, his head straining back on his shoulders and with ripples of agony running along his back. He could not whinny or scream. An operation had been performed on him to ensure that there would be no harrassing interruption to the Yahoo's shouts of "*Mira qué salchichas!*—See what sausages!" It was impossible not to loathe all this, but equally impossible not to thrill to the courage and grandeur of the moment that came later when, the ring cleared of banderilleros, picadores, monosavios and dead horses, the matador was left alone with his furious adversary. There had been plenty to arouse in the bull that murderous fury. First the blinding sunshine that met him when the door of his pen had been opened. To the dazzled bewilderment of that first moment had been added the confusion of voices and the disquieting smell of humans. Then, as he stood hesitating at the entrance of the plaza, there had come a red-hot stab of pain between the shoulders. It sent him out into the ring at a quick trot, tossing his head this way and that in an effort to dislodge the stiletto that skewered in place the coloured ribbons which served the same purpose as a jockey's colours. After that, each additional impetus to his savagery had come quickly—the goads of the heavily armoured mounted picadores, the maddening excitement of that first horn-thrust through tough horsehide, the appetite-whetting smell of spilt blood, the sharp dig of barbed banderillas above each shoulder-blade and the torturing pull of the cruel things as they jiggled and danced in the wounds with every movement. More infuriating than pain was the futility of his wild charges against the twirling, waving capes of red. For the humiliated beast, these inviting, disappoint-ing capes constituted the worst phase of his ordeal. For the bull-fighters this *suerte* was the most satisfying. Every flick of the cape was a *paso* with a name of its own, and every well-executed *paso* brought a deep-throated roar of applause. Now the matador would display his skill, now his banderil-leros would take turns in showing off. Twirling, dancing, doubling, poising, the primitive ballet was played out and the bull was passed from one to another until at last the heavy short-legged beast was worked up into a seething madness of hatred. Only then was he left to match himself in fair battle against his arch-enemy. From now on it would be fury and strength against quickness and skill, animal ferocity against man's daring, two sharp horns against one short sword.

This was the hushed moment when the bull-fight took on grandeur. The stomach had heaved in pity for the horses, and the mind had sickened in disgust for man's inhumanity. Now, matchless courage shut out the horror of what had gone before, and it was the turn of the racing blood and the pounding heart. The blood sang and the heart leaped in salute to the gorgeous little figure that advanced lightly over the sand towards the watching reddened eyes and the waiting lowered horns. There were times when the heart did more than leap. There were times when it left the breast, and vaulted down to join the man with the ribbon-tied cue and the rich white suit with its heavy gold epaulettes, to stay with him and beat with him and share every breathless moment of his danger. This was when the matador was Belmonte, that flame-spirited man with the quiet ugly face which queerly held beauty, and the hunched misshapen shoulder which did nothing to lessen the grace of the slender body and the exquisite silken legs.

To come out of the plaza after the corrida was like coming out of a fever, and the suddenly silent crowds were like sullen convalescents. Always they were taciturn and dissatisfied coming home. When they did open their mouths, it was only to grumble at the poorness of every participant in that Roman show. I used to wonder if this was just a pose, but Rafael assured me that no Spaniard had ever been known to be completely satisfied with a matador's performance.

You have to be bred to strong meat of that kind to be able to stomach it. The distant whiff I had had of it before meeting Rafael had suited me all right. Until he had taken me to the corrida, my only experience of bull-fighting had been to watch from the pension balcony the Sunday afternoon crowds on their way to and from the plaza. Full of anticipation they always were, excited and happy and eager.

"*A donde vás, hombre?*" one would call to another. "Where are you off to, man?"

"*A los toros! a los toros!*" Every word of the loud joyful answer was a peal of bells.

It was a different story with them an hour or two later when they repassed with lagging steps.

"*De donde vienes, amigo?* Where are you coming from?"

A disgusted shrug, an irritable lift of the head. "*De los toros.*" Only three words, but in their disillusion and contempt they managed to convey that the bulls were lily-livered, half-blind heifers too old to moo, that the picadores had qualified ten years since for an old men's asylum, that the banderilleros were only fit to handle knitting needles, and that the matador himself had the agility of a tortoise, the blood of a dried codfish, the courage of a rabbit and the skill of a paralysed gander.

·   ·   ·   ·   ·

I said good-bye to Rafael at the end of June.

He decided one night that we should dine at Casa Botin before going to dance at one of the open-air, lantern-hung inns out by the Parque del Oeste. He took my arm as we went into the queer old-fashioned restaurant that had flourished for centuries on the fame of its roast sucking-pig, and that did not seem to have had a thing done to its white-washed walls and uneven floors since the first crisped bonyeen had been put before a young Governor due to sail on the morrow for Spain's great colonies in the New World. The head waiter who came forward to meet us was so desiccated that he might easily have been one of those who wished that governor *buen viaje*.

There was nothing disreputable about Casa Botin. The highest in the land went there to eat. There was plenty of high society there that night. I took it all in as we stood inside the threshold waiting for the waiter to find us a table —the pale-skinned warm women with their jewels and fine clothes, so carefully groomed that even the ugly ones were beautiful, the fervid men whose Castilian aquilinity gave them a hawkishness even when they were fat. Suddenly I felt Rafael go rigid. I looked at him. He was staring at a table in the far corner where a lady and a gentleman and a young girl were sitting. I had time only for one quick glance at them when his hand tightened on my arm. "Come on, Delia," he said urgently. "I'm sorry, but we'll have to eat some place else." He hurried me out into the street where he hailed a taxi.

"But why, Rafael? What's wrong? What is it all about?" My questions peppered every step of the way.

"I'll tell you—I'll tell you." He helped me into the taxi. "El Hotel Nacional," he told the driver, and got in beside me. Only then did he relax. "Madre de Dios!" he said with relief. "I nearly landed myself in an awkward situation that time. Anyway, Tio Martin should have stuck to his arrangement. He said he was taking them to the Ritz."

"Would you mind telling me who 'they' are?" I asked as quietly as I could. He had me nearly out of my mind with curiosity.

"Did you see those three people sitting in the corner— the lady in black and the young girl with a kind of green dress and the fat man with the bald head?"

"What about them?"

"The man was my Uncle Martin—he is staying with us on a visit. The others are my mother and my sister."

"Really, Rafael?" I was intensely interested. "Your mother is lovely and your sister is very pretty. Now I come to think of it, she is like you. Her hair is the same colour." Bewilderment suddenly returned to oust my interest. "But —I don't understand. Why were you upset to see them? Why did we have to come away?"

Rafael looked at me. We were caught up for a minute in a traffic block and the light from an electric sign shone in on us. I saw embarrassment on his face.

"It's a question of—of etiquette, Delia," he said awkwardly. "The women of one's family—well, a man must respect them. If you and I had remained there, Tio Martin would have had to take my mother and sister away."

A blow in the face would have been easier to bear. There were sudden noises in my head, and my throat started to hurt badly, so badly that for a second or two I could not speak. When I did, the hard dry sound of my voice surprised me. "So it would be belittling your mother and sister to have me eating in the same room as they? I'm so low and common that you daren't let your people see you in my company?"

"Not that, *mi amor*! You must not say such things." He leaned towards me quickly and made to take me in his arms, but I drew myself back into the very corner and held him off. "It kills me that you should speak in such a voice to me, Delia. Don't, love."

He might as well have kept silent. Nothing that he could say had a chance of bridging the chasm that had opened between us. That blow in the face had finished my self-deception. I wanted to hit back. I saw myself at last for the cheap romantic little fool I was. Deep in me I knew that I was being unjust, that it was unfair to hurt Rafael for something I had brought on myself. But not for any man living could I endure meekly such a slight.

Rafael was pleading again. "We have never quarrelled, Delia. Don't let us quarrel now over such a little thing. It is only a matter of etiquette. It has nothing to do with us and our love."

"It has everything to do with it," I said hardly. "If I'm not good enough to breathe the same air as your family, I'm not good enough for you to love."

His quick protest had such sincerity in it that for a second I went soaring up on the seesaw. "Oh, Rafael," I said. "Then you did mean it? About the flat? About us getting married in the autumn?"

"Look, Delia." He shifted uncomfortably, and the two words fell abruptly into the chilly depths of a frightening silence. The silence splashed up around me like ice-water. Humiliation and dismay closed in on me. I sent out a desperate S.O.S. for my pride. It came running to help me. With this grand ally at my side, I was able to subdue those puny traitors, the cowardly tears and the hurting throat and the keening heart. We hung out banners of defiance, my pride and I, and we cheered Bravo, when the tongue found the right jeering words to say and the right common tone in which to say them.

"Well, would you believe it, Rafael?" There was the bright amusement of one who at last sees the point in a joke. "Here was I actually believing that you wanted to marry me, while all you wanted was to make a *cocota* of me. This will be a good joke for you to tell your friends."

He passed his hand over his eyes. "Don't Delia," he begged unhappily. "*Por el amor de Dios*, don't talk like that. I would marry you if I could. But—you see—well, the fact is I have been engaged to my cousin for four years. But it need make no difference to us. We could have the little house just the same. No other woman would ever keep me from loving you."

I looked at him in silence for a second, at the brown pleading eyes, and the mouth that had no happy quirk to it now. I was saying good-bye to Rafael Moragas, and to much else besides. By the time the second had passed and I spoke again, I had grown up. It was not to Rafael I spoke, but to the driver. "Nuñez de Balboa, number one," I told him.

.   .   .   .   .

A queer thing happened to me that night. When I fell asleep in the room, which blessedly I had to myself since Helen went, Gran stole into my dreams. This was the only way she had been able to get near me lately, for when she had come knocking during my waking hours I had hidden myself from her. I dreamt that it was a warm summer night at home, with the moon making a black sheepskin rug of the heather and turning the ash-trees into tall women who stood gauntly with raised arms lifting their heavy crêpe veils a little so as to peep and grimace. I thought I was standing in my bare feet in the stream below Loughlin's Grove. I wanted to get out of the water, but I could not budge because of the way I was fettered ankle-deep in the thick mud. Gran was walking up and down on the bank saying her prayers out of a missal. She did not see me. I wanted to cry out to her to help me but I had to keep my mouth closed because of the millions of darkie-lukers that were leaping about, waiting for a chance to hurl their slimy bodies down my throat. That was the most terrible part of the dream—wanting to shout and only being able to make little whining sounds that Gran could not hear. If only she would look up from her prayers! But she did not look, and I was sinking deeper and deeper into the horribly oozy mud. When I saw Gran shut her missal with a little snap and start away from me down the path leading to Maria Doolin's cottage I could bear it no longer. I beat wildly with my hands at the cloud of darkie-lukers and I opened my mouth and screamed. "Gran!" I screamed. "Don't go, Gran! Help me, Gran!" The next minute I was out of the icy mud and lying some place safe and warm with Gran's arms about me and I hugging her little body. I was crying, and she was comforting me with small whispers. "*Callate, hija,*" she was saying. "*Callate, mi nena, mi pobrecita. Qué le han hecho a mi pequeña?*" It was Heaven to be comforted like this, to be safe and warm. A sudden thought came to me through the dream: How was it that Gran was talking Spanish? My hand on the bony little shoulder felt the soft thinness of a cotton blouse. How did Gran come to be wearing a thing like that? Where was her black stuff bodice with the flannelette lining? I opened my eyes. The light was on, and La Serena was bending over me.

I dropped my arms in embarrassment. "What is it, Serena? What happened?"

She looked down at me compassionately. "Thou wert weeping, daughter," she whispered, using the intimate "tu" for the first and last time in all our knowing of each other. "La Serena came to see if she could help thee. What is wrong?"

"Only," I said slowly. "only that I've found out that you were right in what you said about men."

She nodded sadly to herself. A sudden thought struck her and she fixed me with a bright worried eye. "Tell, daughter," she said anxiously. "*Estás embarazada?* Tell the truth."

For a minute I did not know whether to laugh or be upset. The kindness in her eyes made me answer with gentleness. "No fear of that," I said, "but my heart is destroyed."

Relief flooded her face. "If that is all it will soon mend itself. Young hearts are as easily mended as a tear in a dress." Smiles made her wrinkles seem an inch deep.

I was not at all pleased with her frivolous reception of the news that my life was blighted, and I am afraid I allowed my voice to sound slightly huffy as I bade her good night.

During the next few days I had little chance to nurse my broken heart. The more immediate problem was to find myself something to do that would keep me going until my pupils came back to Madrid. Now that I had come to my senses I regretted not having listened in time to Helen Quinn's advice. I could not find in any of the papers a single advertisement calling for a governess. I was becoming worried when La Serena suggested that I should go to the Reparadoras nuns. If there was a house in Spain that still lacked a governess, they would know of it. I took her advice and met Doña Conchita Lopez.

CHAPTER NINE

"IF the señorita will have the goodness to wait here?
The Mother Superior is engaged. I will find out when
she will be free." The pale child of a lay sister smiled herself out, leaving me in the company of two Popes, a martyr
being stoned to death and a stern-faced Foundress whose
eyes regarded me coldly. They were accusing eyes. They
made me feel unworthy to be breathing the mixture of bees-
wax and yeast-bread-in-the-oven and candle-grease which
is the patented atmosphere of convents.

There was a loud rattle of words and another claimant
for Mother Superior's ears was shown in, a short bejewelled
woman, with her good looks interred under a weight of
scented flesh. The little lay sister smiled and nodded bravely
as the woman bore down on her with an express-train of
words that got their speed from self-satisfaction and their
lubrication from saliva induced by the speaker's pleasure in
the sound of her own voice. "Tell the Mother Superior that
the Señora de Don Juan Lopez wishes to speak to her.
Don't forget the name—Dona Conchita Lopez of Almi-
rante 250. She will remember me—the señora who presented the convent with six metros of white satin for altar
cloths for Christmas before last. And it was I who presented the flowers for the altar in May of last year. Tell her
I do not wish to be delayed, for it is now midday and we
lunch at one." The train came to a stop and the lay sister
escaped.

The newcomer sat down on a chair near the door in the
straddlelegged fashion to which her fat condemned her.
She peeled off her gloves, fished a fan out of her big lizard-
skin bag and, flicking it open, started to fan herself with a
vigour that surely must have given more heat than it took
away. It was a minute or two before she noticed me. When
she did her eyes became alert and she studied me around the

side of the fan. I studied her too—the putty-coloured face with the little embedded features and the hard round eyes and the slack self-indulgent mouth. Her clothes were dear and good: black patent court shoes out of which the insteps bulged in silky pincushions, and a helmet of fine beige felt, the edge of which cut deep into her neck when she turned her head. Her dress of beige crêpe georgette was fascinating. The front of the bodice was decorated with horizontal tucks. The double fold of material in the tucks made them have a restraining effect on the doughy flesh immediately underneath, so that the woman's bosom was as corrugated as a galvanized roof.

As our glances ran over each other they collided. Doña Conchita spoke. "Are you English or French?"

"English," I said, with a mental apology to Ireland's dead.

"Catholic?"

"*Si, señora.*"

"Governess?"

"*Si, señora.*"

"Are you looking for a post?"

"*Si, señora.*"

"Have you your references?"

"La Señora de Valiente, Calle de Barquillo, 58, and la Señora del Dr. Juan Martinez, Carrera de San Geronimo 19."

She stopped fanning and considered me doubtfully for a minute. Then she gave the little resigned sigh of one who realizes that half a loaf is better than no bread. "I would have preferred a more settled person," she said. "And in view of the fact that the boys have had an English governess since they were babies, I would have preferred a Frenchwoman for a change. However, I can see about that when we return to Madrid in September. Will you take a temporary post? The best of food, your own room, bath every week, one hundred and fifty pesetas a month and a half-day every fortnight. Two boys, obedient and well brought up.

Teofilo is eight and Salvador is six. At the end of July we go to Biarritz for six weeks. Well, what do you say?"

"I'll be glad to come."

"Good. You can start this afternoon. Ring that bell for the lay sister. I want to tell her that I have no need to see Mother Superior now. The matter has arranged itself; it was the work of Providence." "It was written by God," was the way she put it.

.   .   .   .   .

It was an uncomfortable household. All the money and luxury in the world was there, but no happiness because of the queer relations that existed between the master and mistress. Towards the maids and me Doña Conchita showed herself a nag and a belittling bully. At mealtimes, in the presence of her husband, she was all meekness and docility. She seemed to be afraid of him, to be always trying to sloother him. It made you squirm for all craven women to see her for ever making up to a man who obviously wanted nothing of her. He was a cold stern little man, hazel-eyed and unusually fair-skinned, and with a breadth of shoulder and a heaviness of paunch that deserved twice his length of leg. When he spoke to his wife it was curtly and grudgingly. Sometimes when that noisy voice of hers started off on one of its directionless non-stop runs, he would give her a look of intense dislike and she would put on the brakes confusedly. They saw little of each other. He had his own room. Sometimes he did not come in until three o'clock in the morning. Some nights he did not come home at all. Lunch was the only meal he had with the family. Immediately he had taken his coffee he was away and out to his big furniture store. The big-business-man strut of him, the value he put on every second of his time and his moneyed cocksureness made me feel I had met his like often before, and when I learned his story I knew why. He was the Spanish counterpart of the returned Yanks who now and again came home to dazzle Ballyderrig after making their pile in the States. Don Juan had gone to the Argentine as a boy. He found work as a shop assistant, helped his employer to work up the business, married the daughter of the house and, on the old man's death, inherited a fortune. Don Juan was not a very likeable man, but he had dignity.

The atmosphere of their home may have had something to do with the boys' behaviour. They were the most unmanageable children on earth. Unless when plotting some fiendish bit of mischief they never agreed for two minutes. "They have had an English governess since they were babies," their mother had told me. They had had twenty governesses. Their kind of temperament may, as some child-psychologists tell us, produce heroes in after life, but it is very trying for any unfortunate girl whose job is to prevent the embryonic heroes from being prematurely lost to the world by sudden and violent death. When, two days after my arrival, I hauled Teofilo to safety from the bathroom window-ledge from which he was contemplating the patio forty feet below, he rewarded me by biting my arm. I felt I would deserve congratulations at the end of September if I had succeeded in keeping the sins of fratricide and suicide off their souls and the sin of infanticide off my own.

It was not an ideal post. I had hoped to be allowed to keep on the lessons with Mr. Yamada and Pepe Blanco, but Doña Conchita considered six hours every second Thursday an adequate ration of freedom for any girl, so from seven to bedtime each evening I had to content myself with trying to catch up on my arrears of correspondence in between remaking the boys' beds, fetching them drinks of water, pulling them down from the tops of wardrobes and digging them out of each other. Their mother exercised no restraining influence on their curtain-devilment. The minute supper was over she retired, locked her door, and was not seen until morning.

The only pleasant occasions of my stay with Doña Con-

chita were the visits to Tia Clara. She was Don Juan's elder
sister, a stout good-hearted little countrywoman, strong-
featured and fair-haired. She was devoted to her brother
and he to her. On his return from the Argentine he had
made her come in from Toledo with her husband and son
and two daughters and had installed the family in a flat over
his shop. He gave the quiet grey husband a job as night-
watchman. He was paying for the girls in a commercial college, and he was having the son, Eugenio, taught engineering. I took the boys there nearly every afternoon for their
merienda of chocolate and cakes. Sometimes Don Juan
would come up from the shop to eat the little cream cakes of
Toledo which his sister made specially for him, and to rest
awhile. He was a different man in that kindly atmosphere,
with the well-kept bits of furniture from his childhood home
around him, and his sister dancing attendance on him and
pretending to be angry if he did not clear his plate. The
sternness left him there, and he laughed and joked with his
sons like any normal father. Doña Conchita never came
with us. The nephew, Eugenio, was the only one of her in-
laws for whom she had any friendship. She was always at
home to him when he came to the house. He was a thickset
youth of twenty with film-star side-whiskers and a pair of
fawn's eyes which he used as if he believed himself to be
Rudolph Valentino. He was doing his military service, and
the walk of him in his uniform gave the impression that if
King Alfonso would only recall his army from Morocco
and send Eugenio out in their place, the trouble with the
Moors would be settled in no time.

He developed a habit of casually walking into the boys
and myself in the Retiro, and of honouring me with his
treacle-dripping glances and a selection from the handbook
on How to Win Hearts and Influence Women which seems
to be issued to Spanish boys with the Ha'penny Catechism.
If he had but known it, Don Juan Tenorio himself would
have been a failure with a woman in my bruised and broken

condition. Eugenio's attentions had the effect on me that the offer of a lump of fat pork would have on someone coming out of a bout of sea-sickness.

When the first free Thursday afternoon fell due, I did not get my six hours. Doña Conchita went to bed with a headache and I had to take the children to the Retiro as usual. I was vexed, for I wanted to see La Serena. I had promised her I would come. Eugenio caught up with us near the Zoo. He sent the boys to buy ice-cream and repeated his offer to take me to the pictures.

"You could easily steal out when the boys are in bed," he said. "I would fix it with the maids, and my aunt and uncle need never know. Once she locks herself into her room with her bottle of anisado the house could be burnt to the ground unknown to her. And you need not fear that my uncle would return to the house unexpectedly and find you out. From the minute he shuts the shop each evening, he occupies himself with a certain little bit of business out in Rosales— a dark-haired, well-made little bit of business." He leered in a man-of-the-world fashion.

The time had come for plain speaking. "Listen, Eugenio," I said. "If you were ten times the man you are, I would not go out with you. I would not walk a foot of the road with any Spaniard living."

His syrupy manner fermented instantly. "Indeed?" he sneered. "And what about the Spaniard with whom you are planning to spend a night in El Escorial?"

What on earth was the fool raving about?

"You may look very innocent but my aunt has opened my eyes to you. She showed me a very enlightening letter which was written to you by your friend, Luis."

Now I saw what he was getting at. Well, of all the dirty-minded prying wretches! So he and his precious aunt had been rummaging in the drawer of my night-table, reading my letters and putting their own bad-minded construction on them!

I yanked the boys home, went to my room and re-read the letter which had given Doña Conchita and her nephew-in-law such a titillation. In the middle of long spiels about Krishnamurti and Æ, Luis had enlarged on the mad sombre glories of El Escorial. "I'd love you to spend an evening here," he wrote. "I think I would be able to help you to discover a new wonder." Into this simple sentence the pair of them had read badness.

Well, there was only one thing to be done, and I did it. I handed in my notice. There was not much use trying to make a fuddled Doña Conchita receive it through a locked door, so I brought it down to Don Juan in the shop. Anyway, I was in such a boiling vindictive temper that I was determined he should be told the whole ins and outs of the affair. First I made him read the letter. "Would you say there is any badness in the mind of the man who wrote that letter, Don Juan?"

"Por Dios, no, señorita! This man writes only of culture and the things of the spirit. But what is all this about?" The poor man was bewildered. "What has your correspondence to do with me?" I told him. He was furious. His face swelled and his eyes became as opaque as green grapes. "*Le romperé las muelas!*" was what he said of his nephew. "I will break his molars!" He was bitter about his wife. Now that the worst of my temper had worked itself off, it was embarrassing to have to listen to the things he said. He asked me not to go at a time when it would be difficult for him to find another governess at short notice. He was unreasonable in expecting me to stay beyond the end of the month. He should have seen that, spirit aside, life in his house would be made impossible for me after this. Doña Conchita would have many a way of paying me out. But he refused to take my notice as final. "Think it over, señorita. It will be only for two months or so. And may I point out that for you it may be as difficult to find a new post as for me to find a new governess?"

After watching the advertising columns of the *ABC* and *El Debate* for a week without results, I began to think that maybe he was right and that after all my big talk I might have to stay on and put up with Doña Conchita's vengefulness for having got her into a row, and Tia Clara's reproachful looks for having got her son into disfavour. I would probably have done so but for a copy of *El Liberal* which the cook lent me when I had nothing to read one night. The paper was new to me. In the "Positions Vacant" column was one incredible, marvellous piece of print:

"Young, well-educated English girl needed for summer post. Three hundred pesetas a month. Send photo with application."

There would be a post worth getting! Three hundred pesetas a month. That was what the governess in the Duque de Alba's house was paid. The size of the salary made me think there would probably be half a dozen children to look after. Even so, provided they were any way normal and ordinary at all, the six of them would be no more trouble than the two I had at present. I typed out my application on the portable typewriter Don Juan kept in the study. To make it more impressive I used the house stationery, with its glossy embossed address and telephone number. Luckily I had a copy of the photograph which Michael had asked me to have taken in the spring. Luckily, too, it was a sedate one and showed me at my most serious. When I sealed the letter I wrote in tiny capitals on the flap, S.A.G., Saint Anthony's Guidance, and that night my prayers were more fervent than they had been for many a day.

At about ten o'clock two nights later, Paquita came running to say I was wanted on the telephone—a long-distance call from San Sebastian. I flew to the telephone and grabbed the receiver.

"Hallo. This is Miss Scully." It was difficult to control the excited tremble in my voice.

"Ramirez here." It was a man's voice, a fruity voice. "You answered my advertisement." He spoke in Spanish but with an accent I could not place. "Say, did you type that letter yourself?"

"*Si, señor!*"

"Would you be willing to do a little typing for me? Not very much—a few letters now and again and some reports."

"Certainly, señor." Hurrah! I would be getting some business experience at last!

"Good. I am staying here in the Hotel Britanico in San Sebastian. We will be leaving for Bilbao the day after to-morrow. Could you come down here by the train that leaves Madrid at eight to-morrow night? I will meet you at the station. Is that all right?"

It was marvellous! I could not believe my ears. Lucky was no name for me. "That will suit me perfectly," I said. A sudden thought occurred to me: those six children I would have to cope with in order to earn that grand salary. It would be as well to know for certain what I was up against. "*Cuantos niños, señor?*" I asked.

He did not seem to understand. "What did you say?" came back over the wire.

"I said: *Cuantos niños?* How many will I have to look after?"

"Oh." A slight pause and then an amused chuckle. "One only, señorita." The operator's voice cut in before I had a chance to ask the age of my charge and there was only time for us to say together, "Until the day after to-morrow, then. *Adios.*"

I could not sleep with excitement. I stayed up packing the yellow dress-basket which was still my only piece of luggage. I made up my mind that my first purchase out of that princely three hundred pesetas would be a real suitcase. The packing done, I wrote letters—to Luis, to my family, to Miss Carmody, Miss Wilson, a boastful note to Helen and to Michael the first real letter I had written him in months.

I was still sleepless, so I switched off the light and went out on the balcony. As I stood there in the warm singing darkness I decided that though Rafael might be as La Serena has said, a liar, a deceiver and a pretender, life held compensations. The wooden frame of the french window still held some of the heat of the day's sun. I leaned back against it and through my thin pyjamas it was as friendly as a smooth larch-trunk. Little lost puffs of wind came wandering through the night and they patted my face and hair with kindness. I thought, as on the night Miss Carmody had given me the dresses: God is nearer than the door.

.   .   .   .   .

Don Juan went out early next morning so I did not see him until dinner-time. He was very annoyed with me for not being willing to put his convenience before my own interests and it was in a displeased tone that he said good-bye. However, he was generous. Although there were three days to go until the end of July he gave me the full month's salary. There was so much to do before train-time that I got no chance to go around to the pension to bid La Serena good-bye. That grieved me, for it was over three weeks since I had seen her. Useless to think of writing to her, either, since the poor old thing could not read or write. "I'll see her in two months' time," I told myself as the train left the Estacion del Norte. "I'll have plenty to tell her then." It was only two days until I saw her. Even so I had plenty to tell her.

CHAPTER TEN

WHEN I saw him coming up the platform I placed him at once as the owner of that opulent telephone voice.

It fitted perfectly his grey-suited, well-fleshed, middle-aged swarthiness. When he found me he raised his curly-brimmed hat of pearl-grey and gave me a smile that showed twice the usual allowance of teeth. "*Es usted la Señorita Scully?*"

"*Si, señor. Usted será el Señor Ramirez?*"

We shook hands, and with a flash of rings he signalled to a porter to take the dress-basket. Chatting genially, he led the way to his car.

As we drove to the hotel I felt dazzled. The heat haze which even at this early hour was dancing on the pavement may have had something to do with it. The uncomfortable night I had passed may have affected me too, for I had travelled in a carriage that was packed like a cattle-wagon. But I think Señor Ramirez himself was the chief cause of my bedazzlement. He glittered and sparkled at every facet. Nature had given him more than his share of shine to start with—black-japanned hair, brilliance of Guinness-coloured eyes and all those flashing teeth. He had added plenty himself in the way of rings and tiepin, a gold watch on one wrist, a gold bracelet on the other, a gold-and-onyx cigar-case, a rosy polish on his nails, highly lacquered tan shoes on his feet and around his neck an unusually deep and extra glossy collar. Without having to say a word he could have stolen the honours in any film calling for a wealthy, juicy Latin. He was more affable and communicative about his affairs than is usually the way with an employer towards the governess. Before we reached the hotel I knew that he was a Chilian, that he was the director of a big firm with branches in every Spanish city, that he would be touring those branches for the next two months, and that in October he would be going to London to visit the English branch.

"We will not be leaving for Bilbao until the afternoon," he told me when we arrived at the Britanico. "I have taken a room for you. You will be tired after your journey, so perhaps you would like to go there now, and rest until lunchtime? Did you have breakfast in the train?"

"No, señor." I had eaten nothing since seven o'clock the previous night.

"I will have breakfast sent up to you at once."

Breakfast, a bath and a few hours in bed—it was an appealing plan, but I felt a little diffident about going to bed immediately after reporting for duty. The least I could do would be first to pay my respects to my new charge's mother. "Would it not be better if I saluted your señora first? And the boy?"

The wide gold bracelet on his right wrist seemed to be hurting him. He twisted it into a more comfortable position. "That will be time enough later," he said then, with a sudden flash of a smile. "We will meet at lunch time, no? Come . . . I will have you taken to your room." My misgivings about him awoke in that moment. As we made towards the lift it hummed down to rest and through its clanged doors stepped a tall spare man with light blue eyes and a clipped white moustache.

"Hola, Mister Malony," my employer greeted him. "What good luck! I wanted to see you. Pardon me a moment, señorita." With his peculiar tiptoed walk, he moved volubly and animatedly beside the grey man towards the office. They stood there talking, a curious contrast in types—Malony a long thin roll of plain bread, Ramirez a big chocolate éclair. Presently Ramirez said something with a backward glance in my direction. He made a half-wave of his arm towards me, an interrogative wave. Plainly he was inviting Malony to be introduced. What happened then humiliated me bitterly. The grey man gave me a contemptuous flick of the eyes and made a little grimace of refusal. Then he turned his back to me rudely and went on with his talk.

"That was an American, a business acquaintance," Señor Ramirez explained when he returned.

"He is a boor and a snob, whatever he is," I thought, rankling.

My employer was waiting for me in the lounge when I came down to lunch. The bath and rest had made a new woman of me.

"Have you rested well?" he greeted me and added immediately, "You are younger than you appear in your photograph. Are you sure you are nineteen?" I assured him was. I noticed that he was looking at me rather uncomfortably. That tight-fitting bracelet seemed to be giving him trouble again, for he fiddled at it. There was no sign at all of his wife and family and no mention of them. The uneasiness which breakfast and a bath and rest had succeeded in chasing returned with reinforcements.

"Look, señorita," he said with sudden decision. "You and I must have a talk. But first we will eat."

It was an awkward meal. Ramirez chatted amiably. He invited me to have a cocktail—"coke-tel," he called it. He kept pressing this dish and that on me. No one could have asked for a more attentive host. Still, I was glad when we finished and he led the way back to the lounge. "Here, I think," he said, selecting a quiet corner. "It is always best to talk in comfort." We sat in the big pillowy chairs. He clipped and pierced a cigar and lit it thoughtfully. When he got it going he studied me for a minute or two through a cloud of smoke.

"Tell me something, señorita." The brilliant eyes were hard and judging now. The voice was very soft. "Answer me with honesty: All this talk about my wife and family—is it an act?" The question was so unexpected and belittling that my face flamed. Hot words got in each other's way and nothing got out but a stutter. He smiled a little tolerant smile. "I know women, you see. Sometimes they are very childish. If they wish to do something they feel is wrong, they will play a little game of make-believe so as to remain in their own good graces. But I prefer honesty. Let us have the truth. Did you really believe I advertised for a governess?"

Many a time afterwards I reconstructed that conversation and with each reconstruction I got new ideas for the grand and dignified retort I could have given if only I had thought of it when it was needed. At the time, unfortunately, the best I could manage was a lame though indignant "*Claro que sí! Of course I did!*"

"But, señorita!" Raised eyebrows, widened eyes, spread palms—they all pleaded with my common sense, my sophistication, my *savoir-faire*. "How is it possible? Does one advertise for a governess in *El Liberal?*"

Whether one did or not, it was as a governess that I had replied to the advertisement and I told him so in plain words. He believed me. "*La creo,*" he said. I was glad he believed me. It was ridiculous, maybe, but in that moment it seemed important to me that I should be believed, more important even than the fact that I had no money and no job.

He leaned forward to drop the thick grey bullet of cigarash into an ash-tray, and the gold buckle of his deep-biting belt hid itself in the fatty crease at his middle. He settled back in his chair and the buckle reappeared. A wavy gossamer ribbon unwound itself from the cigar and he followed it with his eyes. "Let us reach a clear understanding, then, señorita. You came here expecting a post as governess to my children. Unfortunately, that post is already filled. They have a very efficient fraulein. Anyway"—he chuckled, and his eyes invited me to share the joke—"you would have to teach them by post. They are all five with their mother in Chile." There was such good-humoured amusement in his face and voice that I actually found myself smiling in sympathy before I caught myself on. When I did, my face sobered. His did too, and his next words came in a practical businesslike tone. "The position is this, señorita. Though I do not need a governess, I can offer you a very attractive post. I am a man who—well, frankly, the companionship of a woman is as necessary to me as cigars or food. I need a travelling companion for the next two months.

Naturally, I could find plenty of women who would be glad to accompany me." With a wave of his cigar he conjured up long queues of beautiful girls who were aching to keep his journey from being lonely. "But I need to brush up my English for the London trip in October. Couple these two wants and you will understand the exact meaning of my advertisement. Does the proposition interest you?" The tone and words were impersonal, but the eyes were not. I was mad with them and with myself when I felt my cheeks begin to burn. That he should see my flustered embarrass-ment was hateful. He looked at his watch. "It is now a quarter past two. I must go out for a couple of hours on business. At half-past four I shall return. You have two hours in which to decide. I take it you are unemployed at the moment. You could do worse than come with me. I think I could promise you a very enjoyable time. A motor-trip through Spain, the best hotels, some new dresses. Three hundred pesetas is the salary, but in addition there would, naturally, be gifts. I am not an ungenerous man. Well, señorita, will you think it over?"

I did not need two minutes to think over his proposition. If I had been suited to live that kind of life I could have had it with Rafael and with my heart's approval. Annoyance again got the better of my gift for repartee, and I am sorry to say that my answer was on a par with my previous efforts. "*Tiene usted mucha caradura!*" I told him hotly. "You have a great cheek!"

"A pity!" Señor Ramirez lifted his padded shoulders in a shrug of regret. "We would get on so well together, you and I. You have the air of a girl who could enjoy life. You are intelligent. And your knowledge of typing would be very useful, for I have much correspondence. Yes, I like an intelligent girl. Beauty? Pouf! Beauty is nothing. Beauty is easily found and it quickly grows boring. I prefer intelli-gence."

This made me mad entirely. There is not a woman living

who enjoys hearing her brains praised at the expense of her looks. I was stung into finding the use of my tongue. "You make a mistake in looking for an intelligent girl," I said. "I am afraid you will have to content yourself with a dumb beauty, for no woman with ordinary intelligence will have anything to do with you and your motor-trip."

The eyes rested on me thoughtfully. "I am not altogether surprised," he said. "After our telephone conversation the other night I had a feeling that perhaps you were not a suitable type. My doubts increased when I saw you in the station this morning. Your luggage and—you will pardon me?—your clothes and general appearance made me say to myself: This is either a decent girl or a foolish girl."

"Why foolish?"

He shrugged again. "Surely that is obvious. If a young attractive girl is not good and still remains poorly dressed it means that she is wasting herself on some impoverished clerk or student. That is foolishness, no?" He stood up, "Well, this is a very interesting conversation, but I am afraid I must keep my appointment."

Sudden panic seized me. "What about me?" I asked wildly. "What am I going to do? I left a job to come down here. I won't be able to find anything to do until the end of September. What about the money I had to spend on my ticket?"

He smiled down at me, and it was only then I realized the stony hardness behind the lushness and geniality. "Surely that is a problem for yourself, señorita." The voice was a purr. "With such intelligence as yours you must realize that I cannot be held responsible for your misreading of my advertisement. Be reasonable, señorita. I can only repeat my offer of a post that most girls in your position would find very attractive. Perhaps between now and half-past four you may see it in a more favourable light." With a bow and a smile he was gone and I was left feeling really frightened for the first time in my life.

Eighty pesetas my ticket from Madrid had cost. I counted what I had in my bag. A fifty-peseta note and a few oddments of change. Not enough to take me back and hose two long months to face. Mrs. Hansen liked her money in advance. She would never give me so much credit. Even if she did, I would never be able to pay her back. My mind darted here and there, but every road it took was a blind alley. Cable for money to some of my friends? I could not do it. No matter what happened, I knew I could not murder my pride and my independence with a whine for help. Entreat Ramirez to refund my fare? Perhaps. But would he give it to me? As he had pointed out, I had no right to ask it. It was not his fault that I had got myself into this mess. Still, a decent man would feel himself bound to make good my expenses. Then I remembered the Chilean's face and he smiling down at me, and I knew that my speculations were foolish. He had said he was not an ungenerous man. That might be, but his generosity would never be shown in a disinterested way. The pattern of the carpet in the lounge of the Hotel Britanico will remain with me as long as I live. Dark green, with lines of lighter green making diamonds of it, and with a small pink rose in the four corners of each diamond and a large pink rose in the centre. I never see pink roses on a green carpet but I relive the panic of that hour.

"Where is Señor Ramirez?"

I looked up. It was Mr. Malony, the grey American. I had been so far away that he had to repeat his question.

"He is gone out. He said he'd be back at half-four." This was the man who had looked at me so insultingly this morning. It seemed a long time ago, so long that I no longer rankled.

He moved off a few steps and then changed his mind and came back. "You're Irish, aren't you?" His manner was gruff and impatient, but I had so much worry on me that I could take no more and I answered him without resentment.

He hesitated a second and then sat suddenly in the chair Ramirez had used. I had no wish for company. I let him be, and returned to my study of the carpet and of my prospects.

Mr. Malony recalled me. "How old are you? Eighteen?" The words seemed to be coming against his will.

I told him my age. Why couldn't the man go away and leave me in peace?

"What brought you to Spain?" was the next question. "I came as a governess," I said, rudely making the tone of my answer ask: "What has it to do with you?

"I see." The lips were bitter below the tidy white moustache. "And you couldn't stick to your governessing. You had to kick over the traces. Wanted to see life, I suppose. Go on—tell me to mind my own business. I don't know in hell why I don't—except that I get mad every time I see an American or British girl make a fool of herself over a Latin. I can promise you this, you crazy little fool, by the time Ramirez is finished with you, you'll be sorry you ever left Ballyslapguttery, or wherever it is you come from."

The situation needed clarifying. Unreasonably, I was twice as mad with the American as I had been with Ramirez. In two minutes I convinced Mr. Malony that a woman may stand in a public-house without being drunk or having the intention of getting drunk. The unfortunate man became as shy and as awkward as a schoolboy.

"Say, Miss——?"

"Delia Scully is my name."

"Miss Scully. I don't know how to apologize. But I still think you're a fool not to have stayed at your safe governessing job and I think it's a darned shame that youngsters of your age should be sent to a country like this without being told what it's all about."

It was he who was being a fool now, and I told him so. Where would the people of Ballyderrig, or my mother or the Wicklow nuns find knowledge of the things I had seen since coming here?

"Maybe you're right, at that," he admitted. "I wouldn't know. Here, hadn't we better have some tea?" He beckoned a waiter. By the time the tea came, he had the whole story out of me, and I was liking him for the kind way he put his questions. "I shouldn't worry any more about that train fare," he said. "I'll see that Ramirez refunds it. He'll pay your fare back to Madrid too. What are you going to do when you get there?"

It was difficult to find an answer to that. I poured his tea and explained the position. "I'll be all right once September is over. My pupils will be back by then. Anyway I don't mind so much now that you're going to make him give me back my train fare—that will keep me going for a while. Something is sure to turn up. Miss Ivers—she's a woman I used to know—she said there was no fear of me, that Providence looks after fools. Will you put sugar and milk in this yourself?"

He took the cup from me with a nice big freckled hand. No polish on the nails, no rings on the fingers, no heavy gold chain on the wrist. "You have two months to go until the end of September. Can you do anything else besides giving Spanish brats an Irish brogue?"

"I'm not too bad at the shorthand and typing. That's what I want to do. I've been trying to get into an office, but none of them wants a beginner. They won't take you without experience."

With strong deliberate fingers he dropped three lumps of sugar into his tea and stirred it meditatively. He lifted his head with a little jerk and the light blue eyes considered me from under shaggy white brows. "Suppose," he said slowly, "you had three months' experience in my office? Do you think you'd be able to find yourself a job?"

My eyes nearly dropped out on the tablecloth. "Would you"—I could hardly hear myself speak—"Would you say that again, Mr. Malony?"

"I'll have to make work for you of course, for I don't

really need another typist. And I'm going to have a job making it right with Head Office. It would be only for three months, mind. And the salary I can offer won't do much more than pay for your keep. What do you think? Would it help you to get the kind of job you want?"

The man never knew how near he came to being disgraced. It took me all my time to keep myself from making a wild rush at him there in the public lounge. I babbled at him instead. "If I had those three months I'd never see a poor day! Sure, they're always looking for English shorthand typists. And speaking Spanish well the way I do and with the bit of French—I'd have no trouble in the world in getting a good job. It was only the want of experience that was keeping me back. You're too good—I can't thank you——"

"Forget it, forget it. I called you a fool, but you're a spunky little fool, and I like spunk. Anyway, my father and mother were Irish. You have the job. I'm going back to Madrid to-night—we'll travel together." A thought struck him, and his mouth puckered in the rueful grin of a boy who knows he is going to catch it. "God only knows what Miss Leach will have to say about this. She's my secretary. A grand woman, but a tartar."

Shortly after four, His Fruity Magnificence came flashing towards us. "Better clear out for a while," Mr. Malony advised. "I'll manage this better on my own." I gave them half an hour. When I returned they were deep in a business discussion. Señor Ramirez placed a chair for me with as gallant and respectful an air as if I had been the Queen of Spain, and went on with his talk of specifications and blue prints.

Just as he was about to leave he clapped his hand to his forehead in mock self-reproach. "*Ay, que tonto soy!*" he lamented. "Here I was about to depart, and I almost overlooked the expenses which the señorita incurred on my account." He took two hundred-peseta notes from his case and presented them with such conscious integrity that he nearly persuaded himself and me that Mr. Malony had had nothing to do with the matter, and that this kind, good-hearted Chilean would have died rather than let me be at the loss of the money.

When I arrived in Madrid next morning, Mr. Malony told me to take the day off to rest. I went straight to Mrs. Hansen's. I had sufficient money to pay her a fortnight's board at eight pesetas a day. What was left would have to cover tram fares until the end of the month. I hoped to be able to persuade Mrs. Hansen to give me credit for the other two weeks until I would be paid my first month's salary. Surely she would not refuse when I'd tell her of my lovely steady job in an office at four hundred pesetas a month? A job in an office . . . it sounded better every time I said it. I was dying to see La Serena's face when she would hear the good news, and when I got to Nuñez de Balboa I could not wait for the lift to descend, but dashed up the stairs, dress-basket and all, three at a time.

I rang the bell and jiggled with joyful impatience as I waited for La Serena to open the door to me. When it opened it was not La Serena who stood there, but a tall heavy man in a white coat and apron. An unlikeable man. The big flabby face was oyster-coloured. The eyes were mean and calculating and the mouth was surly.

"The señorita wishes . . . ?"

"Mrs. Hansen?" I faltered. "I want to see Mrs. Hansen."

Then he told me. Mrs. Hansen had been dead and buried these two weeks and more. If I had been able to come on that free Thursday which had been denied to me I would have found the poor woman waking.

"Is the señorita looking for a room?" the man asked. "I am the new proprietor of this pension. I intend to turn it into a *pension de lujo*. Already I have made great changes —new divan beds in all the rooms. Next week we start the installation of hot and cold water. The food will be un-comparably better too. I have retired from my position as chef in the Hotel España and I can promise excellent catering."

"What do you charge?" I asked him.

"The señorita can have a room with full board from ten pesetas up. The charge is moderate."

Well, this was certainly no place for me. But I had to see La Serena. "Does Serena still work here? The little old woman?"

"Do you mean the ancient one? *Por Dios* no, señorita! An old one of that kind would be out of place in this pen-sion. I sent her packing." The poor old creature had been thrown out in the street, and not a soul to say a friendly word to her.

"Well, has the señorita decided? Is she going to take the room?" The man's voice was impatient.

"I am sorry," I said. "I can't afford it. Maybe later on. But, please——" he was shutting the door on me—"Didn't the old woman leave any message for me? Scully is my name Did she say where she was going? Please." Paca, the woman who had replaced Maruja, came into the hall from the sitting-room, brush in hand. "Here," the man called irritably. "Did the old one say where she was going?" Paca went on down the hall. Without looking back she said, "She was here on Sunday. Said to tell the *inglesa* she was working in Hortaleza, 225, Pension Camorra."

"Thank you," I said to the man, and picked up my dress-basket.

"Go with God," he said, and shut the door on me.

I went down the stairs without a worry in the world. The problem of board and lodging for the month would solve itself somehow. I knew where to find La Serena and to-morrow I would establish my proud record as the first Irish governess in Spanish history to gatecrash the exalted realm of English-speaking typists. After a year of office work I would be able to go home and get a good job in Ireland. It was a lovely world.

As I stood in the metro waiting for the train that would take me to Hortaleza, I knew I deserved shooting for the doubts that had come to me in the Hotel Britanico while I studied the carpet. Never again, for the longest hour I lived, would I commit the sin of doubting that God is nearer than the door.

CHAPTER ELEVEN

THE street of Hortaleza is like a misspent life. It gets a grand start at the top of the Gran Via. For a few blocks it remains true to its good beginnings, but then it commences to forget itself and to welcome the mean streets that run to it from each side. In their company it grows more shabby and down at heel until finally it comes to a bad end in the Plaza de Santa Barbara.

The dress-basket weighed a ton before I found No. 225 —a gangling slattern of a house with scabby sun-spots on its door and a hall like a gaping malodorous mouth. There was no one in the *portera's* cage. A woman came in from the street, heavy-moving and loose-breasted. She wore a dirty dress of flowered black print and carried a shopping basket. Her coarse greying hair was cropped untidily. When the poor of Ballyderrig came home from the workhouse hospital after a bout of scarlet fever or diphtheria, their hair always looked like that—as if it had been cut with a knife and fork.

She had her foot on the first step of the stairs when I stopped her. "*La Pension Camorra me hace el favor?* On what floor is it?"

The woman shifted her basket so that it was half-supported by her stomach. "On the second right. I am the *patrona* of the Pension Camorra. Are you looking for lodgings?" The words were as toneless as poured flour. Her skin was thick and greasy. She had a broad nose pinpricked with pores, and a mouth that was thin and twisted and colourless like an old scar. The eyes, though dull, were knowing. They were all pupil, with no whites at all to be seen. The stains under them were of so deep a brown that it seemed as if the woman had cried once and that the colour in her eyes had run a little.

"Does a woman called Serena work for you?"

The dull eyes became suspicious. "What do you want with her? Has she stolen something?"

"No, no! She is a friend of mine. I only wanted to see her."

"She is at the market. She will be back presently. So you do not want lodgings? I have a small room vacant, a very comfortable room with a good bed."

"What do you charge?"

"Six pesetas a day for bed, breakfast and two full meals. Five if you take a one-plate supper."

The thought of staying in this woman's house was unpleasant. But where would I get in for so little? Only five pesetas a day! At this rate I would be able to keep myself for a whole month without being dependent on anyone. It was near enough to Mr. Malony's office in Montera to make tram fares unnecessary. It would be only for a month. And wouldn't I have La Serena under the same roof with me?

"Show me the room," I said, and I followed her up the narrow stairs. It was a cupboard of a room with no windows. A square piece cut out of the partition over the door let in the air. There was an iron bed with the mattress rolled up showing a rusty spring. A press, an oilcloth-covered dressing-table with a basin on it, and an enormous old armchair of moulting green plush completed the furniture. A threatening room, but a month would not give it much time to do anything to me. I took it. The *patrona* asked for her money in advance, and I emptied my purse of everything but seven pesetas to pay her a month.

La Serena was horrified when she came in and found me committed for a month to the Pension Camorra. Not even the good news about my job could pacify her. "This is no place for the señorita!" she said, her little face stern. Concern made her bright eyes bigger than ever. "This is not a pension—this is a common lodging-house for workmen. There are people in this house who are not fit for the señorita to associate with."

"What is wrong with them, Serena?"

In quick little whispers she told me. "That Doña Luz, the *patrona*—she is bad. Only a few months out of jail where they sent her for trying to start a little girl of fourteen on the road to Hell. There is another servant, a poor wretch of a Frenchwoman who was *una mujer de la vida* until she got too old and they threw her out. And there is a Galician couple—they have the best room. He is a plasterer, out all day. She has a lover who visits her every afternoon. *Valgame, Dios*, what a house! If only La Serena had been here to warn the señorita before she paid her money." The little thing wrung her hands whimperingly and darted off to her work.

The place was pretty bad, but not so bad as La Serena had made out. The men were hard-working labourers who did not interfere with anyone. They came together only at supper-time. After the first few nights I took my one-plate supper—usually a dish of lentils—in my own room, for the oaths they used in conversation with each other embarrassed me. They could not make the simplest statement without invoking the most intimate part of the female body or an unmentionable lavatory word. At the same time I had to admit to myself that ear-hurting though these expressions were, they were perhaps less offensive than oaths taken by the Holy Name which were frequent enough with my own people at home.

The men's obscenities did not disconcert me nearly so much as the bugs. I could get away from the oaths but there was no escaping the bugs. Even the best-kept and newest of Madrid houses had its share of bugs in the heat of summer, but that dilapidated old house in Hortaleza swarmed with them. La Serena did her best to keep them at bay for me. She stole olive-oil from the kitchen and rubbed the bedstead with it. Any bug with normal tastes would have avoided the bed like poison after this treatment, but the dirty depraved bugs in the Pension Camorra—some of them as big as farthings—were a race apart. They liked my neck and my ankles best. All that sweltering August I had to wear a silk handkerchief around my neck to hide the big red lumps they raised. When I complained to the *patrona* about them I got scanty sympathy. "They never bother me," was what she said. I told La Serena this, and she said she was not surprised to hear it. "That one's blood is so bad that even the bugs won't drink it," she whispered. "The bug that bites her is a bug that dies."

She was probably right. Doña Luz was bad. She was the only person I have ever known that struck me as being bad to the very core like a rotten apple. I remember seeing the evil in her one Saturday evening when I went to get my cleaned white canvas shoes from the kitchen window-sill where I had put them to dry in the sun. It was a horrible littered kitchen. It must have been agony for La Serena to work there. A closet opened off it. Doña Luz kept pigeons for the sake of their eggs and of an occasional little skinny carcass which she roasted on a skewer for herself. She housed the pigeons in the closet, and the cooking smells were polluted by the stench of their droppings. I got my shoes. The *patrona* was peeling potatoes at the table. "I won't be in for supper to-night," I said as I passed her. I was going to supper to a house where later I was to spend the happiest days I knew in Spain. Doña Luz looked up. The right side of her thin mouth lifted itself in a beastly insinuating leer. "The señorita is going out?" She wagged the knife approvingly at me. "That is right. There is always plenty of money in the streets on Saturday night."

I hated her for the way she treated Germaine, the unfortunate wreck of a Frenchwoman. Germaine was forty, maybe, very emaciated and sharp-featured, and with fuzzy dry hair like hay. She had a hard hurting little cough and two burning spots on her cheek-bones. I think the creature was a little bit cracked. She had a nervous flustered way with her, and she giggled foolishly where another would have cried. There was a queer pitiable innocence about that woman, a natural refinement and a childish eagerness to be nice to everyone. She nearly died one day when I came in early and found her trying on the remains of the rowanberry dress Miss Carmody had given me. She must have expected me to fly at her or to complain of her to the *patrona*, for she stood there with terror in her feverish eyes and gave that weak giggle. When I pretended the old dress looked lovely on her and told her to keep it—it was only fit for dusters, anyway—the embarrassing way she carried on nearly made me sorry I had not scolded her instead. Doña Luz gave her a dog's life. Admittedly, Germaine's ways would have taxed the patience of the best of mistresses. Even if she had had the strength to work, she would have been the world's worst maid. She knew nothing at all about housework. She was what my Gran used to call a "slawmeen"—she quarter-did everything. Still and all, she did not merit the abuse she got from Doña Luz. The *patrona* came upon the poor wretch one day when she was making an effort to scrub the passage. Instead of putting her back into it, Germaine was sitting on her hunkers and circling the scrubbing-brush around her like a slow-moving scull. Doña Luz stood over her, her face dark with contempt. "*Agachate, mujer!*" she said brutally. "Get down on your knees, woman! Now that you no longer serve for anything else, down with you and scrub."

All the lodgers liked the Frenchwoman and tried to be good to her. La Serena told me that when Rosario, the wife of the plasterer from Galicia, sent Germaine out to the café each afternoon for a jug of coffee and a plate of buns for herself and her visitor, she always gave her money to buy a share for herself as well. It was easy to believe that of plump Rosario, for her face was full of kindness. She was kind to me too. She knocked at the door of my room one night to offer me a slice of raspberry melon. I was entertaining myself by trying to turn an old dress into a new one. "Give me that," Rosario said. "You don't want to use up all your eyesight after working in an office since morning. I can sew. I have little to do all day. I will finish it for you." She did, too. And she made a very good job of it into the bargain.

Afterwards, when I told Helen Quinn about that house, she said that if I had been a proper girl I would have rushed out of it as soon as I discovered the kind of people I was living with. That I would have put my pride in my pocket and have asked Mr. Malony for an advance, or wired home for money—anything rather than stay in such a place. Maybe she was right. I have never been clear about these things. I only know that with the exception of Doña Luz I liked everyone in that house. Luckily for all of us it is seldom that we are as unpleasant as our sins. The Devil has to have a very strong hold on a soul before its likeness to God is blotted out entirely. So long as even a trace of that likeness remains, no soul is ever frightening.

If the Pension Camorra had been twice as sordid it would have weighed lightly on me that August because of all the grand things that were happening to me. First and foremost, there was the exultation of my job. I had not been a week in it when Luis returned from his Convention and brought me into his friendship again. About the same time I had a warm-hearted telegram from Michael congratulating me on my emancipation, and hard on its heels came a very pleasant surprise in the shape of a cheque for a guinea from a paper called *The Shamrock*, and a letter from the editor saying how much he liked my bull-fight article. I was bewildered. I had never heard of *The Shamrock* and had sent them no article. The mystery cleared when Michael wrote explaining that he had typed out a description of a bull-fight I had written him and had sent it to *The Shamrock* in my name. I thought my future was assured and that from now on I could count on *The Shamrock* for all the guineas I needed, for the editor's letter contained an invitation to submit more articles. Unfortunately, my bull-fight seems to have put a jinx on the little paper, for it died soon after. I have kindly thoughts for that *Shamrock* guinea, not so much because it came at a time when it was sorely needed, but because it was the means of introducing me to Mamá Antonia and Papá Antonio.

Mr. Malony had an agency for calculating-machines. Montera, where he had his offices, was only across the Gran Via from Hortaleza. There were three rooms. First the big general office and showroom where I sat with Señor Ruiz, the head clerk, two other Spanish clerks, Carlos and Amalio, and the office-boy, Guillermo. Through a glass partition could be seen the little room where Miss Leach worked, kept an eagle eye on us, and did watchdog for Mr. Malony, whose office was a big roomy carpeted apartment at the back of hers. It was a grand job. I loved the work and Mr. Malony and my fellow-workers in the outside office, and their pleasant easy-going way of getting through the day's business. Not even Miss Leach's tongue could lash them into adopting the American efficiency methods which she adored.

Mr. Malony had been right. Miss Leach was a tartar. She was an immensely tall bony woman, white-haired, with piercing blue eyes and a pleated mouth that now and again was unpleated to disclose uppers and lowers of white china.

Those girlish dentures were startling in her wrinkled face. Señor Ruiz believed Miss Leach to be very old. He said that in her young days she had earned good money keeping Caesar's slaves in order. She was old, certainly. She had been ten years with Mr. Malony. Before that she had lived in Egypt for more than twenty years, and looked as if she had resided in the tomb of the Pharaohs all that time. The woman was so dry and yellow and mummified that there seemed a danger of her crumbling into dust inside her clothes if she were exposed to the air for any length of time. She must have felt this herself too, for she swathed herself in scarves and veils. She had very long, very flat shoes of soft black leather which she wore at right angles to her legs. The laces were brought up and wound around her ankles in a Highlander design. So long and loose and flapping were the feet that it seemed to be the laces and nothing else that held them on. There was a great courage to Miss Leach. When she went slap-slapping up the Gran Via, her head high, her scarves flying, her straight back scornful of the mesmerized stares of the compact Latins, she was like an indomitable old sailing-ship plashing its way through little bobbing craft. You felt that if those laces broke and the worst happened, Miss Leach would just leave her feet behind her and stump dauntlessly to her goal on her ankle bones.

From the first she showed plainly that she thought I was up to no good. In spite of this she crammed a two-year commercial course into me in less than two months. Maybe she felt that the sooner I learned something the sooner she would get rid of me.

Now and again, Mr. Malony sent for me to find out how I was getting on and to dictate a few letters. Taking dictation was a trial, for I was never much of a hand at the shorthand. Something in me refused to accept those little pothooks and hangers as the equivalents of words. This was particularly so in the case of nouns. I could never associate with those queer symbols the objects they were supposed to represent. Take "ships" for instance. *Barcos, vapores, longa, batteaux*—any of these I could accept as ships, but that a broken-handled reaping-hook should represent sailing-vessels was more than my brain could swallow. Fortunately I had a good memory. Then, as in later jobs, I scribbled away impressively, making doodahs that meant nothing at all, and afterwards I typed the letter from memory. I was taking dictation one day when Mr. Malony glanced at my notebook. He cocked an eyebrow at it. "What shorthand system do you use, Miss Scully?"

"Pitman's," said I, with as much assurance as if I were Mrs. Pitman herself. "I see," Mr. Malony said, and passed a hand over his moustache. He coughed, and I was afraid to look at him.

In those first days, when business language was new to me, having to rely on my memory brought me much embarrassment since occasionally it happened that I remembered only the gist of a sentence and I had to reconstruct it in my own words. One evening Mr. Malony sent for me. He picked up a letter I had typed to a Mr. Isaacstein. He read from the letter: "With reference to yours of the 12th inst., we feel it is little enough cause you have for complaint seeing that you would not rest easy until we added the extra keys to the machine." He looked at me gravely. "Did I really say that, Miss Scully?"

"But, didn't you, Mr. Malony?" I stammered.

"I think," he said, "you had better retype it. Mr. Isaacstein might be confused. He did not enjoy my advantage of an Irish father and mother."

·   ·   ·   ·   ·

If you turned off Hortaleza, down the Arco de Santa Maria, you came into a quiet little tree-planted square called the Plaza de San Gregorio. To the right was a small bright shop with Pasteleria Macia over the door. The window was a delight. Sweets and cakes of every kind were arranged on vivid plates, rounds of sponge soaked in rum syrup and topped with cream—drunkards, they were called, squares of yellow custard as firm-looking and as smooth as ivory, with a deep cap of caramel, big blocks of membrillo, that lovely thick quince preserve that cuts like cake, fruit flans and marzipan and nutty pralines—there was no end to them. Right in the centre of the window there was a big dish covered with gleaming amber cones of nun's cheese, a Catalonian speciality made with ground almonds, lemon, spice, egg-yolks and syrup. I had not tasted nun's cheese since my first days in Spain when I had eaten it in Señora Basterra's house. I promised myself a share as soon as I should have some money.

Early in August I discovered that window. I was drawn to it again and again—not, honestly, through mere greediness, but through admiration for the grand workmanship of the woman who made those cakes and sweets. A mother and daughter ran the shop. I often saw them through the window, the daughter dumpy but very pleasant-looking in a clean countrified way, the mother an elderly woman with a broad kind face. She moved about the shop in quietness and serenity.

The day the *Shamrock* guinea came I made their acquaintance. It was evening when I came and they were sold out of nun's cheese, so I bought two drunkards instead and a glass of *horchata*, an iced drink made with sweetened milk and ground almonds. It was the daughter who served me. Her clipped sing-song accent, so like that of Cork people, confirmed what the nun's cheese had suggested—that she was from Catalonia. A delicate-looking young boy—her brother, obviously—was standing inside the counter studying an English grammar. I spoke in English to him. He blushed and answered me shyly. The bead curtain which hid a room to the left rattled apart and the mother came into the shop. A flush of pride mounted in her face when she heard her boy speaking English, and she stood looking at him with fond smiling eyes. Then she turned and spoke softly to someone inside: "Come out, Antonio. Come out and hear our boy speak English to the foreign señorita." A stocky man came out, a fiercely moustached, bullet-headed little man in a grey smock, apple-cheeked, and with small, good-humoured twinkling eyes. They stood there, the two of them, as I made conversation with the child. A pair of robins admiring their baby's flittings would not have been more rapt. For their greater pleasure I got the boy to read a little from a book I had with me. Badly enough he read, but they were made up with him. When I left that evening I had an invitation for supper the following Saturday.

That was the start of my friendship with a family who will always stand for the real Spain with me, the warm-hearted innocent lovable Spain that I found best worth knowing.

Both husband and wife had St. Anthony for a patron. Mamá Antonia and Papá Antonio, their children called them. After our first supper party, that is what I called them too. They had been in Madrid only two years. In their hard-working Catalan way, they made a good living out of the shop and a coal-carrying business which occupied Papá Antonio from seven in the morning until seven at night. They did not belong in Madrid. Their place was on the little farm they had owned beyond Montserrat, where Papá Antonio had tended his vines and followed his white lumbering oxen over the brick-red fields, and where Mamá Antonia had milked her goats and reared melons of a size *para maravillarse*—to marvellize you. Maria, the daughter, also talked with nostalgia of her home and of the boys she had danced with in the market square on Sunday evenings and the girls she had walked with in the feast-day processions. It was Mamá Antonia's passionate love for the boy José that was responsible for their exile. He was a clever child. The village priest who was teaching him said he was a genius. "Give that boy a chance and he will do great things," he told Papá Antonio. "Send him to college and to the university. But not to Barcelona. In Barcelona the students talk politics all the time. Send him to Madrid." The priest's word was law to the family, but Mamá Antonia would have died without her boy. "Enough," said Papá Antonio whose heart bled when Mamá Antonia was sad. "The matter has arranged itself. We all go to Madrid." The wind that blew them to the Plaza de San Gregorio blew a blessing to me. Even now something happy and excited wells up in me when I think of that home and of the kindness I knew there. I learned plenty from them, too. I learned to say the Our Father and Hail Mary in Catalan. I learned that there was a close kinship between the Catalonians and the Irish. Their long fight for independence, their yearning for individualism as expressed in the way they clung to their language and customs, and their love of liberty as shown in their demand for republican status—all these things made a brother-bond for us. And I learned to make cakes and sweets and yeast-bread. When people praise my *mille-feuilles* pastry, or my yeast rolls, I always say to myself, "Small thanks to you considering the teacher you had." Mamá Antonia was the best hand at confectionery I have ever known. It was a natural gift she had, for she never served her apprenticeship nor read a cookery book. Thinking to make her some little return for her goodness, I bought her a cookery book out of my first pay envelope. The shop was closed for the night when I brought it to her, and she was sitting with Maria in the little room off the shop. A kind of shyness came on her when I handed her the book, and she turned it over in her hands without speaking. "See what is on the fly-leaf, Mamá Antonia," I said. I had written, "*Para Mamá Antonia, la mejor cocinera y la mas bondadosa amiga, con mil amores de su agradecida Delia.*" She did not open the book, but just sat there holding it in still hands. A queer silence was on the two of them. I looked at Maria. She blushed and said in a low voice, "My Mamá never learned to read." Mamá Antonia hung her head in shamed apology. Her humility kept her from knowing that she owned accomplishments which put her above other women though they might have all the letters of the alphabet after their name.

.   .   .   .   .

Before the month was out I met Siemen again.

Juan and Consuelo had been holidaying in Switzerland on the proceeds of a series of cartoons which Juan had sold to a Paris paper. When they returned they gave a homecoming party in their flat in Almagro. They sent me an invitation by Luis. Though more fine-drawn than ever, Consuelo looked well, for she was toasted pale brown by the sun, and she was wearing a lovely Swiss peasant dress that made her look like a child of twelve. It was hard to believe that the dancing flame of her movements and speech and eyes came from a fire that was almost spent. Juan hovered about her, warming himself, trying to drive out the cold of desperate fear, making the most of the fire while he might. Even when he was at the far end of the room from her he hovered.

When Siemen came, he walked directly to where I was sitting. I was glad enough to see him again, but embarrassed because of the rude way I had treated him. He did not reproach me. He only said, "You once promised to dine with me in Ult Heidelburg. When will you come?"

For a moment I considered the wide short face with the greenish eyes and the broad flat cheekbones. Again I noticed that the mouth was kind, and I thought to myself, "Och, why not?" I said, "When would you like me to come?"

"To-morrow evening," he said.

"All right, then," I told him. "To-morrow evening."

Romana was sitting beside me and she overheard. Her eyes made me feel uncomfortable.

When we were going home she and I found ourselves

alone for a minute in Consuelo's bedroom. Romana was sitting at the dressing-table putting on lipstick. "Is Siemen taking you home?" she asked casually. I was standing behind her, peering over her shoulder as I fixed my hat. "He is," I said. Our eyes met in the mirror. Suddenly something blazed in hers. "Hurt him this time and you will regret it!" she whispered fiercely. Then she dropped her eyes and went on smoothing her lips. Only that the finger at her mouth was trembling a little, I would have wondered had I imagined the flash and the whisper. That was the only glimpse I had in Spain of the stiletto-in-the-stocking woman of the novelists. It was the only time Romana ever made open acknowledgment of the tangle that bound the three of us.

CHAPTER TWELVE

THE Señor Ramirez episode had taught me my lesson, and it was in the spotless columns of *El Debate* that I found my new boarding-house. The most straitlaced could not have found fault with the Pension Gomez in the Gran Via. The appearance of Doña Elena, the landlady, was a guarantee of respectability. The woman had missed her calling. The sin-abhorring eyes, the tight disapproving mouth, the bony black-dressed repudiation of everything carnal—it seemed a crying waste to employ such qualifications in the running of a boarding-house. She would have done grand as High Inquisitrix in a home for fallen women.

When the Gran Via started to slash its way through the heart of Madrid some years ago, it was halted by the old church of Caballero de Gracia. The Gran Via was so puffed up with its modern loftiness that it refused to step aside for the venerable church. Instead, it vaulted rudely over it. Part of the church occupied the ground floor of the building that housed the Pension Gomez. A little side-door in our front hall led into it. On your way in and out, you could dip your fingers in the holy water font without losing a minute.

For the first month I had only two fellow-boarders, Senhor Miguel da Veira who was a retired Portuguese bull-fighter, and little Don Leandro Camacho who had a job of some kind in the Prado Museum. I liked Don Leandro. He was queer in the head, but in a harmless way. His madness took the form of a belief that Goya's Maja Desnuda was a living breathing woman. No creature of flesh and blood ever received such love as Don Leandro lavished on the naked sleepy-eyed Maja. He spoke of her in the cherishing way a newly married man will speak of his bride. His meal eaten, the old fellow would rise from the table, looking from one to another of us with his little furrowed face full of innocent delight and his bird-bright eyes childishly and touchingly sure of our sympathy. "*Mi bellota*," he called her, "My big beautiful one. If you will kindly excuse me I will re-turn to her now. She gets lonely when I am not with her." In his enamoured light-heartedness, Don Leandro was a pleasant contrast to the ex-bullfighter from Portugal. Senhor Miguel was a scented manicured man with dull eyes like black seaweed pods set in his putty-coloured face. He spoke little and never smiled. Each evening he dressed him-self very carefully, winding a violet *faja* around his waist, and throwing a violet-lined cape about his shoulders. Then, with his wide black hat set at an angle, he went off on his secret ways until four and five in the morning.

At the end of September we got three new boarders. Helen Quinn returned to Madrid and came to see me. She liked the tone and cleanliness of the place, so she stayed. Rico joined us a few days later. Helen had finally decided that to sell her house property and reinvest the proceeds in matrimony would be a safe venture. She was wearing the bracelet which in Spain takes the place of an engagement ring.

The third addition was Miss Fanning, the blood-haired woman who had jeered my Ballyderrig shoes that day in the Retiro, she whom my first little charges had called "the Parrot of Guatemala." It was neither the long nor the short arm of coincidence that had planted Miss Fanning in my path again. She had stayed in the Pension Gomez before, and was all in all with Doña Elena. She was the only one of us whom the landlady invited to her room for coffee after supper each night. Miss Fanning had not liked me much when she had first known me. Now she liked me less and did not try to hide it. Apart from any personal reasons she may have had, it was understandable that she should have resented me. The freedom I now enjoyed, my luck in having been able to escape from the humiliations of governessing, the ridiculously raised social standing which my office job gave me—there was plenty of cause for resentment here, particularly with a woman who had worked for twenty years in this country as governess and chaperon. Still, I felt she was allowing her resentment to carry her a little too far when Helen Quinn told me some of the things she was saying about me at those monthly Children of Mary meetings in the Reparadoras. "She is going to the bad," Miss Fanning told the other women. "Someone should see about getting her sent home to Ireland. She is going with some kind of a German and stays out with him until all hours." It was a lie about my staying out late. Even if Siemen had wanted to keep me out Doña Elena would never have allowed it.

I have never had that enviable independence of spirit which scorns the dislike of others. Miss Fanning's enmity made me uncomfortable. However, I had plenty to take my mind off her. The night I dined with him in Ult Heidelberg Siemen asked me to marry him. I would have liked to have been able to say yes, but I was still too conscious of his foreignness. I liked him very much for asking me, though. Since the night with Rafael in the Casa Botin, my pride had been in sore need of a tonic like this. We continued to go out together. As they say in Spanish, we had relations, which does not mean what the English sound of the words might make one suspect. Siemen and I were keeping company. There was a thing I discovered through Siemen's treatment of me: men are influenced by convention. Rafael had "picked me up." To him I was a cheap girl without friends or background and he treated me cheaply. It was very different with Siemen. I had been introduced to him as the valued friend of his most valued friend. This coloured his attitude towards me always.

Early in October I got a new job, a grand job in the Banco Zamora in the Calle Alcala. Miss Leach got me the job. She had taught me to manipulate a log, a special kind of calculating machine for the use of banks. When she sold one to Don Alfonso Zamora she managed to sell me with it as a kind of component part. As it happened, the bank's business with London and Paris was increasing and they had been looking for someone to do the foreign correspondence and to take trunk calls. The work was very easy, and the pay very good—six hundred pesetas a month and a double month's salary in June and December. I sat at the switchboard in a little cubby-hole off Don Alfonso's office with the log and a typewriter on a desk beside me. During the Stock Exchange hours, the ups and downs of the pound sterling were telephoned to me at regular intervals. The log gave me the resulting peseta variations in dollars, pesos, francs, marks and the other currencies. I typed out these figures for Don Alfonso who bought and sold money accordingly. There was no shorthand to embarrass me here. Each evening Don Alfonso wrote out in Spanish his confirmations of the foreign transactions of the day, and I typed them out in English and French for Lloyds and Solomon Frères.

There were nineteen other clerks, all men. The Banco
Zamora was a conservative private concern that had been
run by the Zamora family for generations. Don Alfonso
considered himself daringly modern in bringing a woman
onto the staff. Shut away in my cubby-hole I had no contact
with my fellow clerks. The chief himself and Angelito, the
office boy, were the only two with whom I ever exchanged
more than the time of day. The office boy was a knee-
breeched hangdog child with a nimbus of wiry black hair,
a hook-nosed Moorish face and a snuffle. How in that
climate he managed to acquire his succession of colds in
the head is beyond me. I can only believe that the snuffle
was some form of mysteriously imposed punishment for his
thieving ways. Don Alfonso warned me about him when I
first came. He kept on the boy as a form of gratuity to the
father who had been the bank messenger and who had
crippled himself by falling down the stairs leading to the
vault. Angelito, the boy's mother had christened him.
Little Angel, how are you. That child would steal the teeth
out of your head and come back for your gums. Pencils,
pens, rubbers, paper-clips, carbon—from my little cubby-
hole alone he whipped enough to supply ten banks. I would
take my Bible oath that that boy is running a successful
stationer's shop in Madrid this minute with enough stock in
the back room to last him another five years. Once you got
used to his kleptomania, Angelito was a likeable young lad,
obliging and friendly. After snuffling around me suspiciously
for a week or two, he made friends with me. Every Monday
morning I heard a full account of his Sunday cycling excursions. He had persuaded his mother to let him buy a bicycle
on the instalment plan. He gave the bike the devotion he
should have given to honesty. Bicycle is a feminine word in
Spanish. The way Angelito spoke of his bike made me see
it in a blouse and skirt. The wiry black head of him would
come around the door with the suddenness of a sweep's
brush appearing at the top of a chimney. He would snuffle

until he got my full attention. "I took her out to Las Delicias yesterday," he would say then. "She was in great form going out. Coming home her back brake troubled her a bit. I'm going to take her asunder one of these days." The threat seemed cannibalistic, somehow.

The bank made allowance for the way Angelito helped himself. They put him under "Bad Debts" in their balance sheet. If the boy had walked home with the strong-room one night, Don Alfonso would still have felt it his duty to keep him on. There is nothing diluted about Spaniards. They are either one thing or the other. When a Spaniard is kind, his heart is as big as a clamp of turf. Don Alfonso's heart was as big as two clamps of turf. He was a quiet man with a thin worn face and humorous eyes. The humour went out of them when he talked about his daughter who was married to a doctor in Barcelona. She had two children, and had lost her sight through Bright's disease. Don Alfonso blamed the affliction on silk stockings. He thought women were mad in the way they muffled their necks in furs in winter-time and left their legs exposed to the cold. He was always counselling me to wear woollen combinations and lisle stockings in the cold weather. It was not only good advice he gave me. One day he put through a big transaction for a wealthy widow who often gambled on currency. She stood to win thousands. "What will she do with it all?" I said that evening, when I was typing a letter to her from Don Alfonso. "What would you do with it yourself, Delia?" he asked. The hours were long in the bank. I did not get out until seven, which meant that I never had any tea. I was conscious of only one want at that moment. "I'd buy plum-cake," I said. Every afternoon from that out, when Don Alfonso came in from the Stock Exchange, he brought me a half-pound slice of plum-cake from Garibay, the only tea-shop in Madrid where you could buy real English plum-cake. Often too, when he was posting a box of cats' tongues to his daughter he would buy me a similar

box of the smooth little chocolate wafers. On the days that
Angelito had had sufficient forbearance to leave me even a
scut of a pencil to work with, I shared with him. Often I
kept a share for La Serena. Since I had left Hortaleza we
met now and again in a café near the Pension Camorra. She
refused to let me go to the house to see her. She was equally
determined in her refusal to come to the Gran Via to see me.
"They would think badly of you if you had such a visitor as
La Serena," she said, not realizing that she hurt me. I hated
her to be working for Doña Luz. She hated it too. "You
will get a better job soon, *si Dios quiere*," I used to say hopefully. Then she would make a resigned movement with her
little claw of a hand as if to say: "Musha, don't be deluding
yourself, daughter. Where would the like of me get another
job? I'll be working my four bones in that terrible house
till I'm carried out of it."

.   .   .   .   .

Soon after I got my job in the Banco Zamora, Luisita
Juanes and Miss Carmody came back at last from their
travels. My friend and I had tea together in Garibay. It was
good to see her again after a year and a half. My old liking
awoke at the sight of this calm, nice-looking woman who
had befriended me when I had been raw and vulnerable. She
was better-looking than I had remembered, younger and
less withdrawn. When I remarked on this, her pale cheeks
tinged a little and she said it was probably due to the new
clothes she had bought in Paris. After a few minutes the
awkwardness created by our stilted letters melted away and
the old intimacy returned.

"Tell me all you've been up to since I saw you last," she
said. I told her, and I left out nothing. She was stern about
Rafael, shocked about Ramirez and horrified about the
Pension Camorra. "You should not have stayed there a
minute," she said. "You could have wired me for money.
What is a friend for?" I could not share her horror. I felt

then, as I do now, that the only time you need to fear a sin is when you share it. I knew that a girl would have to be a real out-and-out fool before she would stand in danger of big sensational things like rape and violence. Far more to be feared, I felt, were little everyday meannesses and cruelties, for against these there was no defence.

Just the same, I felt rather shamed and dirtied that evening in Garibay when I had told Miss Carmody all I had seen and known since coming to Madrid. As the story came out baldly and without any trimmings, I saw for the first time how sordid most of it was. Miss Carmody's clear grey eyes helped to pull out into the harsh light of truth many things which, at the time of their happening, I had shaded with my own emotions. That was the first time I truly realized that there is rottenness in life.

"Sure, it's a dungheap of a world," I said to my friend, and there was dismay in my heart.

"No, I wouldn't say that," she replied. "The dungheap is there all right. There is a dungheap in the corner of every garden, and the knowledge that it is hidden over behind some clump of laurels need not spoil the flowers for you. Once you know it's there and have learned to recognize its whereabouts by the smell, it is an easy matter to avoid it. Only somebody with no sense of smell will use a dungheap as a garden seat. You stumbled onto it because you were too young and too silly to recognize the smell of manure. I don't think there is any danger of your making the same mistake twice."

That was heartening. But her simile left one thing unexplained. "What about people who have no option but to sit on the dungheap?" I told her about La Serena working in that house.

"Yes—now and then it happens that people are crowded out of the garden and onto the manure. But they don't become dirtied, not if they are clean and good in themselves. Purity of heart is a garment that even manure can't sully."

She looked at her watch—a new one, I noticed—platinum set with little diamond sparks. "We have talked a lot about dungheaps." There was a little wry smile on her lips. "I can speak with authority on them. I landed myself on one before I came out here. It took me a long time to get over the wish to go back to it." That was as near as I ever got to knowing why she did not live at home with her people.

I walked with her down Alcala and along the Paseo del Prado. "You know, Miss Scully," she said, "in spite of this marvellous new job, I still think you should be living in Ireland. What about this Michael boy? Does he still write to you?" She had always had a notion that there was something romantic in Michael's letters, and I put her right. "But I have a boy here in Madrid," I said, and I told her about Siemen. She did not think a Hungarian would suit me. Strangely, that made me want to praise and defend him. "He would make a grand husband for any girl." Siemen gained value in my eyes as I spoke. "You'll like him. Wait till you get to know him well. Next year, when the fine weather comes, we'll all go on trips together to the mountains —you and Luis and the whole crowd of us. We'll have great times."

We were standing at the Juanes door. Miss Carmody stood fingering her glove as if considering the trips. She lifted her head suddenly. "Next year, when the fine weather comes, I expect to be living in Minneapolis. In the spring I am going to Paris to marry an American I met there this year."

Well! I started to say something inane and congratulatory but she cut me short. "A bride of forty-three and a bridegroom of fifty-seven. It does not fit in with your ideas of romance, does it, Miss Scully? No—I'm afraid there is nothing romantic about it." The slight bitterness in her voice left me without anything to say. She was silent a second too. When she spoke again, she was her own calm kind self. "Run home to your supper now, child. Be a good girl."

At Christmas I became engaged to Siemen. For a little while I wore that gold rope of his. Later he gave me a ring with two diamonds and a pearl. His mother wrote me a nice letter and sent me a lovely old Hungarian pendant. It was a heavy silver thing—a basket of flowers with a topaz set in each flower. Something in the silver gave an amethyst shade to the stones. I valued that pendant. I wore it on a fine silver chain around my neck. I wore it so much that something of me must have gone into it, for people used to tell me that it seemed as much a part of me as my hair and eyes. I had it until a year ago when it disappeared off my dressing-table. I was vexed about that. Mrs. Delaney, an old woman at home in Ballyderrig, had her St. Anthony's Treasury stolen on her during the Lenten devotions one time. She was raging. "May the woman who took it go blind from reading her prayers out of it!" she said. Far be it from me to wish a malediction on anyone, so I will not pray that whoever took my pendant may knot it around her windpipe and choke herself to death.

For Christmas Michael sent me a box of heather and a home-cured ham. I gave the ham to Mamá Antonia. She cooked it for the Feast of the Kings and invited Siemen and myself to come to supper. It was a lovely party. On the sideboard was a big dish of *turron*, the almond-studded toffee which is Spain's plum pudding. Mamá Antonia had made another seasonal sweet, a fat snake of marzipan. The crystallized fruits held snugly in his coils made a bejewelled pagan god of him. Doña Elena, my landlady, was annoyed with me for not giving the ham to her, and she and Miss Fanning gave me many a cut about it at meal times. I did not tell Michael about my engagement. I had a fear that he might stop writing. I had to tell him when, in the New Year, he wrote to say that if a filly he had did well he would come to Spain for a holiday. A few weeks went by without a reply so I wrote again and asked him not to let Siemen make any difference to our friendship. That brought me a letter in which he wished me happiness and promised to continue writing as long as I wanted him to.

Early in February Miss Carmody went to Paris. I never saw her again and she never wrote. I hope the American has been good to her.

At Carnival, Siemen and I went with the rest of Madrid to see the "Burial of the Sardine" in the Paseo de las Delicias. A daft scene, a laughing scene, with the whole length of Las Delicias turned into a fantastic fancy-dress ball, men using well-aimed swirls of confetti to bind to them in the kinship of gaiety women they had never seen before, others blessing the ephemeral union with light jets of eau-de-Cologne. The memory of that Carnival is spoiled for me by the humiliating recollection of what happened when we returned to the Gran Via.

I have done many a wrong thing in my life. Seeing that I got away with some of them without shame or blame, maybe I should not feel so bitter at the thought that it was through an innocent religious action I got a bad name with the Irish girls in Madrid. I am told that even after all these years if my name happens to be mentioned in the Retiro or the Molinero or wherever a few governesses are gathered together, someone is sure to say, "Oh, Miss Scully? Wasn't she the girl who was thrown out of that pension in the Gran Via for carrying on with a boy in the church?" God knows I have my share of sins, but sacrilege was never one of them.

On our way back to the Gran Via that evening, Siemen, who was a Lutheran, had been talking about Spanish religious festivals in a way that made me feel uncomfortable. When we reached the door of the pension I said to him on a sudden silly impulse, "Come in here till I put a drop of holy water on you. Maybe it would chase the devil out of you after the things you've been saying." Humouring me, he let me draw him into the hall and as far as the little side-door leading into the Church of the Knight of Grace. I dipped my fingers in the holy water font and was just going to make the sign of the Cross on his forehead when I heard a sound like the hiss of a snake, and there was Miss Fanning beside me. Her face frightened me.

"Oh!" she said, and her voice was trembling. "Doña Elena shall hear of this." She ran for the lift, clanged the door and shot up and out of our sight. Siemen shrugged his shoulder, tapped his forehead, and went home.

When I got out of the lift, the door of the pension opened before I had time to ring. Doña Elena confronted me, arms locked over her flat bosom, eyes ablaze. "So!" she exploded. "You think you are going to be allowed to remain in this decent house? Not another week. You may pack your things to-morrow and go!" Her voice rose to a scream. The woman was so filled with scandalized wrath that she grew enormously before my eyes, swelling like a monstrous wave above and around me. The horror and violence of the attack made me feel suddenly sick and I had to put my hand for a second on the door-jamb before I spoke.

"But what is it all about, Doña Elena? What have I done?"

"Bah! Dissembler!" she actually spat the words and her spittle sprayed me. "Miss Fanning has told me all—she saw you with her own eyes. Tell her, Miss Fanning. Confront the shameless one!" She stood aside a little and Miss Fanning, who had been lurking behind her, pushed forward. Her face was working. In spite of my distress I was fascinated by the way that eyelid drooped until it almost covered her eye. She pointed a shaking finger at me. "Deny it if you can! I saw you with my own eyes embracing a man in the very doorway of the church. You ought to be jailed for sacrilege!"

"You're mad, Miss Fanning," I told her. "You saw me putting a drop of holy water on his forehead."

"Don't you dare deny it!" She became full of scorn.

"Holy water, indeed? Holy water is far from the thoughts of your type. But it was only what I expected, with your lipstick and your dances and your men. I'll take care that every Irish girl in Madrid hears about you."

"Don't believe her, Doña Elena," I appealed and I was crying by this time. "It's a dirty lie—I swear it! She's a bad-minded woman."

But there was no shaking my landlady's belief in my guilt. Even if my accuser had not been her bosom friend, she would have been loath to disbelieve such a thrillingly scandalous story. "*Cochina! marrana! sinvergüenza!*" she called me, and each filthy name was like a blow from a dirty dishcloth. "Out you go to-morrow. I do not keep a house for *putas* who desecrate the House of God!"

If Helen and Rico had been there they would have taken my part. Their opinion of me was not the highest, but they knew I would never have done a thing like that. I had no one to speak for me but myself. I did my best. Though fury made me hysterical, I told them what I thought of them for bad-minded women. They retorted in kind. Our mutual abuse was at its loudest when Senhor da Veira opened his door at the end of the passage. He stood looking at the three of us, his white, pink-tipped fingers patting the violet sash around his waist. For the first time in my experience I saw him smile—an unpleasant smile that slowly twisted his face into a grimace of infinite contempt for the ways of all women. Then he closed his door on us, quietly and definitely.

It was my night for visiting my friends in the Plaza de San Gregorio. Mamá Antonia asked the cause of my red puffy eyes and I told her. "I'll have to take to-morrow morning off to look for a new pension," I said.

Little José lifted his head from the book he was studying and looked at his mother. Maria's soft glance raised itself from her sewing and went questioningly to her mother's face. Mamá Antonia looked at Papá Antonio. He nodded.

She nodded. She smoothed her lap. "We have a room," she began shyly. "A poor room—a small room. If you would care to come and live with us—at less than you were paying in the Gran Via of course. But you would be clean and comfortable. And we would like to have you. Eh, *niños?*" Softly and sweetly she looked around the family, inviting their agreement.

"Another daughter for the house!" Papá Antonio cried, beating the table with terrific enthusiasm.

"Company for me," Maria said.

"We could speak English all the time," said little José.

I could not get out a word. I just sat there like a fool with the tears threatening me. Mamá Antonia saw how it was with me. "Enough, then," she said. "It has settled itself. Delia comes to us to-morrow."

Papá Antonio raised a short stern finger. "All is not settled yet. Now certainly you must have a maid, Mamá. Someone to help you and Maria in the house. No, no! do not speak, woman. No longer have you the excuse that it would not be practical. With the money we shall rob from Delia in exchange for poor food and that small room you will be able to pay a maid without fear of making us bankrupt."

Mamá Antonia moved her shoulders unhappily. "I do not want a maid," she said worriedly. "How many times, Antonio, have I told you that these smart young Madrileñas frighten me? With one of them in my house I would not be happy."

"To-morrow you get a maid," Papá Antonio said stubbornly, hard for once.

I gripped the edge of my chair. "Would you"—I was nearly afraid to say it—"Mamá Antonia, would you take an old maid? She is a friend of mine. She comes from the country. A very old maid, but a hard worker and very clean and good. You would like her—I know you would. A good cook, too. She can brew tisanes like a doctor."

Interest awoke in Mamá Antonia's face. "Was it she who sent the recipe for the borage tisane when José's breathing was bad last winter?"

"The same, Mamá Antonia! She came to your shop once with a book I was lending to José."

She nodded. "I remember. *Una criatura decente, simpatica*. And a splendid tisane. It improved José's breathing in two days. Yes, I think we might get on well together. Tell her to come to see me to-morrow."

.   .   .   .   .

I had plenty to thank Miss Fanning for after all, and La Serena had reason to pray for her too.

CHAPTER THIRTEEN

IN the spring of 1928 a private radio station started sending out rebel propaganda. It called on the people of Spain to overthrow the dictatorship. In May, Juan Negrin was arrested on suspicion of being connected with the station. There is no doubt that Juan was doing useful work at the time, but it is unlikely that he was connected with that station. However closely allied he may have been with its purpose, the man's dignity would have prevented him from having any association with propaganda that relied chiefly on scurrilous stories coupling the names of highborn ladies with Primo de Rivera and his tools.

After Juan's arrest the bright lovely flame in Consuelo dimmed and burned low. She was brought to the new sanatorium of Tablada in the Guadarrama mountains. Luis, Romana, Siemen and myself went out there to visit her every Sunday. Those excursions would have been very pleasant but for the pain of seeing Consuelo lying so still and quenched in her bed on the long veranda. Every Sunday the bed-clothes were flatter and the hollows in her cheeks and temples more deeply shadowed. In the old days, Consuelo's eyes had been one of the joys of life. Everyone she smiled on was given a share of the happiness that shone from them. It was from this happiness they got their beauty, more even than from their size or the milky blue of the whites or the irises flecked like bronze chrysanthemums. Now the happiness was all gone and they held agony of soul. Consuelo was torn with religious fears. Though Juan was an unbeliever, she had remained a Catholic. Now that she was dying she was tortured by a fear that her going would end everything between them. Luis would try to comfort her. "You will be together, Consuelo. Don't doubt it. Links forged by the spirit are not sundered by death. Juan and you have been together in previous incarnations. You will be together again." But Consuelo's beliefs rejected this kind of comforting, and the big hurting eyes would travel from one to another of us, begging wildly for comfort that we did not know how to give. Sister Celestina was the only one who could quiet her in such moments. If she were about one of us would beckon and she would come hastening down the veranda, her big rosary rattling, her white veil flying out behind her, a tall, straight young nun, fresh-faced and calm-eyed. She would lay a quiet hand on Consuelo's forehead and talk to her soothingly. "Our Lord Jesus Christ is all kind," she would say. "He gave you your good husband as a sign of His love—like a keepsake a father gives His child to console her while she is away from home. When He brings us home to Heaven we no longer have need of keepsakes."

The little panting voice of Consuelo would protest at that. "I will always have need of Juan. He was more than a sign. He was God's love itself."

Sister Celestina did not reprove her for breaking the

First Commandment. Instead she said, "In that case, you are sure of meeting your husband in Heaven. God never takes His love from us."

But Consuelo needed further comforting. "What about the words in the Catechism: Outside the Church there is no redemption?"

Sister Celestina would pretend to grow really impatient. "Such a doubting woman!" she would say. "First she doubts God's love for her and now she doubts her husband. You will be calling to Juan from Heaven, Consuelo, telling him that you need him up there with you. Is it likely that he will refuse to hear and to take the road that will bring him to you?" Then the nun's voice would falter a little as if she were frightened by her own daring as she added, "Anyway, how can any one of us say with certainty that another is inside the Church or outside it? The relationship between a soul and its Creator is too intimate even for a wife to penetrate. It may well be that those we think farthest from God are nearest and dearest to Him. One thing is certain, Christ died that we might all live with Him in glory." The gentle voice would go on murmuring and the gentle hand stroking until the agony left Consuelo's eyes and she lay quiet as a spent bird in the bed. But it was better not to remain sitting there while all this was happening. There was always the danger that the aching throat would give passage to the demanding sobs and that the stinging eyes would release the tears. Better stand up and walk to the railings of the veranda and find reprieve from Consuelo in watching the patients who walked with their friends in the bright terraced grounds. Their tragedies, because they were only outlined, were less hard to bear. A professor from Madrid University was there that summer, a tall man with thick tossed white hair and a face dyed chocolate by mountain sun and pine wind. Every Sunday his class of fifteen young men came out to see him. For the whole two hours of visiting time, they had one of the wide

flower-bordered walks to themselves. Up and down they
went, up and down, he talking and explaining and teaching,
they listening with the reverence of the Disciples. They
formed themselves in a circle around him and so as not to
miss a single gesture of the master or a flicker of his eye, half
the circle walked backwards all the time and never seemed
to tire.

Sister Celestina had broadmindedness in little things as
well as in big. I had not known that the sanatorium was run
by nuns. At our first visit I was embarrassed to meet her
for I was wearing a suit of boy's dungarees. They were the
only possible protection against the dust and grease of a
pillion-seat on Siemen's motor-cycle. I apologized to the
nun for wearing trousers in a convent. "What else would
you wear on a *moto*, girl?" she said. "Before I left the
world I often rode pillion with my brother. If Mamma had
allowed me I would have worn trousers."

I was terrified of that motor-bike. Siemen had had it only
a few months. It was a French make, a Lucifer. It was
not misnamed. It reared and bucked like a possessed jennet.
I had many a toss off it. It had not a proper pillion seat,
only a luggage grid on which I used to tie a little cushion
that La Serena made me. Sometimes the cushion slipped its
moorings, and then the bars of that grid went to my heart.
I dreaded the Sunday rides to and from Tablada, but Siemen
had a Prussian contempt for physical cowardice, so I had to
hide my fears. The rides had compensations. Once the city
was left behind and we were on that powdery road that
wormed itself up through the baked fields towards the mountain top there were things to see that one missed in the train.
A quiet little hamlet with laneways and streets radiating
from a yellow church like ribbons from a maypole. Small
barefoot boys in blue cotton trousers playing at bull-fights
outside the church and a long-robed priest, breviary in hand,
black furry soup-plate on his head, picking his way among
them. A tall woman out of the Old Testament gliding away

from the fountain, a pad of blue cloth on her black head and
on the cloth a heavy red pottery vessel of water, one lovely
olive arm raised carelessly to the vessel, the other crooked to
her hip. She was very willing to let you drink from the
pitcher. The water came from it as icy and fresh as from
our pump at home. There was an art in drinking from the
pipe-like spout. It would have been the height of bad man-
ners to put your mouth to it. You tilted it above your head
and let the thin stream run down your throat. No lip movements, only an opening and closing of the throat. One day
the Lucifer barked its smelly way into a scene of great excitement. Everyone in the place, the *parroco* and his breviary
included, was gathered outside the church. In the middle of
them were two gipsies and a dancing bear. As a cure for
human pride there is nothing to beat the bored contempt in
the eyes of a performing animal. One of the gipsies held a
wooden spoon in his teeth and beat out a muffled tune on it
with a piece of stick. The big shaggy fellow at the end of a
chain shuffled his feet and moved his arms in time to the
tune. The crowd cheered and shouted and laughed, and the
dancer's eyes flicked one after another of us with their belittling indifference. It was a relief to get away from them.
Siemen was glad too. Dancing bears were a sore subject
with him. The Spaniards have a fixed idea about Hungarians
just as the French and English have a fixed idea about us
Irish. Every Irish parlour has a pig. Every Hungarian makes
his living out of a dancing bear. Sometimes a Spanish friend
would say teasingly to Siemen, "Where did you leave your
bear?" It always ruffled him.

Sometimes we stopped at an inn that stood back from the
road, a red-and-white doll's house, with iron tables and
chairs set out among the vines and flowering creepers. One
day a big luxury car was drawn up at the entrance and we
had to wait until the occupants got out. We had to wait a
good while, for the woman in the back had to be lifted out.
She had two artificial legs—they stuck woodenly out as the

chauffeur lifted her. She looked to be about forty, beautiful girlish clothes on her, her hair bleached yellow and with too much rouge on her thin face. She was so small and slight that she was like a child in the arms of the thick-set young chauffeur. As they passed us, she rubbed her cheek against his and he smiled down into her face with real affection. A fat old *señora de compania* wedged herself out of the car and waddled after them into the inn. I wondered would the chaperon inform the woman's family and get the chauffeur dismissed. It would have been nice to have been sure that the crippled girl was independent and answerable to no one but herself.

Nearly always, a big wine-coloured car with a crest on the door passed us out before we reached Tablada. Before it vanished from us in a cloud of dust we had a glimpse of a dark lovely girl sitting in state in the back. I knew who the girl was. She brought a memory of Rafael and of my star-crossed love affair of two years before. She had been one of the dance hostesses in the Alcazar cabaret, a well-built girl of eighteen with splendid eyes and a wide good-humoured mouth. She dressed in a more *outré* fashion than the other women, higher heels, more flashing jewellery, more exotic hair styles. Rafael told me that she was the most fashionable *cocota* in Madrid and that she had been working in the Alcazar since she was fourteen. I missed her from the cabaret after a week or two, and learned that she had gone to live in a villa in the suburbs with an elderly and wealthy nobleman. She never missed a Sunday at the sanatorium where her mother had a private room. One Sunday when the Lucifer was out of order we had to go by train. The girl was in our carriage. She sat back in the corner with her eyes closed and the stiff lashes meeting the beauty patch which she had fixed on each cheekbone. The knife-pleated skirt of her white crêpe de Chine dress fell in little fans each side of her crossed silken legs. Her hands lay in her lap, short thick hands to which the most expensive lotions had not been able to impart breeding. The finger-nails were exaggeratedly long and were lacquered crimson. On the crimson of each nail a little letter was stencilled in gold. Her name, Paula, was spelled out on each hand. The girl was saying her rosary. For the length of that journey, a mother-of-pearl rosary beads slipped endlessly through those incredible fingers.

Siemen was cynical about that. I felt he was wrong. Sister Celestina had put into words for me what I had always felt: that it is the greatest impertinence in life for one of us to assess the spiritual rating of another.

I was lonesome for Ireland that summer. Michael had written to me in June: "Johnny Moore of the Bullring was here this morning to threaten the law on me. It seems that my mare leaped a five-barred gate and had a fine time in his wheatfield. I went to inspect the damage. It did seem a shame that even such a small patch of his wheat should have been trampled and cropped. Growing wheat is a sacred thing."

Travelling to and from Tablada between the arid Castilian acres I had a great longing to rest my eyes on the rich freshness of an Irish wheatfield. Brilliance of sun and sky and overcoloured landscape are little addition to someone who is hungering for the gentle shading of the bog. It eased me to write a poem. "Ballad of an Irish Wheatfield" I called it. I sent it to Michael, for it was based on his thought about the sacredness of wheat. A few months later he sent me an Irish magazine with my poem in it. This is it:

Walk softly, O man, past an acre of wheat,
   With awe in your heart and your face.
Walk humbly, O man, and with reverent feet,
For strength slumbers here—can't you feel its heart beat?
And beauty's own couch is an acre of wheat,
   And holiness dwells in this place.

Breathe gently, O breeze, on the grain-heavy ears
  That drank long and deep of spring rain.
O breeze, ripple gently the yellow-tipped spears.
Our little ones, caught in the rush of the years,
Need growth that is stored in the wheat's golden ears,
  All mother-ripe now with smooth grain.

Sing sweetly, O birds, as you skim the rich field,
  And sprinkle your hyssop of song,
For here in each silken-caped kernel is sealed
The secret of living. The liberal yield
Will strengthen and quicken, O birds of the field,
  And comfort the earth's hungry throng.

Shine kindly, O sun, keep it warmly alive,
  On this field lay a tender caress,
For here is the reason men struggle and strive
And strain, sweat and anguish and battle and drive,
And life's spent for wheat just to keep men alive.
  O sun, let your rays kindly bless.

Walk softly, O man, past an acre of wheat!
  O birds, mute your silver-splashed mirth!
O breeze, hold your breathing! O sun, shed your heat!
For here is the Food that God gave us to eat. . . .
The Body of Christ comes from sanctified wheat.
  Thrice-blessed be this fruit of the earth!

Before the big bell which summoned visitors rang out
from the sanatorium, there was always a couple of grand
hours for us in the pinewood. Romana and Luis joined us
there when they came off the train. We ate our picnic lunch
together—the good food that Mamá Antonia had cooked
and La Serena had packed. A loaf as flat and as round
as a griddle-cake, split and buttered and with a thin savoury
omelet sandwiched in it; fresh crusty rolls stuffed with

lettuce and delicate fillets of veal; marzipan Jesuits: little
triangles of thousand-leaf pastry corpulent with moist almond
paste. Luis and Romana brought bottles of beer and cold
coffee and a basket of fruit, grapes and apricots and peaches.
When we had eaten we lay on the thick carpet of pine-needles
and talked. Usually, it was only Romana and Siemen who
talked, for Luis liked to wander off by himself among the
trees, and I was often too lazy to do more than lie on my
tummy—a position made advisable by the luggage grid—
and put in a word now and again. I remember thinking one
day as I lay there half-dozing while Siemen and Romana
chatted, how well they got on together, far better than he
and I. We had been engaged now for a year and a half, and
sometimes I had a panicky feeling that we were strangers.
In May, Siemen had said that it was time for us to fix our
wedding-day. He had promised his people that he would go
home for good at Christmas and he wanted us to get married
in November. I had been to see Helen that afternoon.
Helen was now Señora Cortes with a beautifully kept flat
in Zorilla. The kitchen was wonderful. Linen runners with
hand-worked crochet edging on every shelf, a shiny white
ice-box, a gas stove imported from England and a charcoal
range as well, a kitchen-table like a butcher's block with an
enamelled top that lifted up to show a zinc-lined washtub
beneath. She had a sewing-room with a machine and an
ironing-board. And she had a little maid in a cap and apron
who said when she opened the door, "I will see if my
señorita is receiving visitors." Helen was expecting a baby.
She was very proud of her pregnancy, for Rico's two elder
sisters had been married for years, and not a sign of a child
with either of them. Although it would be the end of the
year before the baby would come, already she had enough
clothes for two children—baby-clothes the like of which
are not to be seen outside Spain where children are more
valued and cherished than in any other country in the world.
Little soft padded dressing-gowns no bigger than a hand-

kerchief, with satin ties on the shoulders, chemises of crêpe de Chine with embroidery as fine and as delicate as anything ever turned out by Chinese hands, dolls' dresses covered with smocking, and petticoats with fine lace edging put on with veining. Every stitch in every garment was done by hand. There was enough in that flat to turn any girl green with envy, and that is why I agreed readily enough when Siemen suggested November for our wedding. Once it was settled I ignored the misgivings I had known before. It was the big difference in our natures that had caused them. It kept us from talking companionably in the way he and Romana would talk. When Siemen and I were not making love we were quarrelling. Quarrelling is not the word, for he refused to quarrel. That is an aggravating thing: to be itching to fight with someone who is too nice to fight back. "Not now. Let us not discuss it now," he would say with quiet kindness. "You are upset now. We will discuss it when you are calmer."

There was always something to discuss, a fault on his side or on mine, but mostly on mine. I had plenty of ways that warred with his stern Lutheran upbringing and his inability to budge from any policy which, after careful reasoning, he had adopted as right and proper. One of his policies forbade the giving of indiscriminate charity. It was inevitable that this should cause friction between us in a city like Madrid where one cannot walk two yards without being asked for alms. Siemen would go to great trouble in explaining patiently why almsgiving should be done through trained almoners. I could not see it. He was probably right. Others than he have told me that my approach to these matters is sloppy and sentimental, but I cannot change it. I lack the intelligence or whatever it is that enables one to take a detached view when the pity is assailed. Show me a hungry wretch and I will go without my dinner for him as readily as anyone. Show me Shaw's *Intelligent Woman's Guide to Socialism* and I will go to sleep. Some of my friends and acquaintances were upsetting to him, too. Coming from a big city he could not be expected to understand that where I came from there had been only one class. I remember upsetting him very much one night. We were walking along Barquillo towards the Plaza de San Gregorio. It was a bitterly cold January night, about nine o'clock. We had got as far as Price's Circus when there was a quick patter of steps and an urgent voice at my elbow. "Señorita Delia! Let me walk a little with you." It was Maruja, the girl who had gone to the bad after leaving Mrs. Hansen's. "We are not supposed to be out before ten," she said. "There is a policeman watching me. Let me walk with you. If I am accompanied he cannot charge me." She walked with us a good way. Siemen was silent and disapproving. I was embarrassed, but Maruja's naturalness soon put me at my ease. When we reached a point where it was safe for her to be alone, I stood and talked to her for a few minutes while Siemen waited impatiently a little distance away. When I joined him he reproved me. I hardly heard him. I had learned a shocking thing. Maruja's heart was not broken to be leading that life. She liked it. I knew then I had been unjust to Huxton in blaming him so bitterly. The girl would probably have arrived where she was if she had never known him.

. . . . .

Siemen had only one fault—his unreasonable jealousy. By the way he carried on, one would think I was Helen of Troy, Cleopatra and Salome all in one, and that any man who set eyes on me yearned for me at once. Because he liked me himself, he imagined every other man had the same taste. He really convinced himself that I had the attributes he ascribed to me. Men are queer. They grow to manhood with a notion in their heads of the kind of woman they want to fall in love with. She rarely or never materializes. They grow impatient waiting for her, and impress the image of their ideal on a substitute. They end up by persuading themselves that the substitute is the real thing. I do not claim this as my own original theory. I agree with it absolutely, but a Frenchman called Chateaubriand thought of it before me. I read it in a book which poor old Miss Myers lent me that time she was trying to improve my mind up in Bilbao. What Chateaubriand said was: *Le beauté des femmes n'existe que dans les cerveaux des hommes qui les aiment.*

At first it was very flattering and thrilling to be engaged to a man who wanted pistols for two every time another man looked in my direction. I was touched that he should estimate so highly my charm and good looks. I was so touched that I broke into verse about it after an incident that happened in a café one night. Siemen had spent the night glowering and sending murderous glances at a decent respectable man who sat sipping a matrimonial glass of manzanilla with the wife of his bosom. Siemen insisted that the man was ogling me. Anyone but himself would have seen that the way the unfortunate man's eye was riveted on me did not betoken any base design. The poor creature had an atrocious cast in his eye. I gave Siemen the poem the next evening. It went like this:

> Chateaubriand it was who vowed
> That woman's beauty is a work of art,
> Created by her lover's wishful heart
> And that her every grace is love-endowed.
> So, if I walk with conscious air
> And ape the queen,
> Conceitedly toss back my hair
> And prink and preen,
> Carry my breasts with royal thrusting lift
> And act as if the world were in my gift,
>   'Tis not through pride of anything in me,
>   But pride, my dear, in your ability—

Pride in your skill, which could create
A vision that would satisfy
And rule your willing heart in state
From such poor shoddy stuff as I.

Siemen read it. "Well, what do you think of it?" I asked
him. I thought it a rather good effort myself, and I wanted
my self-congratulation confirmed by his praise. No bard
was ever so disappointed. "Let me see, now," he said. "It
might be quite good but for this line here. Don't you see,
Delia, it is rather coarse? We will find another line instead."
He took out his pen and, after thinking for a moment or
two, he crossed out the ninth line and substituted "Carry
my head with proud and royal lift."

It was only at first that his jealousy flattered me. It became something to be resented when I saw to what lengths
it could carry him. In my desire for a peaceable life I let
him blackmail me into doing the most ridiculous things. In
two years I changed my job four times, and all because he
imagined I stood in grave danger of being seduced by men
who thought no more of me than of the desk at which I sat.
In a misguided moment I told him about Don Alfonso's
gifts of plum-cake. Into the old man's kindness he insisted
on reading a subtle Latin technique. Don Alfonso was saying it with cake instead of flowers. He gave me neither
peace nor ease until I left the bank. I cannot say that
changing jobs meant any hardship for me. I liked variety,
and at that time an English shorthand-typist with fairly good
Spanish and a smattering of French could find herself a new
job every day in the week. Later it was to be the turn of
German and Italian girls, but in 1928 an English queen was
still on the throne and everything English was still popular.
English electrical fittings were being installed in all the rail-
ways, English and American machinery was coming in by
every boat. There were English specifications and hand-
books of instructions to be translated for the use of Spanish

mechanics. The demand for clerks was greater than the supply.

When I left the bank I went to a firm that sold electrical supplies. From there I went to a pet post in a foreign legation. Finally, through the good offices of Luis, I got a job on a newspaper. Thinking back over my time in the newspaper, I have a great regret that I was not intelligent, that I did not take an intellectual interest in what was happening around me. The design Spain took in after years was shaped in that newspaper and though I was in the very middle of it, I noticed nothing. People are like blotting-paper. One, the more worthwhile kind, will absorb clearly the good black ink of intellectual impressions. The other, the cheaper kind, smudges everything but the red ink of emotion. I am the cheaper kind. When I hold the blotting-paper up to the mirror of memory, the black ink impressions are blurred and indecipherable while the red ink tells a clear story. There is nothing worthwhile or important there—only the face of Juan Negrin as he watched Consuelo on the night I first met them—the desperate eyes of Maruja as La Serena brewed the tisane for her in Mrs. Hansen's kitchen—Tomasina, the wet nurse, walking proudly along with the Marquesa's baby in her arms—the droop of Miss Fanning's eyelid when she accused me of sacrilege—the gentle ashamedness of Mamá Antonia because she had never learned to read.

There is another picture, if I could bear to look at it. I saw Consuelo die in Tablada. Juan was released for her funeral.

CHAPTER FOURTEEN

ON August 26th the customers of the Pastelleria Macia in the Plaza de San Gregorio had to go without their cakes and quince preserve and nun's cheese. Mamá Antonia decreed it a holiday of obligation and said that no one in the house was to do a stroke of unnecessary work. It was the feast-day of San José de Calasanz who was the patron of her son. There was good reason for making the boy's *santo* a special holiday this year. José had won a scholarship. He and his family insisted that his splendid marks in English had won it, and they made me take the day off from the office to celebrate with them.

Such a hot day, a happy day, a sick and sore and sorry day! After Mass in Las Salesas we walked to the Hipodromo to drink vermouth and soda under the trees, glad Mamá Antonia linking her tall thin son in front, Maria and myself behind with proud fat Papá Antonio in his best black suit and *boina* between us, the sun shining and everyone smiling, and I nearly dead from having to talk and smile while that drum of pain throbbed in my head. Carlitos, Maria's sweetheart, was there when we got back, a decent typical young Madrileño, resplendent in pointed shoes, pink shirt, nutmeg-coloured suit with padded shoulders and flapping trouser-legs, a very polite young man who always addressed me as "Señorita Miss." Siemen would have been there too but that he had gone to Bilbao for his firm. La Serena was ready for us with the best cloth on the table and, stretching down the length of it, the bottles of claro and tinto and anisado which Carlitos had brought. There was a feast of macaroni soup, with calamaries cooked in their own black juice, and chicken with rice. A big tray of olives, sardines, anchovies and sliced sausage to fill up odd corners. Afterwards, tutti-frutti ices and coffee and little eggy cakes soaked in perfumed syrup. A lovely meal, but a torture to me because of the way every scrap I swallowed was hurting my throat. Even the macaroni felt like chestnut burrs. We had speeches and congratulations and giving of presents. Mamá Antonia made gentle admonishing faces at Papá Antonio when happiness and wine started him singing a funny impolite little song about an old miller who could find no one to marry him. There was nothing but good humour and laughter, and I with my eyes burning and my bones aching and my backbone like ice.

The siesta brought release. It was Heaven to get into my small dark room and to close the door on joy and companionship and on having to pretend to be part of it. I knew then why animals always crawl away by themselves when they are sick. My hunger for the bed was too great to let me fold Mamá Antonia's yellow silk bedspread as it should have been folded. I drew it down and draped it as creaselessly as I could manage over the wooden footboard. For a while I lay half-dozing. Now and again my eyes opened onto El Greco's San Geronimo which hung opposite the bed. The emaciated suffering of the saint became confused in my mind with my own sickness. The confusion filled me with a queer foolish pity for the man. God help you, I thought, and you having to sing hymns with your poor throat so sore. Give yourself peace, I begged him. Don't be trying to concentrate on your prayers and you with that terrible pain in your head.

La Serena had noticed. She came to me. Her hand on my forehead drew me out of San Geronimo and back to myself. "Are you not well?" she whispered.

"A headache, Serena," I told her. "And my throat is hurting me."

She nodded. "You have a little quinsy as you had in the spring. It will be nothing. Wait. La Serena will make you something." Presently she returned with a glass of greenish water that smelled of *flor de malva*. "Drink this, daughter. It will make you better." I got it down. She took the glass and stood there looking at me, struggling with herself about something. "You will feel better now." There was supplication in the way she said it. "You will feel better in time to go with them to the *romeria*, no?"

To-night, in the avenue leading to the Plaza de Toros

Madrid would be honouring San José with a *romeria*—booths and sideshows and music and dancing. We were all to go. It had been arranged for weeks, the high spot in the celebrations. In the *romeria* there would be noise and glare and the lonesomeness of feeling sick among happy healthy people. Here, between the four walls of my room, was a great peace, and the bed was a kind little island of protection. "Must I go, Serena? Must I?"

The old mouth puckered and the bright black eyes were harried. She was sorry not to be able to spare me. "José's *santo*," she said sadly. "José's *santo*." That was all her lips said, but her eyes were speaking as well. "The child has won his *concurso*," they said. "This is the happiest day in his mother's life. It is her justification for having uprooted her husband and daughter from their little farm—for the exile they have known in this strange city. If you tell them you are sick and cannot go to the *romeria* with them, Doña Antonia will insist on staying at home with you. Then Don Antonio will stay to keep her company. For little José there will be no happiness in the *romeria*·without his mama and papa. No enjoyment for Maria and her *novio* if they have to entertain José all the time. Would you let your little attack of quinsy spoil everything for people who have been so good to both of us?"

"Yes!" my selfishness was shouting. "I would! I would!" But La Serena still stood there looking at me. I turned my head away, but her eyes continued to plead. "You are feeling better already, *verdad*?" she whispered.

"Yes," I said reluctantly. "I am."

"Good." There was great relief in her voice. "There will be no need for the señorita to dance—she can say her shoe is hurting her. And to-night La Serena will make her a plaster for her throat. Now she can rest a little longer. Presently she will drink some *esencia de café* and then she will be able to get up and dress."

Her prophecy was right. The tisane worked on me. I

slept a little. When I awoke the drum in my head was still there, but I was filled with a wild elation that mocked at pains, and a singing energy ran through all my veins. When La Serena brought me the coffee essence I was up and dressing. It was a burning-eyed flaming-cheeked stranger who looked at me from the mirror, but she did not worry me. Nothing, nobody could worry me. Not the stranger, not the anxious way Mamá Antonia looked at me during supper when the elation made me laugh loudly, not even the hollowness inside me nor the inner trembling of my bones.

The drunkenness saw me through a great part of the *romeria*. I went through the sideshows with the rest of them. We saw the unfortunate dwarf men who wagged their big round heads at the girls and gestured obscenely at us with hands as broad and as short-fingered as the forks for serving salad. We paid our *dos reales* to watch the performing fleas in their white paper skirts. They danced and kicked football. When each plump jet actor had done his turn, the grey-haired woman-trainer picked him up in a tweezers and rewarded him with a meal off her arm. From elbow to wrist, that mottled arm was sucked to the dryness of a withered stick. We went into the Hall of Hell with Papa Antonio leading the way before us three women, and José and Carlitos behind. Mamá Antonia said a woman should never go into those places without the men of her family. A dark terrible place, the Hall of Hell, with trapdoors that went from under your feet and let you drop two inches that felt like two yards, shutters that shot back to show dripping and awful decapitated heads, and skeletons that leaped down in front of you, grimaced a second and then shot up in the air again. Worst of all were the startled screams of the people who had paid money to have their nerves ruined by these sights. It was a relief to get out into the *romeria* again. This was Hell too, but a more bearable hell. A hell of noise— shouting and laughter and music, shots from the rifle range

and the cries of water and lemonade sellers. A hell of smells
—acrid oil from the *churro* and doughnut stands, sweat and
brilliantine and eau-de-cologne from the crowds, and the
cloying smell of boiling sugar from the booth where they
sold the *almidon*, sugar cooked and spun into white fluff.
Papá Antonio bought us all a bag. For twopence you got
what looked like a bale of cotton wool, but which could be
stuffed into a bag no bigger than a prayer book.

During the dancing I sobered. The elation went and I
became hot and shivering. The drum started to beat merci-
lessly in my head. "I am going to be sick," I thought, and
I tried to fight away the sickness. We were standing watching Maria and Carlitos dancing a paso-doble. Maria was
wearing her manton of black silk that was covered with roses
of every shade from pale pink to crimson. She was twirling
in the dance when suddenly she was no longer Maria in her
lovely shawl, but a rainbow coiling in on itself, coil upon
coil, coil upon coil, flashing, dazzling, terrifying, and I was
caught up in it, twirled with it, hurled with it . . . out . . .
away . . . through the screaming air . . . then down, down
into a sea of still soft blackness. . . .

      ·   ·   ·   ·   ·

I was like a Red Indian next morning. They sent for the
doctor. He was a tired-looking dried old man with a chalky
voice. "She has scarlet fever," he said. "Would you like
to have her removed to hospital?"

"No," Mamá Antonia said firmly. "She got it while
living in my house. In my house she shall be cured of it.
In any case, if we are to take it, we will take it."

"Maybe you are right," the doctor said. "I believe myself that if a bug has a message for you he will deliver it
though you spend your life in a soup tureen with the lid on.
On the other hand, if the message is not for you, he will
pass you by." As it happened, that bug's message was for
myself alone.

That was the last intelligible conversation I heard for many a day. Faces and voices broke now and then through the delirium, but they could not hold me. Siemen came and looked at me anxiously. He took the medicine La Serena was trying to give me and gave it to me himself. I heard La Serena whimpering and saying she was to blame, and later I heard Siemen telling Mamá Antonia that he had arranged for a night nurse. That night and every night after, a little black crow of a nun came to mind me. Luis came often, and Romana came once or twice. But I was ungrateful. I did not want to see or talk to any of them, not even to La Serena. They were all part of this place, and of the heat and thirst that were burning me. I spoke to them for a minute or two and then I ran away into the cool green places that were calling me.

·   ·   ·   ·   ·

I was picking nuts in the wood with my brother Joe. We were mitching from school. He was wearing his brown corduroy breeches with jags of the lining falling down over his knees and his grey jersey that buttoned on the shoulder. He was in his bare feet and so was I. I had on my first Communion dress with the three net frills around the hem. It was dark and very quiet in the wood, but there was nothing to be afraid of and no loneliness. The squelchy moss was cool to my bare feet, and the little threads of it were nice and scratchy between my toes. Joe was up in the tree throwing down nuts to me and I was filling them into Gran's black leather handbag. It was not a tree of single nuts, such as you might find anywhere, but a tree of muckelties—lovely clusters of four and five nuts together. "Catch," Joe called. "Here's a muckelty-six." He threw it, but I missed it and it fell among the brown and orange leaves at my feet. I groped for it, and Siemen's engagement ring slipped off my finger and rolled away. Joe got down to help me look for it. I knew Siemen's mother would give out to me for losing it and

I was crying. Joe stopped searching. "I hear Don Alfonso calling for the exchange figures," he said. He lay down and put his ear to the ground. His hair was cropped tight with a long tuft left in front for a fringe, and the white scalp showing through the black stubble made his head look grey. I lay down beside him to listen.

"This is bad," Don Alfonso was saying. "We'll have to get down her temperature. Give her a vinegar bath. Or tell the nun to give it to her when she comes to-night."

"I'll give it to her myself," Mamá Antonia said. "Serena here will help me." I was back in Madrid and Mamá Antonia and La Serena were bathing me, a little scrap of me at a time, with vinegar and water.

I could not wait for them to finish. I went back to Bally-derrig and hurried up the boreen. I had to hurry, for Gran was calling me in to my tea. She was standing at the door with one hand over her eyes to shade them from the sun. With the other she was beckoning me on. I raced across the yard, but when I got to her it wasn't Gran at all, but the sergeant. He frightened me by the way he looked at me. "I am going to summons you," he said. "I am going to summons you for the way you carried on in Spain. How many Sundays, when you were going to see Consuelo in Tablada, did you miss Mass?" "Three," I had to tell him, and my face was burning and my heart was thumping with fright. "You'll get three months for that," he said. "On Monday we'll be holding the court in the room at the back of the post office. Father Dempsey will give you three months, surely." In the middle of my fright I remembered something against himself. I turned it up to him. "What about yourself?" I said. "I was watching you on Holy Thursday in the Church of the Calatravas when you were guarding the Blessed Sacrament. You were standing with the other *guardias civiles* and you dropped your rifle. I saw you drop it." The sergeant's mouth opened and his fat red face paled and narrowed. It paled and grew bony, and the little blue eyes became big and dark and burning until it was no longer his face I saw, but the white hollow face of San Geronimo.

"Take this," he said, and his voice was no longer threatening, but kind and coaxing. "Take this. Try to take a little of it." I was back in my room in Mamá Antonia's house and Siemen was trying to make me drink something. He was wearing a green shirt with an open collar. His neck rose strong and thick and young out of it. The dark green looked nice with his tawny hair.

"Have you a new shirt?" I asked him.

"No," he said, "this is an old one. You often saw it before. Don't you remember I wore it this summer going out to Tablada on the bike?" He dipped a spoonful of thin soup out of the cup in his hand. "Come on, Delia. Take this. La Serena says you have been a bad girl all day. That you wouldn't take anything for her. Come on and take it."

I could not swallow it. My stomach rebelled against everything that was put to my lips. I had been swallowing sips of things to please them, but nothing remained in me for more than a few minutes. I was tired of trying. Anyway, his mention of the bike had brought the reek of motor-oil into the room. I closed my lips to the spoon, and I closed my eyes to Siemen's face. I pretended to be asleep, and then I was asleep and dreaming that Siemen and I were going to a dance in the Temple at home. We were going in Gran's pony and trap and Rafael Moragas was driving us. The road was hard and white, and the hedges were glistening under the moon. The air was clean and sweet like the taste of a russet apple in November. It was a bright night. I could see away down over the fields to where the canal lay still as a strip of steel. Granny Lynn came hobbling through Loughlin's meadow. She waved her umbrella for us to stop. She was coming to the dance too. "Stop and we'll give her a lift," I said to Siemen. He did not want to stop. "How many times," said he, "have I explained to you that it is a crime against the state to encourage children to beg? If you refuse them they will learn that begging is not a lucrative profession, and they will be forced to earn their livelihood in a more useful and honourable way." We quarrelled then, and I lost my temper. Rafael looked back over his shoulder and laughed at the two of us. I said I would not go to the dance with either of them. "Very well," Siemen said. "We will go when you are calmer. You are upset now." I made Rafael draw up the pony and I got down, and they drove away around the bend at Mitchell's forge. Granny Lynn opened the gate of the meadow and came over to me. "Never mind," she said. "We'll get a lift. There's someone coming now." There was. It was Michael. I could see his face in the moonlight. He was riding a poor old hack of a bullring horse. The creature was so old and tired that it could only lift its hooves with dreadful slowness. When they struck the road, they made the smallest little rattling noises, not like hoof-sounds at all. As I stood listening to them and waiting for Michael to catch up with us, Granny Lynn started to say a Hail Mary under her breath. "*Dios te salve, Maria. Llena eres de gracia. El Señor es contigo. Bendita tu eres entre todas las mujeres, y bendita es la fruta de tu vienete, Jesus.*"

I came out of the dream. The whispered prayers continued and the little rattling sounds went on. I turned my head and saw Sister Mary John of the Cross kneeling bolt upright in the middle of the floor. She was saying her rosary. She felt my eyes on her, and she blessed herself and got to her feet. She came to my bed and looked hard at me for a minute. Then she put her hand on my forehead. This was the first time I had really seen her since she had come to me. A broad plain face, sallow against the white of quimp and coif, but sweet-mouthed and with peaceful eyes. "*Gracias a Dios!*" she said fervently. "*Gracias a Dios!* Your fever is gone." I knew it. The minute I had awakened I knew it. My throat no longer hurt, and the sore muddle had left my head. "How do you feel, child?" the nun asked me.

"I'm dying for a cup of tea, sister," I told her. I was aching for it.

The nun's face grew troubled. "Is it English tea?" she said. "If it were camomile tea, or herbal tea. . . . I never made English tea." There was nothing surprising in this. Often in a café when I had asked for tea they had brought me a jug of tepid water and a little packet of musty tea grains. "If you direct me I will make it," she said.

I directed her. I had my own tea-making apparatus, for not even La Serena nor Mamá Antonia, with all their cooking skill, could make a decent cup of tea.

Sister Mary John of the Cross lit the spirit lamp and put a saucepan of water to boil. "A little biscuit with this will do you good," she said. I wanted bread and butter, and she went out to the kitchen to look for it, and to find milk and sugar. When at last the meal was ready, I was ready too. From my dream I had brought back with me a longing for thin slices of soda bread with plenty of freshly churned salty butter, and a good cup of strong tea with fresh cream in it. The tea I got that night was watery and it smelled of methylated spirit. It was coloured with boiled milk, for Mamá Antonia always boiled her milk the moment it was brought into the house. The bread was a thick split roll with a scrape of unsalted butter on it. If the meal had been strictly in accord with my longings I could not have enjoyed it more. I drank every drop and ate every crumb and then I lay down and slept peacefully until two o'clock the next afternoon.

Siemen was there when I awoke—he had been coming every day at lunch time—and the doctor and Mamá Antonia and La Serena. They were all so delighted with me that they made me feel I had done a very noble and praiseworthy thing in responding to their care.

"In a few weeks you will be as well as ever," the doctor

said. "But you must take great care. A little holiday, first of all. A change of air. In Santander, say. You will need the sea air."

"We will be getting married shortly," Siemen explained to him. "We could spend our honeymoon at the sea."

"An excellent idea. What do you say, señorita?"

"No," I said, and it was only as the words came out that I realized my mind was made up. "We will have the honeymoon wherever Siemen says, but first I am going home to Ireland for a holiday. I want to say good-bye to my people before I get married."

Siemen looked startled, and no wonder. It was the first time he had ever heard me express a longing for my family. It was the first time that I myself was conscious of wanting to be with my own. There were eight brothers and sisters of us, and we might just as well have been strangers. I had often been ashamed of this. I had often envied Siemen the great love that existed between his two brothers and himself, and the constant letters they exchanged. My family hardly ever wrote to me, nor I to them. Even Joe, my favourite one, who had gone to America since my coming to Spain, had written me only three letters in all my time here. But now I felt an urge towards them. I wanted to be with my own flesh and blood, to warm myself at the fires of home before going into a cold new country among black strangers.

Siemen tried to dissuade me, but it was no use. "I'll go in the beginning of November," I said. "I will have a clear fortnight at home. That will see me back in plenty of time for our wedding on the 27th."

While I was convalescing I had time to solve the problem of how to find the money for the trip. I am ashamed to admit that of all the good money I had been earning in the past two years, I had not saved a single peseta. A palmist read my hand once and said the wide spaces at the bases of my fingers are where the money rolls through. The biggest

regret of my life is that I did not come into the world as
web-fingered as a duck. My salary was mounting up for me
while I was away from the office. My chief knew that I
would be leaving them in November. It made no difference
to his generosity. Every Friday he sent a clerk with my pay
envelope. He even raised my salary, and sent a little note
saying that he had done this because he realized that sickness
meant expense. I would be ungrateful if I did not say that
this good nature was typical of every office in which I
worked in Spain. My salary was mounting up, but I could
not touch it for my holiday at home. What was left after
paying Mamá Antonia had to go to the doctor and the
chemist and Sister Mary John of the Cross. Not that she
set a price on her services. She belonged to an order that
nursed for the love of God. But if I who could afford something did not pay what I could, it might mean that there
would be no little nun to nurse some other girl through
scarlet fever. I remember well the morning she held her
crucifix to my lips for the last time. I thanked her and
offered her my contribution. "Post it to the Reverend
Mother," she said. "The rule forbids me to handle money."

Our Boys brought me home. In between visits from
Siemen and Luis and Helen and my other friends, I sat up
in bed and wrote twelve more stories for them, this time
stories of my own with a Spanish setting. Luis took them
away and typed them for me. The editor accepted them
and sent me a cheque for twelve pounds by return. I sold
an article on Catalonian politics to a Dublin daily paper for
a guinea and a half. Papá Antonio gave me the data for that,
and from Mamá Antonia I got material for an article on
Spanish cooking which an English woman's magazine
bought for three guineas. I had enough for my return fare
and a little over.

In October I wrote to Michael: "I am starting for home
on the 1st of next month. I want to see Ireland again before
I get married. And I want to see you, to thank you for

what your letters have meant to me these three and a half years."

.   .   .   .   .

I said good-bye to La Serena in the house, for she refused to come to the station in the taxi with the others. It was in the kitchen I said good-bye to her. "Are you not going to wish me *buen viaje*, Serena?" She stood there gripping one of my hands in both of hers and not a word out of her. "I'll be back in a fortnight, Serena," I said. She did not speak. She kissed me, and her kiss was like the cold sweet little kiss of a child. But she never said good-bye to me.

They all came to the station to see me off. Luis, with his brown face full of friendship and a bundle of books under his arm for me, Siemen with chocolates and the little air-cushion for travelling which his mother had given him when he left home, Papá Antonio with the gorgeous pigskin case which he said was José's gift to me in return for the English I had given him. Maria with a basket of fruit, and Mamá Antonia with a basket of cakes and bocadillos and a flask of coffee. They settled me in my carriage with their gifts around me. We said good-bye. The train drew out and I leaned from the window to wave to them.

"Come back soon to your friends," Papá Antonio cried.

.   .   .   .   .

I never went back. Michael was waiting for me at Dun Laoghaire. When I saw him I knew that I could never go anywhere again unless he were with me.

Siemen married Romana. They have one little girl. We have two.

VIRAGO MODERN CLASSICS
&
CLASSIC NON-FICTION

The first Virago Modern Classic, *Frost in May* by Antonia White, was published in 1978. It launched a list dedicated to the celebration of women writers and to the rediscovery and reprinting of their works. Its aim was, and is, to demonstrate the existence of a female tradition in fiction, and to broaden the sometimes narrow definition of a 'classic' which has often led to the neglect of interesting novels and short stories. Published with new introductions by some of today's best writers, the books are chosen for many reasons: they may be great works of fiction; they may be wonderful period pieces; they may reveal particular aspects of women's lives; they may be classics of comedy or storytelling.

The companion series, Virago Classic Non-Fiction, includes diaries, letters, literary criticism, and biographies – often by and about authors published in the Virago Modern Classics.

'A continuingly magnificent imprint' – *Joanna Trollope*

'The Virago Modern Classics have reshaped literary history and enriched the reading of us all. No library is complete without them' – *Margaret Drabble*

'The writers are formidable, the production handsome. The whole enterprise is thoroughly grand' – *Louise Erdrich*

'The Virago Modern Classics are one of the best things in Britain today' – *Alison Lurie*

'Good news for everyone writing and reading today' – *Hilary Mantel*

'Masterful works' – *Vogue*

Printed in the United Kingdom
by Lightning Source UK Ltd.
110777UKS00001B/4